FAKE REWARD

a puzzlingly different murder

———∽———

by

N N Wood

Also by N N Wood:

FOUND LOST

SKILLS HIDDEN

(available on AMAZON)

Copyright © N N Wood 2024
This book is sold subject to the condition that it shall not, by way of trade or otherwise, be lent, resold, hired out, or otherwise circulated without the publisher's prior consent in any form of binding or cover other than that in which it is published and without a similar condition including this condition being imposed on the subsequent publisher.
The moral right of N N Wood has been asserted.
ISBN: 9798327018112

This is a work of fiction. Names, characters, businesses, organisations, places, events and incidents either are the product of the author's imagination or are used fictitiously. Any resemblance to actual persons, living or dead, events or locales is entirely coincidental.

to Gill

Acknowledgements

Many friends have been supportive in lots of different and helpful ways. I am especially grateful to Derek, Giles, Gill, Jan and Tania for helping me set the right direction and tone. Any and all of the errors and inconsistencies are, of course, all down to me.

I wish to state that at no stage in the writing and production of this work of fiction has there been any use of any kind of AI (artificial intelligence).

CONTENTS

PART I SUMMER 1
PART II PREVIOUSLY 155
PART III RESOLUTION 196
PART IV EPILOGUE 231

PART I

Summer

One

Sally and Graham had, at last, taken the afternoon off work for their long-planned lazy boat trip round Bristol's Floating Harbour and up the River Avon. Their picnic hamper, handed down through generations of Sally's family, was laden with bottles and food exactly right for a late lunch and an early wine o'clock, and later for whatever came naturally. Mike, the boatman, had put himself at their disposal for his usual fee, and the handsome tip on top made him smile at his clients. He was getting paid for what he liked doing best in the world – just messing around in his boat. His instructions were to saunter around in no particular hurry in the brilliant early May sunshine. "Idyllic", for all three of them, was the right word, with the bustle of the Bristol traffic kept well in the background. Graham opened a bottle of fizz, and Sally laid out the smoked salmon sandwiches on brown bread with, as she pointed out, the crusts cut off. They toasted each other and chatted about their recent party celebrating their birthdays, coincidentally only a few days apart. Mike yelled a warning that they were about to veer to the left, adding his off-repeated old quip about port not being just a drink, bringing the boat round in a full circle and then to a standstill.

'That's a strange looking bundle. Just there – look.'

They did both look. It was a very strange looking bundle: oblong and well wrapped in polythene sheeting. Mike took what looked like a punt pole and prodded the bundle until it flipped over.

Sally and Graham put their hands to their faces and gasped. The bundle was clearly a male corpse, visible through the translucent polythene.

'I think we better head back to base,' Mike said. He took out his mobile and made a call.

Two

Mavis Smith was poring over her usual data on correlating bicycle thefts with the Bristol postcodes just as Chief Inspector Brandon strode into the general office.

'What are you girls up to?'

'Women,' Mavis said without looking up.

'Well, that's as may be but today you're neither. Stand up, *Detective Sergeant* Smith, and congratulations. You deserve it.'

'Sir! Wow! Gosh, thank you. I didn't mean any disrespect; I was deep in thought.'

'Not a problem. I'm pleased for you, and your previous heads agree with me; they have all given their approval. Now, that also means work, and we've just had a call in about a body in the harbour. Forensics are there, and I'd like you to get over and take charge of the situation. There'll be crowds and the Press. I'll see you later.'

The newly appointed DS got up and left the office.

For all her comparative youth, Mavis was now in her mid-twenties, and she had had plenty of experience learning the hard way in South London. Then, she had a posting to rural Sussex and, more recently, a move to Nottingham. When the vacancy at her (then) same rank popped up in Bristol, with vague wording about possible promotion, she had applied straightaway and, after a few interviews and some tests, Brandon had decided she was easily the best candidate. He was also reassured by the snide accusation from Bradley at Nottingham that he was poaching his staff. Brandon promised he would settle this matter at the golf club next time they met.

Mavis walked over to the harbour. She was smiling inwardly about her promotion. It had not been promised, but her friends and her old mate Clive Drewett had each said in their own ways that a step-up was not far off and a transfer might help. She was sorry to move away from her boyfriend Philip in Nottingham, but they had vowed to do alternate weekends, work permitting, and see where they got to. She had told him that he could be an auctioneer anywhere to which he replied, 'Police, ditto.'

*

A small crowd had already gathered around where Forensics were hauling the wrapped body out of the dock. Adrian, the local uniform, was trying his best. Mavis introduced herself as DS Smith and got a 'Yeah, we've met,' response. Together, they shepherded the crowd well back, and, with the help of Forensics, put up some temporary barriers. Hugh Cranston, the senior pathologist with many years' experience of fishing bodies out of rivers, lakes and harbours, as well as all the other routine work with the police and hospitals, was a tall, kindly man who took life and death as they came. Mavis sought him out.

'Hi, Mr Cranston. What's it look like so far?'

'Early days, but I'm afraid it's very much just what you can see in front of you: a dead body of a male wrapped in polythene sheets. Probably a lethal bash to the head before being wrapped up and dumped. I'd like some dredging done please, around where the body was found and also at the quayside from where the body was presumably dumped. Can you get the CCTV downloaded to help locate precisely where that was, let's say over the last twenty-four hours? Then we'll do a search for clues there. More when we've got the body on the slab.'

Mavis spoke into her mobile and then asked Adrian to go round all the local CCTVs. There were plenty of pubs, cafés and restaurants in this busy and sociable area, and she was hopeful of faces and vehicles yielding some evidence. She made to go but was confronted by the local Press wanting to know what, when, who, why, how, and was this connected to the current local crime wave, *et cetera*.

'Thank you for your interest and concern. It is obviously very early days yet but when we have further information, we will give a Press conference asking for your help and that of any witnesses. Until then, please let us get on with the job.'

With that, she brushed the Press aside and strode quickly back to the station to give a debrief to Brandon. He didn't waste any time in deciding what to do next.

'It's a start, and thank you, that's helpful. I'd now like to see you take charge as much as you can with Alec Robertson as the formal SIO. He's back tomorrow and then the two of you can take this forward. We need identification, witnesses, CCTV, whatever.'

One minute you're promoted, the next you're in it up to your neck.

Three

Peter Vernon was a good citizen; all those words like "safe", "sound", "reliable", "trustworthy" that would immediately come to mind without the need of a Thesaurus were mentioned in the warm tributes about him at his retirement party. Needless to say, he had qualified as an accountant in quick time many years ago, and after ten years in private practice had joined a bank as an internal auditor. He found he warmed to the forensic side of the profession, particularly with this now single client to get to know in depth. All this might have made him out to be someone you'd slip away from after a few minutes' conversation but that would be wrong; he was an *interesting* man in the best possible interpretation of that word. His strength in life and in his job had always been to drill down until there was a complete and logical explanation. At work, a former colleague had remembered him, and often recalled him, tackling two versions of some aggregate figure. If two departments had a discrepancy of, say, £5 between them, Peter wanted to know where the difference was. *Intense* would be a good word, too, and all with his trademark charming and unthreatening manner. That is until there was proof. His classics degree at a provincial university might have seemed an odd choice but the apparent precision of language in Latin and Greek had fascinated him. His roundedness was completed with a happy marriage to Barbara, a homely suburban house in Surrey, and a son and a daughter, now grown up. He was an adoring husband and father who had nevertheless always managed to retain a certain aloofness in matters domestic.

He had not been, nor wanted to be, Head of Internal Audit. The silo management structure always conveyed to him that the heads spent far too much time on office politics, speculative strategic ventures, salaries and car parking. Nothing was better than an apparently unresolvable problem like a mysterious deficit or, best of all, suspected skulduggery.

Another former colleague referenced Peter recalling an old case of what was then a very large sum of money which went missing. The bank had got the drains up on that one, and every department had to answer to the Audit Committee, of which Peter was a long-standing and respected member. It was never resolved and the bank later kitchen-sinked the amount along with some other dubious debts. Peter on the other hand had never entirely given up on it. Whenever he had a spare afternoon, he would get the files out and try to progress his work on it. He wanted to rely on that quote from S. Holmes: "When you have eliminated the impossible, whatever remains, however improbable, must be the truth." But Peter had always felt this case was different because there was nothing that was impossible.

His few, all very close, friends and former colleagues had paid him the best of compliments and wished him and Barbara a happy retirement. They both thanked them all warmly, asking them to keep in touch. Peter had kept his files on several old cases in his study which even for his dear wife was a strict no-go area. Now he had the time in retirement, he would solve one of those cases if it killed him; something else to do as well as golf and bridge.

Four

Mavis was at the pathology laboratory with Hugh Cranston for his first debrief. He did not exhibit nor indulge his superiority to the young officer.

'Male, mid-fifties, head bashed in before entering the water, likely to have been dumped in the small hours, and was dead at least twelve hours before that. There were some stones added but not enough to sink the body. I'll do an autopsy on organs, food, alcohol, drugs, all the usual stuff, Mavis. Congratulations, by the way.'

'Thank you, Sir.'

'Hugh, please.'

'And any clues on the clothing, wrapping, quayside evidence?'

'Of course – all in good time; come back the day after tomorrow, and hopefully you'll have some CCTV output to show me.'

Mavis left, not feeling much further forward. She would chase Adrian about the CCTV. Then there was her first meeting with the SIO. And she'd call or message Philip.

*

Alec Robertson was in his office when she got back to the station.

'Good morning, DS Smith. Congratulations by the way! How is this murder case going?'

'Thank you, Sir. There's very little other than the obvious at the moment. Head bashed in before being well wrapped up in polythene sheeting and dumped. Adrian is collecting all available CCTV and Mr Cranston will have a fuller analysis the day after tomorrow. I'm getting an updated list of missing persons; so, in short, more soon, Sir.'

'Okay, I'm going to let you run with this, Smith, and I'll just keep an eye on developments as they happen. Message me or pop in at the end of each day with the day's activities and results. But first, we need to know who this guy is. That'll give us leads on family and contacts, etc.'

'Exactly so, Sir, will do.' Mavis left.

Robertson was Scottish by place of birth and family roots but had lived around Bristol for most of his life after university. He had risen up the ranks, not rattling any cages, and was surprisingly laid back. Mavis realized that he was giving her rope and would pounce on any shortcomings. It was ever thus, she thought, and she hoped Adrian had got something.

He had and he hadn't. The dumpers had chosen a quayside spot where CCTV was switched off between 2 am and 5 am. At least that placed limits on the timing and the location for potential forensic findings. The surrounding area had more possibility in filming traffic but there was nothing out of the ordinary in the random stream of lorries, vans, cars and taxis, and even a night bus.

'At least there's enough to put out a release for any information within time and place. Sorry Adrian, but please get all these photos blown up for registration and faces.'

'There's a lot.'

'I know, but it's all we've got at the mo. We have to check them out. Ask Celia to give you some help.' Mavis had noticed the two of them chatting at the coffee machine.

She phoned Forensics and asked to meet at the quayside where the off-loading was suspected of happening. It was clear why they had chosen that particular spot – it was deserted, with no overlooking warehouses, offices or dwellings. Mavis looked back at the city skyline; yes, there were some tall buildings with a direct sighting. All it needed was some weirdo night owl looking out onto the harbour in the small hours and noticing one or two people dumping a bundle into the water. She made a note of the buildings.

Five

Clive Drewett was stationed at "W-town" in the West Midlands. That's the name he gave it when he was posted, well over a year ago now, up to the West Midlands where nearly all the places seemed to start with the letter W. Apart from Birmingham, obviously. He had formed a local relationship with Amy which had gone nowhere and was now over for good. Although he was in his early thirties, he had not formed as many relationships as he thought he should have, but with this recent one he was more than glad it was over. Nothing wrong with being single and biding one's time, he tried to convince himself. He had always had a soft spot for Mavis Smith ever since they had worked together on a tricky kidnapping case way back in Sussex. She had been his junior, though they had worked together as colleagues quite easily. He hoped he had helped her career, and was pleased to read of her promotion down in Bristol. Not that far away, but she was attached and, in any case let's be honest, she was way out of his league. He was pleased that they were now the same rank and felt absolutely no superiority over her. They were equal but she was better. She would get promoted again, and he wouldn't. There was no rivalry between them, and for him work mostly came first. Relationships were okay but they could get in the way; and relationships at work definitely got in the way. He was most likely a career copper and that is what he would concentrate on the most.

Inspector Bolton called Clive in and asked him what he was up to.

'The usual, Sir, you know - mainly cars, domestics, break-ins, and pub closing times.'

'You need something meaty to, er, get your teeth into.' They both smiled at his accidental joke.

'Yes, Sir.'

'There's an old cold case of mine, never happy about it, felt I could have done better, you know what I mean. Then I was taken off the case and it was filed.'

'Sounds like it's up my street.'

'I hope so. It's fraud but nobody could pin down what or on whom, but Geoffrey Faulks was involved, very definitely involved. The file's here somewhere; dig it out and in your spare time or gap time, see what you can do. There's no criticism if you can't solve it – after all, I didn't', Bolton said grimly but with good humour. Clive thanked him and went down to Janet in Records.

'Hi Janet. Does Geoffrey Faulks mean anything to you?'

'Clive, don't. Bolton was like a bear with a sore head on that one, and everything was a dead end. We gave up. I'll find what I can and bring them up to you.'

'Bolton has handed the cold case to me; I'll do what I can but if he couldn't, how can I?'

'You're thorough, Clive, but let me give you a tip. If you get anywhere, let him have the credit.'

'Janet, stand for politics some time. Noted; but he did give me the case.'

Six

Mavis reported in to Pathology and went straight through to Hugh Cranston's office. He was at his desk rather than in the laboratory, and with a sheaf of papers in front of him.

'Morning, Mavis. I'll let you have the report later but I'll run through the main points. He was in fairly good shape, no obvious physical failings. His last meal was at least nine hours before he was killed and it was some sort of Chinese takeaway – noodles, prawns, chicken, chilli – and taken with a lot of wine. Alcohol level high and I could be pushed into saying that he was forced to drink rather more wine than he wanted. No drugs. He had been tied up with strafing on the wrists and ankles. No mask or mouth covering, and the blow to the head was clearly from behind, probably when he was tied up, and he would not have been aware of the violence coming from behind. We can tidy up the front of his face for a photo ID but everything is quite ordinary, average height and weight, High Street store clothes, a few fillings, no shoes or socks so they had both been removed. No papers or wallet or mobile; all pockets empty. And organs normal for a man of his age.'

'Thanks, Hugh. Looks like we'll have to depend on missing persons and a good picture of his face. Will the skull fracture show?'

'Not at all. It's the one mistake they made: you will have a good photo of his face, I'll see to that. Sadly, the site you suspected for the dumping yielded no evidence. Whoever it was probably just reversed up to the quay edge, opened the rear doors, tipped him out and drove off. It's back to any CCTV for that.'

'Nothing covering the area at that time of night, but we are going through the neighbouring streets for vehicles and faces. Not much in the small hours.'

'Quite. Oh, there is one thing. The polythene was wrapped round the body many times. It was therefore a big sheet or taken from an even bigger sheet. Industrial size and industrial thickness; not from a standard DIY warehouse, so there may be a technical lead there.'

She left having got a promise that a good photo would be a matter of hours. She reported this to Robertson with Adrian sitting next to her.

'Adrian, what's the progress on the CCTV?'

'I've got pics of 97 vehicles, of which 43 have readable number plates, six pedestrians and a face or two on the night bus. I'll concentrate on the vehicles first as there is a hope we got them when they drove off.'

'Okay, follow those through; that leaves photo ID, missing persons, and I suppose a Press conference, Mavis.'

'Yes, and the industrial strength polythene. Will you be doing the Press conference, Sir?'

'Yes, of course, and I would like you alongside me, and Brandon too. We'll do that as soon as we've got a decent photo.'

They agreed that would be the next day at midday.

Seven

'Hi, Philip, how are you?'

'Missing you, of course. How is Bristol and the upper ranks of the police force down there?'

'Ho ho. I should be able to come up this weekend before this case mushrooms after the Press conference. Then it would be best if you came to Bristol the following weekend.'

'Got you. My, you are in masterful form. Yes, that's all good. I've got theatre tickets for Saturday evening, plus a kedgeree for breakfast. Experimented with it the other day; I hope you like it. We had a brown furniture sale last week; I kid you not the highest price paid was less than a decent bottle of wine; the buyers went away excited, the sellers didn't.'

'Okay, your job sounds safe enough. Listen, it's too far for me to travel Friday after work as I can't get away earlier like I used to. I'll leave crack of dawn Saturday and I'll have to leave Sunday evening for the same reason. Sorry, Philip.'

'I understand how it is; we are where we are. Let's enjoy the weekend and we can sort out me coming the next weekend; I can get off early. Where are you living?'

'I've taken a short rental but I think I'm going to try to buy a flat. I need somewhere that I can call my own. I'm about a mile from the centre and that's where I'm looking to buy.'

'Sounds like you're putting down roots. Perhaps we can look at a few places ...'

'Got to go now, Philip, take care.'

'Bye, see you soon.'

Mavis ended the call on her mobile. Philip's a sweet guy, she mused, but she wasn't sure where this specific relationship was going. They got on okay on the surface and the amorous side of their brief times together was good too. But – there was a "but", and she didn't know how to express it, even to herself. She wanted, and needed, to build her career and that took time and application. The physical distance between them meant that logistics kept creeping into their arrangements as the upcoming weekend showed. And she had to see her mum and dad more often now that she was nearer to them.

Her father had been a career civil servant and had served in many departments but mostly in those involving travel, which he loved. So, the Foreign Office, Trade, Overseas Development and even Defence had taken him all round the globe. He had met his future wife in the Caribbean and they had travelled together, with her picking up local work wherever he was assigned. Finally, he took early retirement and they found a bungalow in Devon and had lived there ever since. Mavis's sister had decided to stay on in the Caribbean and build her future and family there. They would each alternate travel to be either here or there.

Eight

Robertson wanted an update on the CCTV vehicles before the Press conference. Mavis and Adrian assembled in his office.

'You said 43 out of 97 had number plates. What have you found?'

'I've contacted 19 of the 43 by phone, and the standard response is that they were just driving home after a late evening. They assumed I was accusing them of drink driving or vehicle theft. None claimed to have seen anything around that particular quayside. I've noted the vehicle and the driver, plus any passengers, the time, and the chat. At the moment, it feels like I'm having to make a personal assessment as to whether they are being truthful, hiding something or sounding a bit shifty.'

'And the pedestrians?'

'Nothing. That'll be down to face recognition, local knowledge on the beat. Definitely something for the Press conference, Sir.'

'Mavis?'

'To get a breakthrough, we need people, at least someone, to come forward. It is their own town, sorry, city, after all and it's in everyone's interests. The Press conference can give a summary of the facts as far as we know them, but it's much more an appeal to the public to come forward. We have the photo of the victim, plus I think actually mentioning that we know at least six pedestrians were in the vicinity and asking them to please come forward would be a good idea, Sir.'

'I don't want to admit that we've got nothing.'

'No, agreed, but you could emphasize that anyone with absolutely anything that could help should come forward to assist our investigations.'

'Close to saying we haven't got anything. But, yes, I agree, putting the victim's face out there, plus the fact that we have extensive CCTV should get some response. Here's the photo Hugh has, er, sorry, mugged up. You'd never guess he'd been dead nearly 48 hours and been in the water. Looks more like an actual recent live photo.'

They both looked at a man in his fifties, a rather pinched face, brown hair flecked with grey and a few spiky bits sticking out, brown eyes, stubble just showing, skin slightly pock-marked.

'Not the prettiest boy in town but a great achievement. Will the Press ask where the photo comes from?'

'Quite. I'll have to handle that one.'

The Press conference was well-attended. Brandon, Robertson and Mavis were on the top table, and Brandon introduced Robertson as the SIO on the case. Robertson gave the bare facts clearly and concisely, including the suspected time and place of the dead body being dumped in the harbour. He made it clear that the victim was dead before being dumped.

He then outlined how the investigation was proceeding, including a mention of DS Smith, forensic analysis, CCTV, and other clues. Finally, a strong appeal to the public to help identify the victim and anyone who was in the wider area, on foot or in a vehicle, between 2 am and 5 am that morning to come forward to help the police with their enquiries.

The local and national Press were represented.

'Is it now safe to go boating in the harbour?'

'Is this connected to the other murder last week?'

'Is he one of the missing persons?'

'Why is there no CCTV of the incident?'

'What do you know about the victim?'

'Where did the picture of the victim come from?'

To each question, Robertson gave a downbeat official answer, and to the last question he said it was a professional artist's depiction of the victim's face. He finished by repeating his appeal and saying that the victim had a family and friends, and he would hope they would come forward with help from the Press and the public.

Brandon said there would be a further release as the investigation proceeded. They retired to Brandon's office.

'Well done. It's a start, not much, but at least a start, though as of now, we have nothing.'

'Yes, Sir, true. It's down to steady police work now, working through whatever we've got. Smith has a good track record of sleuthing, and I'm happy for her to lead the day-to-day work.'

'Thank you, Sir, I'll do my best.'

'You will, you will.'

Mavis returned to her desk. She knew she had got what she wanted so she had better get on with it.

Nine

Janet knocked on Clive's door and staggered in under the weight of two armfuls of files which she off-loaded onto Clive's desk, then brushed herself down.

'There you are, Mr Clive, that's all we've got on the honourable Sir Geoffrey Faulks.'

'Was he titled? I didn't know.'

'Of course not; he's a rogue, but the way Chief Inspector Bolton went on and on about him, he might as well have been. I hope you can close the case, and can I stress again that not only would Bolton be thrilled if you did but you should give him lots of the credit because it was his case.'

'You've already said that, and yes, of course I would. Thank you Janet, you are now my very own psychologist and adviser.'

Clive thumbed through the files: pages and pages of routine stuff and searches. He thought he would start at both ends, which would cover early days and the most recent of any clarifications along the way. This was not his normal logic but it would at least save having to plough through previous work in the middle of the many files.

Faulks was a dealer. Straight after leaving school, his first job at a betting shop had given him an insight into risk levels and human nature, and more importantly how to handle money coming in and money going out. Seeing a healthy profit on the 3.30 at Market Rasen, whatever the result, was a monetary paradise. From the betting shop, he had moved on to a second-hand shop with a business partner. They bought and sold literally anything with only two constraints – would it sell at a good price and would it sell quickly. A regimental jacket or a chest of drawers that didn't move was a waste of time and space; cut the price, call it a special offer, and move on. It seemed a natural development for someone like Faulks that he would move on to deal-making of any kind and anything that worked. This had led him into deals that were not to everyone's taste, as were his various colleagues. Shady deals with shady people.

Clive got the feel of the guy after a few hours file reading. Faulks had not broken the law otherwise Bolton would have been on to him immediately, but it was all too obvious that he sailed very close to the line between legal and illegal. He needed to find the man and meet him for a chat. He put in for a few searches which would take a few days to come back. He also clicked on to local police files and had a peek himself.

Ten

Philip welcomed Mavis back to his flat in Nottingham. She had driven up early Saturday morning and was more than ready for his coffee.

'Great to see you again; it's been ages and I've missed you. Coffee's ready and there's chocolate brownies.'

'On form, Philip, you know how to spoil me.' They kissed and hugged. He congratulated her again, and she expanded on what had happened.

'And I've actually been given my own case. Well, not quite – I have to report upstairs but he seems pretty laid back about it. Too laid back, I think, though I'm keeping that to myself.'

'Don't go imagining demons where there aren't any. He wants you to do a good job so he can take the credit.'

'Yeah, I'll buy that, thanks. Now, what's the day looking like?'

Philip outlined the day. Do the city centre, minimal shopping, lunch at a bistro on the river, perhaps a leisurely afternoon, and theatre in the evening. He thought that would give openings to some bedroom gymnastics later and maybe in the morning as well.

'It's a classic – *Hobson's Choice* – and the theatre company is good; I hope that's okay?'

'I think I've seen the film so, yes of course, thank you and a good choice.' She ruffled his hair affectionately. She said he could tell her all about his job and life as they walked into the city. They set out twenty minutes later, and Philip droned on about his job. He was shaping up to be a personable auctioneer; he liked to think his part of the regular auctions were at least as well attended as those of his bosses; in truth, he was stuck on brown goods which meant bookcases, wardrobes, sideboards, tables and the rest, which none of the others, his seniors, wanted to do. His gentle, likeable nature tended to mean he also got prices that they wouldn't ever get but he would like a change now and again. The other side of brown goods was house visits, and this he found fascinating. How people lived and the state they died in was an insight to humanity that only a few close friends and family knew about.

'Imagine, there's ... what, thirty million households in this country, and almost every one of them have brown goods, some old, some even antique, some new, some stylish, some utilitarian,' he said, "utilitarian" a word he often used for "rubbish".

'The thing about auctions is that you can sell anything, given a good audience, internet connections, and no stupid reserves.'

'Yes, Philip, I get all that. Let's move on. Have you met any new friends?' This was abrupt and rather direct so she softened her words with a smile and held on to his arm.

'Er, yes, I suppose so. There's the team at the office obviously, and we do have some evenings where we take life less seriously. I go to the leisure centre as you know and do badminton and some gym. There's my sister Christine and Tom – they have a few friends. Life ticks over, you know.'

Mavis thought that sounded steady and stable but not exactly exciting. It seemed little different from when she had previously worked up here in Nottingham – which had also included badminton with Christine and Tom. She wondered about the relative pace of their careers. Even though she was struggling to make a go of it, at least her career appeared to be going forward with fresh challenges all the time. She wanted to delve into Philip's make-up. She did not particularly like this side of herself which questioned whether the relationship was going anywhere. Was it time to call time and if so, when?

'It certainly does and always will, but we have to make things happen, don't we?'

'Yes, in theory. Here's the bistro by the way. Love this spot.'

It was pleasantly warm and the outside tables on the terrace gave on to the towpath and the river. Rowers were straining, passing the leisure boats which were clearly not straining. It brought back the Bristol case to Mavis that rivers and water hide ugly matters. Philip continued.

'Let's sit here and order. I work for a family firm and they reward talent, which I hope I have. A partnership or directorship is a very real prospect after putting in the work and building up trust and profit. I'm realistic about that. And I'm realistic enough to know that it's not going to happen this year or next, and that it's not automatic. Maybe it is unrealistic to assume that hard work and loyalty will be rewarded, but I work in an area where trust is built up and rewarded.'

'Ok, Philip, sorry if I sounded heavy. I know you are good at your job and you like it. There's nothing wrong with that.' They relaxed and chatted over some drinks, light pasta dishes and puddings to die for.

'Shall we go back to mine? We can put our feet up.'

Mavis consulted herself: it won't be just our feet, and I'm not ready for that in any case – maybe later.

'Come on, let's enjoy this sunshine! We've got theatre this evening so let's stretch our legs, not rest them.' She laughed and made light of the moment. 'I used to live here, remember, and not all that long ago actually. Let's take in the best of the city.'

Philip had to agree and felt he better switch into an energetic gear. They did do the city, found a street market, bought some silly things, enjoyed the street musicians playing violin, guitar and saxophone, and the voices that sang along. They strolled back to Philip's flat holding hands and feeling better about each other. Philip put on some lazy blues and jazz and they twirled round his flat, and slowly got changed for the evening. Philip came over to Mavis to help her change into her evening wear; she pushed him away as kindly as she could with a 'not now, Philip' and a kiss.

The air was warm and Philip suggested they walk up to the theatre and maybe go to a tapas bar when they felt ready for it.

They enjoyed the play, a classic, and Mavis recalled seeing the black-and-white film on TV with Charles Laughton and John Mills.

They dallied, one might say romantically, on the way back, chatting about the play, and stopped at a late night café bar for another drink so that by the time they climbed the stairs to Philip's flat, it was all they could do to undress each other and collapse into the big soft double bed and sleep.

Eleven

Adrian was struggling. He had decided that since there was nothing on this weekend, and Celia was off to see family in London, he would take work home and plough through the CCTV photos and number plates, and the six individuals plus two people on the bus. He just couldn't face it on Friday evening so he stocked up from the supermarket on the way home with the good intention of starting with a clear mind on Saturday morning. After a good night and then fresh coffee and croissants, he did.

A number plate yields the type of vehicle and the person who is the owner or keeper, not necessarily the driver. The owner/keeper person can be traced via police methods and one would hope to get a phone number. If not, one had recourse to the address which was more labour intensive. After a couple of hours, he had collected fifteen more phone numbers to go with the photos. These were in addition to the nineteen already phoned, though he had marked some of those queries as shifty, also to be followed up. He changed where he was sitting, made fresh coffee, and started phoning.

It was monotonous. First, someone had to answer the phone and be willing to talk. Usual diversions were shopping, kids, sports, music, ballet, pilates, whatever. But he thought that if he did happen to contact the real criminals, then they would talk so as not to look guilty without sounding shifty. He introduced himself, without at that stage making reference to the Press conference the other day, and then stating, for example, that a vehicle owned or kept by them had been noticed near Bristol Harbour at 3.30 am on that day; could they state the purpose of and reason for their journey?

The reasons given were a microcosm of the state of the nation and family life: I had to sober up after closing time and I knew I'd be okay by then; I was picking up the son/daughter from a late night party; it was my dad's 70th and we stayed on a bit; I was setting off early to get the ferry at Holyhead/Dover/Portsmouth; I'm a taxi driver, it's what I do; it's none of your business, is it – which probably meant an affair and they didn't want wife/husband/partner to know. If they were straightforward with no hesitations or sounding natural, that was okay with Adrian. He had to get at the very least a short list for DS Smith and Robertson. He chased up the ones who said it wasn't convenient or didn't answer first time. So, one way or another, he had covered 34 vehicles, leaving the rest for other methods and the eight faces to go to face recognition.

If, a big if, there were two of who'd lugged the body into the water, would they go back together or split up? The vehicle would have significant forensic traces so 'they' would have to get it well away to scrub it down or destroy it. Destroying it would still leave a frame even in a metal body crusher. Adrian's double hunch was two people: one of them drove the vehicle some way away and hid it in a shed; the other person followed in another car to pick their friend up at the shed and then they drove back together. He wondered how a request for CCTV from M5 north and south, M4 east and west between 2am and 6am would go down. Or maybe they garaged it close by and left it for months. Too many possibilities; we have to stick to what we've got until more evidence comes to light.

By Saturday late afternoon, he had produced a primary shortlist of five vehicles and a secondary shortlist of ten more. No more work this weekend; off now to see some mates at his friendly local pub Ales4Sale. He would summarize these fifteen cases to DS Mavis Smith on Monday morning, seeking guidance on how to proceed with the rest and the eight cases for face recognition. It was all too much.

Twelve

Peter and Barbara Vernon were starting to get an understanding of what retirement meant.

To Barbara, it meant Peter was always around; it was better when he was wrapped up with something in his study. She knew he had what he called "unfinished business", without knowing quite what that meant. If he had left work and retired with his pensions, what could possibly be unfinished? He did go out sometimes in the day, mumbling that he was off to see old so-and-so for a pub lunch, and he was getting to appreciate the advantages of playing casual golf once or twice a week at the club. The rest of the time he was moping around the house and garden during the day, before adopting the same type of evenings together that they had always spent when he got in from work – dinner, family chat, TV dramas, and the news. Apart from having Peter around some of the time, she did not want to change her life – her recreational golf, her walking group, her book club, her simple bridge evenings with a wide circle of friends that she had cultivated over the years of bringing up the family. Their two children, Nigel and Alison, had their own lives now with their own partners and families. She visited them often as did they her. Retirement also meant that Peter could now be more involved with the family.

To Peter, retirement meant simply not going to work and getting stuck into the challenges or routines of the day. He had his files, of course, and now that he didn't go into work he felt he could concentrate more fully on that old fraud case that he still felt had harmed his reputation at the bank. The rest of the time, he would hope to improve his golf, keep up with some old friends either with pub lunches, or exchange dinner evenings as a foursome. Barbara and he would also hopefully add in an extra holiday to fill the time – and enjoy it, of course. But that old fraud case was going to haunt him.

After a few weeks of trying to get used to the new domestic routine, Barbara formally announced at breakfast that clearing up his study was long overdue.

'What are you keeping all that stuff for? Can't it all go now? It's a nice room and we could try to make something more sociable and inviting for the grandchildren, like an extra lounge or bedroom, even a games room for them. What do you think, dear?'

'Well, that's fine in theory and there is of course logic to what you say. Please may I tackle it in stages? Some of it can go straight out, I totally agree, but there are one or two matters I have to resolve, for my own benefit and sanity. I promise I'll make a start this morning.'

Barbara was very pleased and surprised at this response. Peter returned to his study after breakfast and tried to take in the big picture. Yes, she was right; an awful lot could go immediately. 'Department away day trip to Brighton'; 'Accounting – the new regulations, Harrogate'; 'Banking acquisitions pros and cons, Edinburgh'; and 'Family holidays'. Many other similar files could all go straight off to recycling, and he piled them up in the hall. But there were a few other files, much more personal to him, some resolved most unresolved, and a few protracted cases including his old fraud case and anything remotely connected to it. He retained one filing cabinet in which he placed these files and other corresponding material. This would mean that he could show Barbara he had cleared some space, though he did remind her that it was still his study.

Thirteen

It was Monday morning and Adrian was proudly going through his weekend findings and phone calls with DS Smith. Mavis wanted to be receptive, but it was a sharp reminder that she had done nothing on the case since leaving the office late on Friday. She had driven back Sunday early evening after a lazy day with Philip, all rather close and personal, a traditional Sunday roast at a local pub, and finally a brisk walk along the river discussing their future, or more precisely their futures. That had not been as romantic as the rest of their time together. She would have to dwell more on this on her own during the week.

Adrian sought guidance on the fifteen vehicles and the six plus two for facial recognition. The latter was easier – send them round the usual outlets including the Press as people who'd been identified to come forward to help with enquiries. Mavis wanted to drill down to discover how Adrian had determined these fifteen vehicles.

'Of course, I respect your judgment call Adrian, but it has to be more than an inspired speculation.'

'It is, or I hope it is. After each phone call, I listened back to it to try to detect anything shifty or illogical, or anything slightly mysterious in their account from their tone. Did they sound guilty? These five plus ten are the premier division if you like. I could have brought along another nineteen and I've still got pics of 50 or more without any number plate legibility.'

'Ok, Adrian, I didn't mean to devalue your thinking, and that's a fair explanation. These fifteen plus the Press conference, plus these six plus two we're hoping will come forward might give us some clue as to what happened in the early hours. Failing which, we drill down more. So alongside these, keep at your list, at least an hour and a half a day. Now tell me more about these shifty ones.'

They took each in turn. Mavis began to understand him a bit more through his work and she could hear the awkwardness in some of the conversations. She came round to him.

'We need to interview all of these people, some here, others at their homes. Can you and Celia set them up over the next week? I'll interview with you, and it'll be a case of either elimination or suspicion.'

Mavis went into Robertson and gave him a sitrep. He asked how over sixty vehicles could be traced, because the statistical likelihood was that the perpetrators were among them.

'Possibly, Sir, early days. Let's see if we can get any leads from these fifteen first, which may yield some clues, then on to the next batch. Meanwhile, Adrian is working away at interpreting more.'

'Okay, but don't lose any of the data or lose sight of the probability of criminal action being with the larger number who've not been contacted.'

'Sir.'

She went back to her desk and read the Forensic report again. Polythene. She needed a walk and fresh air, and some decent coffee. She left the station and walked to the nearest sizeable building supplies trade counter. Bristol seemed so much nicer than Nottingham, wetter but nicer. She reached 'QuickBricks – You need it, we've got it!', and bought a coffee at the trailer parked outside. She went in and asked to see the manager, and was introduced to a Mrs Shirley Brindley. Shirley had been in the business for more years than she would want to admit but she had not lost her approachable manner.

'Hello, Officer, how can I help? What have I done wrong now?'

'Mavis Smith. Nothing that we know about, Mrs Brindley.' They smiled at each other.

'Shirley, please. Go ahead.'

Mavis showed her a specimen of the trade polythene taken from Forensics.

'Where would someone buy or get hold of at least 16 square metres of this?'

Shirley felt it, almost fondled it, and thought for a few moments.

'Since you're here, I'm guessing it's not been used to line an extension or greenhouse. For a trade sale, we would need to know the buyer. It's going to be us or the opposition on the other side of town, or any of our other stores, or theirs. There are of course independents but they are more likely to buy from us or the competition.'

'You need to join us with your sleuthing. What about farms? Could it have been taken from a farm?'

'No, this sample is not what they use on the fields or for baling. A patch as big as that cut from a field would be too conspicuous, methinks.'

'So, if I wanted to trace all sales of at least the size I mentioned in the last, say, two months, could you list them?'

'That's not retail and there's a minimum size for trade. Yes, Officer Mavis, we could and, though I don't rate them, I think the opposition could as well.'

'Good. I don't think my, er, clients would want more than a minimum order so that specifies the goods quite nicely. Be prepared for a request for all sales in the last two months prior to a week ago: date, time, any details as to buyer, etc. Do you have CCTV by any chance?'

'We do, sadly, because the trade does occasionally have to deal with some rough types; rougher than you, Officer Mavis.'

'Great. Please secure the last two months of tapes or files or whatever, if you can. Our request will have to go to all your outlets through HQ I suppose?'

'Yeah, that's right, but I'll do ours here because maybe your crime was local, shall we say?'

'Indeed. Many thanks.'

Mavis left, relieved that, out there, there really are people willing to help the police and that Shirley was just like her … well, nearly.

She walked back to the station, picking up lunch from Munch'n'Mange, and drove round to what Shirley called the opposition. The manager was not in Shirley's class but the outcome was about the same. Later she communicated with their two head offices and formalized the request for information on any sales of trade polythene in the preceding two months. Slowly, she felt some sort of triangulation was being set up. The big glaring gap was who the devil was the corpse?

Fourteen

Clive was not feeling good about life. He felt his job was drifting; not downwards, but not upwards either. Just floating along doing this and that. He was pleased Bolton had given him the Faulks case, to which he would keep returning and with some energy. Perhaps it was his social life. His usual group was Anna, the colleague who had introduced him to Amy, and her partner Ray. The four of them had formed a good social group for parties and drinking, and the inevitable badminton. Since the split with Amy, who had now disappeared to the other side of town, they didn't meet up so much for obvious reasons. He occasionally went to the leisure centre by himself, did some gym, and offered to play badminton if a partner was needed. This was drifting and he wasn't comfortable with it. He had thanked Janet from Records for her work on Faulks, and even went out for drink with her after work. But it was perfunctory; his self-diagnosis was crystal clear: he missed Mavis, not just the working colleague bit but the meeting of minds bit. However, she was taken; he needed to get over it and her, and move on. Faulks might lead somewhere, and he would try a bit harder with Anna and Ray's group. After an office coffee and chat with Anna, and not pushing himself forward, she had suggested he come along to their next group social.

'End of the week. We're joining forces with another group for a quiz night at the Forge & Foundry. Why don't you come along? Amy won't be there and you'd be most welcome.'

'Love to. How is Amy by the way?'

'She's fine; she's hooked up with someone just like her, and we hardly ever see her or them. You're history.'

'I'm okay with that and pleased for her; yes, I'd love to come and thanks for the invite. My speciality subjects are cars, cricket and composers, all at a superficial level. Sorry.'

They returned to proper work and by mid-afternoon this for Clive seemed to come to a natural end; yet it was far too early to slope off.

So, he decided to review the Faulks case afresh. He had been looking at files in reverse chronological order. Now he would review the searches he had asked for and then make a new start at the beginning to see how, where and when Faulks started to arouse Bolton's interest.

The searches were not helpful. No current address, nothing current from DVLA or DWP. However, these all confirmed a last known address in Portsmouth which was over five years ago and nothing since. Bolton had previously contacted Portsmouth Police, and there was a note in the file to say that they knew of him, couldn't pin anything on him, and he didn't respond to anything. He might as well have not existed. Clive knew from experience what was needed: nosey neighbours. Bolton was acceptable to two away days sleuthing. 'One day will count as holiday, mind,' and Clive was off.

He left early the following morning, stopped inevitably en route for coffee and a bacon sandwich, and was outside 19 Hardy Close by 9.30 am. He knocked on the door. It opened slightly, but the chain lock stayed on.

'Who is it, and what do you want at this time?'

'I'm really sorry to bother you. My name is Clive and I'm down from the West Midlands Police. I'm looking for a Mr Geoffrey Faulks who I believe used to live here.'

'Show me your ID.'

After a perceptively long pause, the door opened.

'You better come in.'

The cautious resident was a man in late middle-age, medium height, thinning mousy hair, not apparently in the best of health, wearing a cardigan and slippers, and clearly living on his own. He introduced himself as Robert Jenkins. 'But call me Bob as everyone does'.

'Thank you, er, Bob. What, if anything, do you know about Geoffrey Faulks?'

'Very little. Please sit down, I'll move these magazines. I bought this place off him just over five years ago now, after my divorce. It was somewhere I could just about afford and I settled down. He was tight on price, screwing an extra thousand out of me to make the deal, and then he wanted more for fixtures and fittings which the agents had said were included. It was all rather unsavoury; we met only once, and for me that was once too much. And I had to replace things after I'd moved in – not my favourite person, sorry.'

'That's quite okay. In fact, it fits in well with what little we know of him. Did he leave a forwarding address for you, or the agents or the postman?'

'Nope, nothing, and no post came for him after I moved in.'

'Did you live round here before buying this place?'

'No, I'm comparatively new to the South. I'm from Norwich and I'd lived there all my previous life.'

'Now, Bob, this is the crunch question. We think he lived here for a number of years.'

Bob nodded.

'And so he must have struck up with some of the neighbours round here, even in Hardy Close.'

'Let me think now … they would still have to live here now to be any use to you. There are two who I pass the time of day with and who are kind enough to comment that I'm better than Geoffrey. They might know something. He's at number six and she's at number eleven. She might be more useful because I think they went out for the odd meal together – odd meaning occasional, not the food.'

'Here's my card, Bob. If you think of or remember anything, and I mean *anything*, to do with Geoffrey Faulks, please do get in touch.'

They parted with a handshake and a smile. Clive thought Bob had welcomed the company. He strode down to number eleven and rang the bell. The door opened to reveal a well-dressed lady of uncertain years and an appearance that strongly suggested a forthright manner.

'Good morning. Mrs Palmer, I believe? I'm Clive Drewett from West Midlands Police. This is purely a research visit and I'm sorry to have disturbed you.' Clive realized that he was talking in a deferential manner to match her bearing. Scary.

'Well, you'd better come in.' She led him into a neat and tidy drawing room with the possibility of a sea view in winter. 'Coffee? I'm making some anyway.'

'Many thanks, straight black, please.' Clive wondered if Bob had phoned ahead but decided definitely not. The room had some family pictures, but there was no indication of anyone else living here.

'How can I help?'

'It's about anything you know or can remember about a Mr Geoffrey Faulks, a former resident of number nineteen. Mr Jenkins there was kind enough to mention that his time there coincided with yours here at that time.'

'Well, I suppose Robert was doing his civic duty. Yes, I do remember Geoffrey. Who wouldn't? He had a certain style that was almost charming. He took me out to dinner once and then said he'd left his cards and money in another jacket, so could I pay? Two weeks later, he posted an envelope with cash through the door for half the bill. Yes, he was a rogue, no question.'

She brought the coffee in with two chocolate biscuits.

'What else do you recall?'

'Hardly any visitors; would go away for days at a time; did nothing to the house. I feel sorry for Robert in that respect. He was outwardly charming but utterly unlikeable if that makes sense.'

'It does. Now, do you have any idea of where he went when he left? We're trying to trace him.'

'It has to be London. He was always going up there on the train or by car.'

'He could have been going anywhere. Why do you say London?'

'Well, he told me all his business was in London. The so-called clients and colleagues were London-based and his place down here was just a bolt-hole to escape to.'

Clive left his card with the same request as he had told Bob. He went away thinking less of Geoffrey, but knowing that he was still not really any further forward. He walked over to number six and tapped on the door.

'Yes, coming! Who is it?'

'Mr Standen, I believe? I'm Clive from the West Midlands Constabulary, making a routine enquiry – not about you, I hasten to add.'

Mr Standen opened the door. Clive looked at the fit, youngish man, probably mid-thirties, with a cheerful manner, light brown hair, jeans and T-shirt with the slogan, 'I am therefore I think'.

'Please, Clive, come in. I'm Mike and it's tea and scones mid-morning, about five hours too early. How can I help?'

'Well, thank you, Mike. It's about your former neighbour at number 19 – a Mr Geoffrey Faulks. Mr Jenkins there did say that you were here when he was there, if you follow me. Do you know anything about him or his whereabouts?'

'I do actually, though that may surprise you.'

'It does, but do go on, please.'

'We share an interest in darts. We met in a pub years ago. We were both skilled, pretty accurate, but he was always in it for the money. He could do the maths in a trice. "Double twenty and a seventeen, or a treble nineteen if you're up for it!" he'd shout straight off. His betting know-how was useful. As well as beating opponents, I think he confused them as well, which upset their game.'

'So, you were a couple of hustlers, then?'

'That's a bit strong. It was mild and a bit of fun at first. Then he wanted to do more of what you're suggesting. I bowed out and told him he needed a better partner. We met at the same pubs now and again, and we would have a few games. By then he always beat me and I would get him another pint. Our contact became more casual and occasional.'

'OK, I get the gist. The key questions for now are: where is he, where does he live and what is he up to?'

'In truth, I don't know. What I do know is the names of his favourite haunts, and I think I've still got the photo of him and me winning the All-Comers Cup way back before we were banned.'

'Photo would be great, please. But why were you banned?'

'We weren't giving the locals a chance. The Rules Committee came up with the cunning plan that you could win the trophy only once. Help yourself to another scone. I'll have a hunt around upstairs.'

Clive recognized some small progress. Photos could be matched; surely someone at these old haunts would know something about

Faulks? Some ten minutes later, Mike came downstairs with a photo and a Press cutting from a local paper with the heading "The Dynamic Duo Do It Again". Clive read the date of the cutting and saw that it was consistent with Mike's apparent age.

'That headline was out in the local Press before the Rules Committee had been got at and before they came up with Rule 22 (b). Geoff wasn't too bothered. It proved we'd won it twice and he actually handed the cup back – a year later! Ha ha!'

'You've been excellent, and thanks for the scones. Do please get in touch with literally anything you can think of. And I want the names of those pubs and clubs.'

Clive gave him his card, pausing to look at the cutting again.

'Plus the names of anyone you recognize cheering or booing you two.'

Mike sat at the table and carefully wrote a few things down after some thinking time.

'There you are, Mr Clive. I hope that helps. Your card is safely on the mantelpiece. Good luck.'

Clive thanked him and left with a spring in his step. He returned to his car and made a call on his mobile.

'Hi Neil, it's Clive. You're not doing anything this evening, are you? How about we go to a couple of pubs round your way and renew our acquaintance with the dartboard?'

Fifteen

Peter Vernon found that retiring to his study following a limited chat over breakfast was therapeutic. Getting some files out and revisiting unresolved problems from his days in the city gave him something to think about as he took a fresh look at those old problems. *You never know what might turn up*, he thought. This morning he would dig out Corinthian Catering Ltd, which became insolvent some years ago. He had underlined all the directors' names and had assembled brief profiles of each of them. His internal report to the bank, which had lost money, was condemning of the bank's lack of monitoring its debt and the cavalier behaviour of some of the client's directors as they went to extreme lengths to get new catering contracts with big companies. The expense claims at various restaurants and clubs with the same date suggested high living and low life. Towards the end, the contracts they got were for minor single events, and the income did not even cover direct costs. One of the directors' names was Geoffrey Faulks, which Peter had cross-referenced to the insolvency of another company: Winning Wines Ltd. There were directors in common with Corinthian Catering, and indeed invoices to and from each other. His handwritten cutting comment was: *They don't know their business and we don't know ours.* The bank lost heavily on both. The directors disappeared but he had wanted to find this Geoffrey person as being one of those responsible for the two downfalls.

Barbara bustled in with some coffee and remarked that it had been a long time since she was "one of the office girls", keeping things in order. The way she said "girls" made her recall those early days when it was always "men and girls", never "women", perhaps, even worse, "female staff". The passing years and the social changes, coupled with her natural grace and maturity, had increasingly meant she was now referred to as a "lady" or Mrs Vernon. Peter was always methodical but he did have his moments, particularly if he got a wasp in his trilby, one of his phrases that she had come to love.

Peter smiled and thanked her, and then picked up the phone to discuss his cases with one of his contacts.

Sixteen

Adrian had lined up the fifteen of what he liked to call the premier division for DS Smith, and glided up to her desk.

'The nine nearest are coming in today and tomorrow; the other six I said we would call in at our convenience. There's Bath, Avonmouth and nearby villages. Is that okay, Miss?'

'I think you can call me Mavis at work, Adrian. Thank you for that, let's see how we go.'

They interviewed the five for today together. The first two were hopeless. One thought they were being helpful, but was actually over-forthcoming, the other thought they were being treated as a suspect, which led to curt and vague responses. For the rest, Mavis therefore decided that they would just treat them normally, as members of the general public from whom they were seeking any information that would help with their enquiries. This proved to create a better dialogue and resulted in more information. The last couple that day were Fred and Betty who gave an outpouring of helpful information.

'We have a photo of your car proceeding at 3.45 that morning. Please tell us about your journey.'

'Well, it was one of those nights, or should I say mornings. We're usually sound asleep of course but the phone went at midnight and it was our Julie saying she thought she might be starting. Well, Fred said we must get over there and so we went straightaway. She was fine – it was just a false alarm. We didn't want to or need to stop the night, so we drove back and slept in till eleven. Then Fred said a fry-up was called for, which he's good at, so I suppose you could call it a late breakfast while we chatted about out nocturnal adventure.'

'Thank you for that. I hope Julie continues to be okay. Now, when you were driving back around 3.30, did you see any other vehicles or people, or anything at all odd?'

'Betty's given the reason we were on the road. It was very late, or early if you like, and we were tired. It was mainly deserted but I think I followed a car between the traffic lights and beyond for a bit of a stretch, and there were a few lads hanging around outside the pub along there.'

Adrian consulted his laptop to see if there were two vehicles together.

'Would it be this one, Sir? We have a photo of it just ahead of yours at about the same time.'

Fred and Betty looked closely at the 4x4 hatchback with a driver and no passengers.

'I know where that is by that shop in the background. It's between the traffic lights. Could be, Officer, could be; but I couldn't swear to it.'

'Anything suspicious about it?'

'Tricky. Driver could tell we weren't the police so I did think he could've got a move on at that time of night. No overtaking places, really.'

There was a little more and then they left.

'Well spotted, Adrian. What is that car in front?'

'Sod's law; it's one of the ones where we can't read the number plate.'

'It would be, just like Robertson said. Tell you what, send the film through for advanced enhancement. It's just possible it might show something more interesting.'

The four the next day produced similar discussions. They decided to wait to see the others until the photo enhancement came back.

'Aren't we banking too much on this one?'

'Probably, but it's all we've got at the moment. We've still got ID of victim, Fred and Betty's observations, the polythene, the high-rise city centre buildings which I shall explore, and all the other vehicles. What do I do next, Adrian?'

'Celia said pray for a breakthrough.'

'Celia's right. You two getting along?'

'Please, Miss.'

Mavis contemplated that evening how she and Philip were getting along. The tree with branches growing from friend to good friend, to boyfriend, to partner, to commitment, with alternative branches at each stage back to "just friends" or dumper/dumpee, was not at all clear with Philip. Clearly he was very much more than a good friend to her and she knew that he would think of her as his steady girlfriend. Neither of them was seeing anyone else but the consequence of that would be a slow drift further along the branch path as above. If you're not sure of the destination, are you entitled to enjoy, or even endure, the journey? "We are where we are" is at least factual, and anyway, one's days could end abruptly tomorrow – so does that condone the journey with no destination? Tricky, or just too over-thought? If she peered into the future, she could imagine Philip as a middle ranking auctioneer, specializing in some aspect of the sale room, herself as a middle ranking detective, well-respected, with either two or no children. Men can drift, but women have to balance life, career, children, partner. The twenties and fifties plus don't look too stressful, but in one's thirties and maybe early forties, the balance of those four pulls seem to matter greatly and, in her view, unfairly. Her mother was just a broken record on this subject. Fred and Betty were clearly very happy with life and each other. She knew that she didn't like drifting; everything had to be for some purpose, even men. She remembered Clive; they got on well, but allowing for some pluses he was unambitious, happy with his lot, and a bit too serious. He would be happy with someone like that Amy he had moaned about. And he would have been happy with her …

She drifted off to sleep. In the morning, it was straight back to work, taking life as it came.

Seventeen

Neil Poole was an old mate of Clive's going back years. He had helped Clive out on at least two other previous cases. He operated over north and central London so he was always a useful contact for Clive whenever he happened to be in town. He had never connected Clive with darts so there had to be a real or better reason to meet up. Clive had suggested the TAle & TWine at 8 pm in north London, and at 7.55 Neil nonchalantly sauntered into the pub, prepared for darts and score keeping. Clive was ahead of him and thrust a pint of TAle's Special into one hand, firmly shook the other, and motioned them both over to a corner seat. The pub was half full and, indeed, there was action at the dartboard in an alcove.

They had caught up with each other in five minutes, after which Clive effectively gave Neil a debriefing on Faulks and everything Mike Standen had supplied, including the photo and the Press cutting.

'I didn't think I'd be here playing darts after a day of arrests, burnt out cars and deportations.'

'Me neither. Things happen, Neil.'

'How do you want to play this? No pun intended.'

'I suggest we look interested in playing darts and see if anyone wants to join in, or they leave us alone to play. Either works. Are you any good?'

'Er, no, but I've an eye for accuracy.'

'That'll do; let's go.'

There were two couples playing each other 501 down and they were over half way, the difficult half they heard one of them say. Neil and Clive chatted, made approving comments, tact personified. When their game was over, the two young women in the couples said they had had enough and suggested the four boys play. After some fake manners, it was resolved that Neil and Clive would be on opposite sides. They chatted while they played two games, and then Clive offered to get the four of them another pint and whatever the girls were having. While he was at the bar, Neil thought it best to protect Clive's position and make the going on Faulks.

'We play locally up in the Midlands, and one of the gang produced this photo and cutting from a friend. We think it's here, so we thought why not call in as we were down here. Mean anything to you guys?'

The two of them and their girlfriends studied them very closely, quite fascinated. It took a little time for a response.

'Yes, it's definitely here and it's before the bar was redecorated. I'd say well over five years ago. Yes, there is a cup but there's not so much interest these days so it tends to be when someone's got a special birthday so as to get the drinks in. Why are you bothered?' The taller of the two was direct.

'We think we know this guy and there was a bit of unfinished business up our way. I'd rather not say more. What about these other faces?'

'We're too young; you need Wilf. He's over there, no need to hurry he'll be here all night.'

Neil softened the tone, and they chatted sociably for a while longer, then thanked them and made their way over to Wilf. Clive thought they should just concentrate on face recognition; at this stage of the evening, Wilf was unlikely to be as adversarial as the others. Wilf was well into retirement with thinning grey hair, a welcoming smile, and a brushed cotton check shirt over an old pair of maroon cords. Everybody seemed to know him.

'You must be Wilf, kind sir. Ready for another? Someone told us you know everyone around here.'

'That's uncommonly decent of you gents. If you say so, yes please.'

Neil went to the bar this time, and Clive plunged straight in.

'Here we are. What do these old pictures remind you of? Better times or not?'

Wilf took out some old reading glasses and studied the pictures carefully.

'Oh yes, that was before my dear Susan went to Heaven. Happy times; I still think of her here every time I raise a glass; so sad. But here, these are old photos – what you doing with them?'

'They were in a friend's scrapbook and we knew they were taken here, so we thought some of you guys would remember the cup and the players.'

'Yes, well, that's Geoff winning with a mate. Could be Mike, but I think he came along later.'

'And the other guys? And the lady of course?'

'That's Mandy. Oh my word, we had some times with her!'

Clive thought they better move on swiftly.

'And these gents here – any still around?'

'Oh yes, that's me there, and George looking serious; that's George over there by the fire; feels the cold now.'

'How would we get in touch with Geoff, Wilf?' Neil took the plunge.

'He had a house in Portsmouth, a flat here, and then he disappeared. Folks said Wales as he needed to get away but I dunno. George! Over here if you please.'

George took his time; he had been explaining the offside rule to one of the young women; they were pleased he was called away. George could have been Wilf's older brother, but smarter.

'Now George, look at these photos … that's you looking very spry, I might say. These gents here who got me a pint …' Neil took the hint and went over to the bar for two more, '… were asking where Geoff might be these days. You were closer to him than me. Well?'

George took two slurps and studied the photos closely.

'Wilf, you're not wrong, that's you and me and that is Geoffrey. Did a bunk to Wales where his sister lived. They both followed rugby and she went to all the games there; so, my guess would be Cardiff.'

'Is it a guess or do you have a clue? We'd really like to catch up with him,' Clive said.

'You two coppers or something?'

'Now, now, George. The mate who gave us these photos said he'd got some new darts for Geoff as a present for a special birthday, I think. Said he'd treat us if we could find him.'

'Sounds a bit suspicious to me. No, it's just a vague memory of him saying we go to the big matches and we get the bus back after a few drinkies. Got to be Cardiff, hasn't it?'

Clive and Neil took their leave and headed for a curry house. They checked they were not being followed.

'Maybe not go there again until we've some authority; your version of the truth is flexible.'

'Sorry, but there was no way we could be identified as police. And you were just as bad.'

'I work round here.'

They discussed what they had. Mike Standen's account stood up. The bunking off to Cardiff explained leaving London and moving out of Portsmouth. Clive would do searches on Faulks in Cardiff, either Faulks or née Faulks for the sister.

'Why are we doing this?' Neil asked.

'It's a cold case of my boss's – alleged fraud and skulduggery, case not closed.'

'And how is Mavis? I know you want to talk.'

'Moved to Bristol with a promo to DS and has a boyfriend back in Nottingham.'

'Last I knew you were going up to see her in Nottingham and have an evening out at the theatre.'

'Yes, we were; it was to celebrate some case we'd been involved in. It never happened, something got in the way, and that was that. I congratulated her on her DS and she sent a sweet reply.'

'Meaning, I want to see you again?'

'I don't think so, Professor Poole. She's in a good place and I would be in the way.'

'Clive, you're plain stupid and that's telling you. I've seen you two together, don't forget. You're made for each other. Go for it! All's fair in L-A-W.'

'L-A-W?'

'Love and war.'

'Thank you, Neil. Any chance I can crash at yours tonight? Else I'm taking a risk finding somewhere to bed down.'

'Yes, provided you make a positive effort with Mavis; you can't just let her go.'

'Yes, Neil.'

They had late night whiskies with more philosophising about life. Clive got up early, left a note, drove back to the Midlands and started the search for Faulks's sister in Cardiff.

Eighteen

Peter Vernon returned to his files on Corinthian Catering and Winning Wines. Sadly, he had been dwelling on them while doing other things and was wondering how to dig out something new. He felt he knew that Geoffrey Faulks was a common factor and he had an additional file called GF, which was of a more personal nature.

Peter's internal notes made entertaining reading: *GF at any meeting would be the sanest, most plausible vendor of common sense and good advice, but out of sight cannot be trusted. If he said he would do something, he didn't. If he agreed to an amount or a date or a course of action, none would happen. He could turn trust into rust, advice into vice, correct into wrecked. I could go on. The fool simply cannot be trusted to deal with anything involving a company, an agreement, money, any third party without turning it solely to his own personal advantage.*

On top of that, unsurprisingly, I don't even like the man.

He read on. The proceedings of winding up CC and WW did divulge some action taken with the police involvement of an Inspector Bolton in the West Midlands. He had kept the phone number so he phoned it. When he mentioned the name Geoffrey Faulks, he was told that a named officer, Clive Drewett, was dealing with it and he was put through straightaway.

'Drewett speaking. How can I help?'

'Good morning, Officer. My name is Peter Vernon. Although I'm recently retired, I've been going through some of my work files and been reminded of a certain Geoffrey Faulks with your station's number, so I rang. Sorry to be a nuisance.'

'Not at all. It's what we call a cold case, so any new info is priceless. What have you got?'

He gave a description of the files on the two companies and also the personal one on Geoffrey Faulks.

'I'd like copies of the lot, please. If you could possibly go into your nearest police station, they will digitize the lot and send them to me. I'll give you a reference number which will help oil the wheels. If I need more, that is if there is more, I'll get back to you.'

They exchanged numbers and rang off. From what that Clive Drewett had said, clearly something was going on and it might come to something. Peter suggested a cabernet sauvignon to Barbara, to go with dinner that evening.

Nineteen

Adrian appeared at Mavis's desk.

'Is it convenient?'

'Of course it is, my hard worker. What have you got?'

'Ta. We've got an enhanced image of the car that Fred and Betty were following. We know the car make and we've got some of the reg, so I'm getting a search on that. Fred did say it could have gone a bit faster, so maybe they didn't want to draw attention to themselves;

in fact, the steadiness of the speed has had the opposite effect.'

'Okay, come back on that one. And another?'

'One going in the opposite direction; a hatchback ideal for the dump, but I was fobbed off with "just driving home", and not too pleasant with it.'

'When you've got more on that first car, we'll go and see the driver, and we'll visit the unpleasant owner. Please find where home is.'

Mavis's phone rang, and she accepted the call.

'Officer Mavis, it's Shirley about the polythene. We've got three buyers in that time period. All three were private purchasers, not builders, so I'll send their details to you. Bye.' Mavis smiled at her style; you had to like her.

'Right, Adrian, we can now start cross-checking cars, drivers and polythene. Isn't life exciting?'

'Why is there nothing from the public about the man? Surely somebody should be missing him.'

'There are a lot of single lonely people out there; but you're not one of them, are you Adrian?'

'We're going to an Italian this evening.'

Mavis winked at him and indicated she had to move on. After he left, she phoned the other building supplies warehouse but they had nothing to report. Robertson was out so she went out for a stroll to find the high-rise block overlooking the harbour dumping site. After two tries, she located Brunel Mansions, a high-rise block of apartments where the upper floors would have the right view. She took a lift up to the top floor and rang the doorbell of the flat that would have a direct view of the harbour. No response, so she went to the flat directly below on the next floor and knocked on the door. A boy – or young man – answered; he was exactly what an ageing journalist would describe as a "spotty youth".

'Yeah?'

'Hello, I'm Mavis Smith from the local police; don't worry, I'm purely fact-finding. I think you have a good view of the harbour. May I come in?'

'It's a bit of a mess. I'm Darren.'

'I'm here for the view, not to do your cleaning. Nice to meet you, Darren.'

He let her in, and she marvelled at the panoramic vista in front of her. Yes, if anyone were to be looking at the right time, they would see everything that happened.

'See that bit of road that backs on to the harbour? We think two people dumped a body in the harbour from there a week ago, between two and five in the morning. I was wondering whether any of you night owls up here might by chance have been gazing out at the night view?'

Darren came to life; he wasn't being picked up for his light-fingered approach to shopping.

'Yeah, right, the top three floors have the same view. Him upstairs is weird, and I sometimes think he's a peeper for the ladies undressing. Yep, definitely a hopeful. Sorry, I may look like a night owl but I'm either out at a mate's or solid gone here. Mum and Dad ditto – they go to bed after News at Ten. Downstairs, she's a bit wacky, you know, men coming at all hours, so maybe she would be looking at the ceiling rather than out of the window.'

Mavis had to smile at his humour but tried not to let it show.

'Darren, you've the makings of a detective with your observations. I could use you. What's the name of him upstairs?'

'We had some of his post once, I think it's a Jeremy Hyde, with some letters after. Could you – please, Miss – could I come on patrol with you?'

'Absolutely not; but I do sometimes want some footwork so give me your mobile number and keep me posted on the goings on upstairs and downstairs, and we'll have to see. Have you got a job?'

'I help out at the Media Centre. It sounds good but I'm just the go-for.'

'Good luck with that, and try learning on the job from the others. People are always interested in themselves and what they do. I'll see myself out. Thanks for your help.'

She went upstairs but there was no response again; she went

downstairs and passed a middle-aged man ringing the doorbell. Mavis took the lift down and walked back to the station.

Shirley's email about the polythene buyers had come through; she passed the details to Adrian, requesting that he triangulated people/cars/polythene. Data was starting to come through but not really any breakthroughs. She googled Jeremy Hyde and the lad was quite right – he had letters after his name and had had a distinguished career across Whitehall and industry. His penthouse flat had clearly come about through his connections with the construction industry. She put in a call to him and left a message that she wanted to liaise about "the recent murder in the harbour and his direct sightline with that part of the harbour". Sure enough, twenty minutes later he returned her call.

'Good afternoon, Smith. Hyde here. How can I help?' His voice was authoritative and patrician. Mavis gave a brief outline of the circumstances of the body floating in the harbour and asked if he had observed anything from his vantage point.

'Well, you are correct on one point. Yes, I do have a direct view of the harbour and I am in the habit of looking out over the city when I have a call of nature in the night, but on that particular night, early morning even, I have no recollection of murky misdeeds. But I may be able to help you in a surprising way.'

'Please go on, Sir.'

'My nephew loves playing around with my telescope, purely for astronomical and other viewings of course, and what he captures is connected to some sort of recording device which he then looks at the following morning. I'm not saying he happened to record that particular early morning in question, but you never know he might have done. Can I get back to you on that?'

'Thank you; I think we will have to borrow the device, as you call it, so that we can absolutely capture the morning in question or, sadly, rule it out as *not* covering that morning. I would like to send a colleague round now if that is possible, Sir.'

Mavis thought she might as well be direct and immediate to avoid protracted discussions with this pompous individual. Jeremy Hyde for once was caught off-guard and stumped for coming up with a reason for not complying. His honours were forcing him to do the right thing.

'Er, yes, of course, Officer. I'm in for the rest of the afternoon though I'm dining out with an investment group this evening. Please get him or her over sharpish. Thank you, good bye.'

Mavis called over to Adrian.

'Adrian, uniform on, top flat, Brunel Mansions. Jeremy Hyde's got a recording device, get all he's got, be polite and call him "Sir". I want to see you gone in five minutes.'

'Yes, Mavis. I've got a date this evening at the Italian, so I've got to be quick. Bye.'

Twenty

Peter Vernon was true to his word. The next morning, he telephoned the local police station and explained Drewett's request. He was able to quote the names of DS Drewett and Chief Inspector Bolton of West Midlands Constabulary, and eventually these seemed to register. He gathered all his notes together and put them in a buff folder. "Local" police station actually meant a twenty-five mile drive, so he decided to make it a shopping trip as well.

He was expected on arrival, and Janice showed him into a meeting room where he laid out the material. Janice said the copying would take a little while so it might be better if he came back in an hour. That suited Peter just fine and he went off to find a newspaper and a decent coffee place.

When he returned, Janice said it had all gone through to DS Drewett and that he had already acknowledged receipt with thanks. Peter took the buff folder with the notes inside and headed home. He was pleased he'd made what might be some progress; indeed, he had done his civic duty, and immensely looked forward to hearing any outcome.

*

Clive was equally delighted to receive Peter's files seeing as they came from a former bank insider. It was an advance from Bolton's efforts, and he hoped his dual attack from both the darts info and the bank info would lead somewhere. He finished his ordinary day's work and got stuck into Vernon's notes. Faulks's disappearance to Cardiff, or somewhere else in Wales, followed his failures at Corinthian Catering and Winning Wines. The bank and their solicitors' attempts to track down Faulks had also failed.

The search on Faulks's name in the Cardiff area did not reveal any Geoffreys, but there were three ladies of about the right age with the maiden name of Faulks. He went into Bolton's office at the end of the day.

'Sir, there's progress on Faulks. A retired bank auditor has contacted us – Faulks is mentioned copiously in his notes, including police interest, namely a certain Bolton in the West Midlands. Also, and separately, together with a London colleague of mine, I've tracked down his interest in pub darts and his winnings.'

'That's good, Drewett, well done. I knew you could build on my previous findings. What now?'

'A man in the darts pub thought he bunked off to Wales to his sister's; my guess is to hide. I've traced three ladies née Faulks in Cardiff – permission to go tomorrow, Sir? I'm up to date with routine stuff.'

'Okay, lad, we have spare hands here and I'd like you to conclude my case. Off you go.'

Clive winced inside at the phrase "my case" in recognition of the politics. He told Janet he'd be off to Cardiff tomorrow, with mobile on.

'You've put a smile on Bolton's face for sure; have a good day.'

*

His routine for day trips was to set off early, breakfast at a greasy spoon, and arrive at the start of business hours. He did just that and was knocking on the door of Mrs Brenda Noakes (née Faulks) at 9.45 am. No answer. Neither did Miss Kathleen Faulks at 10.45. At 11.45, he approached No.15 Gareth Lane. Mrs Megan Morgan answered the door and, after his introduction, said that he had better come in. Mrs Morgan was a quietly spoken lady of late middle-age, and dressed demurely.

'This is purely investigative, Mrs Morgan, but we are attempting to locate a Mr Geoffrey Faulks, believed to be in the Cardiff area. My searches have taken me to a few other houses where there are Faulks living. In your case, it's your maiden name I believe.'

'You are quite right, Officer, in everything you say. Geoffrey is my younger brother.'

'I'm very glad to hear it and to have the opportunity to catch up with him.'

'Geoffrey came down from London to live with me a few years ago. He was on his own, never really had much luck finding a nice wife. He said he was in trouble and needed to lie low for a while. I naturally asked him what sort of trouble, and he said he hadn't broken the law but that he was on the wrong side of company disputes in two or more insolvencies. I asked him if he was in debt or being chased for debt, and he assured me it was all down to the companies' failings. He was quite depressed about it all but, Officer, let me say I am open to the idea that he had brought some but not all of it on himself. Dear Geoffrey had always had an adventurous side to his make-up.'

Megan was starting to get tearful and Clive knew that there was more to come.

'Can I get you a glass of water or something, Mrs Morgan?' She nodded and when Clive returned from the kitchen, she continued.

'Geoffrey did lie low round here in the Cardiff suburbs. He went for walks, he went to the pub to chat and play darts. He was a very good darts player, you know. Then one day, a foul, wet and windy day, I received a knock on the door and learned that Geoffrey had had an unfortunate accident. I was beside myself. He'd been walking up in the hills and slipped and fell down a cliff edge onto the stony beach below. Bones were broken so he had been taken to A&E at the big hospital here. The report said he could have died but there were no suspicious circumstances. The path was slippery – one tiny false step and over he went, apparently. Because of his state of mind, I found this totally credible. It was a terrible period of my life, having lost my dear Richard only two years before and then this, my happy-go-lucky brother. There's only the two of us left in the family now. Sorry, Officer, I'm getting upset and I don't mean to be. The choir, the bridge and a women's group here have all been wonderful, and

I've thrown myself into all of them to try to move on; but moments like this bring it all back. I'm sorry. But that's not all, Officer.'

Clive did not feel too good about himself at this particular moment but he realized this was a step forward. First, he would comfort Megan and see what more she had to say. Gently he said,

'When you're ready, Mrs Morgan, please continue.'

She composed herself and took a few sips of water.

'When I said that's not all, I meant it. After leaving hospital, he convalesced here and because we spent days together chatting, doing crosswords, watching TV, we got as close as we had at any time in our lives. Then he disappeared.'

'I'm sorry, what do you mean?'

'He had got most of his health and strength back, even to the extent of more walks with the help of a stick and going to the pub. Then he went off, leaving a note. I've got it here.' She opened a drawer in a sideboard and took out a white envelope with "Megan" written on it. Inside was a notelet which Mrs Morgan gave to Clive to read:

My dearest, dearest Megan,

I'm so sorry but I have to go as I can't stay here. It's not you or your house or your hospitality and care in taking me in. It's my business and I have to go. I'll let you know when we can catch up with each other.

With fondest love, Geoff x

'How long ago was this? What did he take? What did he leave?' Clive found this all rather strange.

'It was about two years ago, and from what I could work out from his room, he took a hold-all with most of his clothes and papers. There were no papers left behind. You could say that he took his whole identity with him. He took his mobile, but it is permanently switched off. I never looked at his papers, so I don't know what he had. What was left here were things that weren't worth taking. I reported this to the police and all that seemed to happen was that he was added to the list of missing persons. I have not heard anything since, nor have the police.'

'Mrs Morgan, please know that I do not wish in any way to distress you. I'm sorry I had to ask these questions and of course you are in no way involved in our investigations. Can I call a neighbour or make a cup of tea?'

'You're too kind, Officer, but I'm fine. It's choir tonight and I'll get myself ready for that and all will be fine. In the space of just two years, I lost Richard and apparently Geoffrey. The memories remain of course but the feelings at the time subside. Please, just let yourself out. I wish you well in your job, whatever you have to do.'

Clive sympathized, left a card and went back to his car to make a few calls before heading off to the local station a few miles away. He wondered whether Bolton had known Geoffrey had disappeared.

He was greeted warmly by a Welsh policeman. 'We don't get many English coming down this way – you're from Birmingham, then?' Clive did not engage with this and got straight to the point.

'A few years ago, maybe three or four years, a Geoffrey Faulks had an accidental fall over the cliffs. He was hospitalized, convalesced and then disappeared. His sister says she reported him as a missing person. Please may I have a look at the files?'

'Well now, you'll be needing our Nerys over there, she won't be a minute.'

Nerys was efficient, and within twenty minutes Clive had the file and a mug of tea. He was surprised how thin the file was. He jotted down the relevant facts, date of the accident and Geoffrey's disappearance. The accident was recorded as due to "a walking mishap", nothing suspicious noted, and a subsequent reporting of a missing person. Routine enquiries were put out, there were no active bank accounts, and the case remained as a missing person. Clive was left with the overwhelming impression of a man at the end of his tether, gone to ground first in Cardiff and then elsewhere, leaving no evidence of his tracks. The only suspicion in Clive's mind was that all this was at variance with his apparent gung-ho lifestyle back in London. He wondered what Faulks was wearing and what the weather conditions were like on the day that he fell: the file recorded him as lightly dressed for a summer walk, suitable for the prevailing fair conditions.

Bristol was nearer than W-town, so he put a call into Bristol to see if Mavis was around.

Twenty-One

Adrian was at his desk, playing around with the recording device he had collected from Jeremy Hyde the previous evening. Mr Hyde had been officious with Adrian, treating him loftily in his patrician manner. He demanded a receipt of the equipment taken which Adrian wrote out on some office stationery. Hyde wanted it returned at the first available opportunity, "for my nephew, of course". Adrian said that they would rush it through.

It was not obvious what to do with the device until Celia came up to him, smiling with a mouthed "thank you for last night". She put the end of one of the wires into a socket at the back of a desk top, clicked on a few dialogue boxes, and there in front of them was a view of Bristol Harbour. Adrian said they needed the date and time.

'Patience is a virtue. Look at the bottom left-hand corner: it's got date and time in a backwards format.'

'Okay, smarty pants, scroll backwards to 02:00 early that morning, if he's got it.'

It was awkward and slow but she did find the date and slowly crept forward in time, starting at midnight. The nephew must be something of a night owl as the recording was not just set up and left to run; true, Bristol Harbour was the main theme, but it was interspersed with American football, some porn, a repeat of the World Cup final, until … there it was, at 3.48 am: a blurred 4x4 or hatchback reversing up to the edge of the harbour wall. Two get out and heave an elongated package from the back of the car into the water. One of them gets back into the car and steams off; the other quickly disappears into the shadows. There did not appear to be anyone else involved or even hanging around at the time.

'Gotcha!' shouted Adrian then screamed, 'Mavis!' at the top of his voice. She hustled over and asked what was going on.

'Wait till you see this.' Celia scrolled back and replayed the viewing from 3.48 am. Mavis peered closely at the screen until both the criminals and the car had departed; she paused for thought.

'We've done well on this, that's including you, Celia. It puts Fred and Betty in the picture as key witnesses. So, now, Adrian or Celia, I want the highest possible enhanced image of that total scene from our local experts, plus multiple copies. I'll deal with Hyde, and have words with this nephew fellow. When you've got a timing for when the enhanced image will be with us, get Fred and Betty to come in for a private viewing. I better see Robertson. Well done both.'

Mavis scuttled off to Robertson's office.

'Convenient, Sir?'

'For you, always,' he said with cheeky smile. Mavis recounted the Hyde visit, the Hyde nephew, his recording, scene retrieval of dumping, and its cross reference with Fred and Betty.

'We can be certain that the body was dumped at 3.48 am that morning.'

'Sounds good, but don't get ahead of yourself. Cross-check that the clock time on the recording matches the clock time on that wall; secondly, there could be multiple dumps that morning, eh?'

'Time check will be done. Yes, of course, there's only been one body found in the harbour, so unless it's lead weights or rocks they're chucking in, it seems a fair bet it's the body. The enhanced image should give a better indication of the size and how the two miscreants handled it, similarly its weight.'

'I agree. Why has no one come forward yet? Missing persons?'

'Don't know, Sir, but we are increasingly homing in on the perpetrators. Next step will be triangulation with the polythene purchase.'

'Okay, I think we need another Press announcement with what little new info we've got so far. The longer he's left unidentified, the more likely it is that this is an out-of-area job; always a can of worms in my experience.'

'Sir. I'll get on with Hyde now; please let me know when you're having the Press conference. Can I assume it'll be the same set-up as before?'

'You can, Smith, but with more info this time.'

Mavis left his office and checked with Adrian that the recording enhancement was underway.

'It is, Mavis, it is. Celia took it off my hands and was on the phone faster than you could spell her name.'

'That's delegation, Adrian. Well done, keep me posted, we're making progress. I'm off to see your friend Hyde.'

Mavis decided to walk round to Brunel Mansions as it was late lunch time and she wanted some fresh air and time to think. Robertson had a point about out-of-area. What if nobody came forward? All we've got is the body of a man. We need to get his face on the national TV news. She picked up a carton at a juice bar and sat on a street bench to drink it. Darren plonked himself next to her.

'Hello, Miss, out on patrol? Can I come?'

'Nice to see you too; no, you can't, but I am on my over to Brunel Mansions to see Mr Hyde and his nephew.'

'Pity – another time maybe. They're not in. The nephew, he's Charlie by the way, works at the media centre near me. I can take you there if you like. It's only a couple of minutes down the road there.'

'That's decent of you, Darren. Okay, yes, I accept. I will have to have a private chat with Charlie. He's not under investigation, just some info needed. And you're not to big yourself up, or me, for that matter. Just let me deal with him.'

They set off. Darren used a card to gain entry to the media centre and asked reception to let the police, i.e. Mavis, in. Mavis showed her ID and asked for a private meeting room, and for Mr C Hyde to be shown there.

Charlie Hyde was a Darren replica, though the description of "spotty youth" would be unkind. Jeremy Hyde had seen to it that his younger brother's son was a well brought up kid.

'Do come in, Mr Hyde. May I call you Charlie? Darren has told me about you. You are mates?'

'Yes, we are, but I haven't done anything wrong, I promise.'

'I know that; in fact, you've done everything right and I wanted to thank you.'

'Oh, thanks.'

'Your Uncle Jeremy told us that you do recordings of the view over Bristol Harbour and he lent us your device to investigate some murky goings-on on one particular night. We've viewed them and they are proving to be immensely helpful. We will have to keep the device for a few more days yet. I'm sorry about that, but can I check a couple of details with you?'

'Okay, I'm sorry about the porn, it sort of just happened.'

'No worries; I had a good laugh over it as well. No, what I need to know is how do you set the date and time? You'll understand that police work has to be precise.'

'Got you. I reset the date and time every Sunday morning for the week. The most difference I've ever seen is a couple of minutes, like a clock or watch that runs a bit slow or fast.'

'Exactly; and can you confirm that you did precisely that these last few Sunday mornings?'

'I can, Miss. Uncle Jeremy likes to do a fry-up on Sundays. He calls it a full English. He does it for him and his friend, and while I'm waiting, I reset the recorder.'

'That's all then. Many thanks. We may need you to make a statement as evidence in due course. We'll let you know. Tell your uncle that he and you have been very helpful, and we'll return the recorder in a few days.'

Charlie slipped out and she noticed he went straight over to Darren.

She was walking back to the station when her mobile pinged.

'Hello, Mavis, it's Clive here.'

Twenty-Two

'Clive, what a surprise. What are you up to these days?'

'A cold case led me to Cardiff, and I thought Bristol was nearer than the West Midlands so …'

'True. So?'

'I know it's cheeky and short notice, but I wondered if we could meet up and I could crash out on a sofa or something?'

'That's assertive of you, young man. Let me think. First, am I available given my hectic social programme? Answer: yes. Second, I have a blow-up mattress and a blanket which together would fit in the hallway. Third, the fridge is empty so it might have to mean a visit to the Italian down the road. Fourth, would I like to see you? Answer: yes. Does that meet your requirements, DS Drewett?'

'It does, DS Smith. Time and place?' Mavis gave him some details and rang off.

Mavis reflected on the last time they had worked together – she in Nottingham, he in the West Midlands, with some interaction in the Peak District and Oxford; a strange case of dubious burglaries, valuable stamps, and an exotic couple from London and two brothers who had been keeping apart. They always got on well, different ways of thinking, but always in tune with each other. Yes, her instincts had been right; she would very much like to meet him this evening. She must call Philip.

Mavis strolled back to the office and filled Adrian in on the Charlie meeting, telling him that the timings were correct.

'We're getting enhanced images in two days' time,' he responded. 'And Robertson has called a Press conference for later that day. I've put it on your schedule.'

'That's fine. I hope something comes back on the polythene. In order for the public to get involved, we've got to give the lead to get them involved with some meaty evidence and some sort of story to go with it. Robertson's right – why has nobody recognized his face or reported a missing person? It's uncanny. Anyway, I'm off now as I've got an appointment this evening.'

'Is he nice?'

'Not as charming as you, Adrian. Bye.'

She walked back to her flat and phoned Philip on the way. It went to voicemail and she left a simple message: *Tried phoning you, am out this evening, catch up tomorrow, not sure about this weekend.* She thought she didn't sound very loving but to change it now it had been said would look ridiculous; better to make it up to him tomorrow. She also decided to dress down for Luigi's, the Italian where she was meeting

Clive.

Dress down meant cut-off trousers, flat shoes, T-shirt and a light jacket, reasonable colour coordination and minimal accessories. She twirled in front of the mirror in her bedroom and mouthed, 'just right'.

Clive was already there when she arrived and sitting at a side table.

'Mavis, promotion seems to suit you, you look great.'

They touched cheeks tangentially, and Mavis responded.

'Not bad yourself – that is for someone just coming off duty out of area.'

Clive ordered drinks, a bottle of beer for him and sparkling water for her, and started off.

'Well, what are you working on? You've got some autonomy now, not some geezer like me breathing down your neck!'

'Clive, stop it, you were never like that, not in my memory. Yes, I have, actually; I've been given my own case and have to report upstairs every now and again. And it's a murder. We never did one, did we?'

'Nope. Good for you. Can I give any pointers? No – silly question; you never needed any input from me. I think we both always had separate insights and then merged them to go forward.'

'I'm fine actually. Body dumped in the harbour; no missing persons; no recognition, so at the mo we're have to go on supporting logistics and forensics. Even industrial strength polythene, Clive.' She smiled with this, and he took in the humour.

'I've been given a cold case which I think this trip to Cardiff has brought to an abrupt end. He disappeared after falling off a cliff during a coastal walk while not in the best of spirits. Broken bones, convalesced, then disappeared.'

'Never believe those myself; bet you he was pushed. Cliff-top footpaths don't go near the edge and there's always something to grab hold of. You heard it from me first.'

'Well, like every suggestion I've had from you, I'll give it consideration, of course I will.' And he meant it. 'So, how's the other world? Your young man, Philip, the auctioneer, isn't it?'

'You know it is. We're fine. Never sure about distance relationships, but we'll have to see. And your good self – Amy?'

'Well remembered, but no. It felt like gentle me meeting desperate her, so it had to end. Not one for me. Let's order, I'm famished.'

Clive ordered big, Mavis ordered light, and she continued his thinking for him.

'It's good you brought it to an end if it wasn't right for you, but do you know what *is* right for you? Would you recognize what was right?'

'Doubt it; in fact, I'm happy burying myself in work so …'

'So that something might happen without having to make any effort to make it happen, you mean. Do you want a partner or not? Sorry, that's a bit blunt, but it's meant to be helpful.'

'I know it is, and you're not wrong. I do dwell on this subject from time to time, but my inner thoughts seem to be wildly at variance with my external life.'

'I get it, I really do, having worked with you, but perhaps try to be a little more outgoing and express your thoughts socially without sounding self-centred or me-me-me. You're not like that anyway. I'm not into therapy, absolutely no way, but sometimes giving is reciprocated in receiving, and a response would be at your level.'

'Wise words, Aunty, and thank you. I do hear you, by the way, and I didn't cross the Bristol Channel to sound like Clive from W-town on the personal problem page of the local paper. Here comes the food; is that enough for you? I can order an extra side if you want.'

'It's fine, just fine, and you're not a problem, you're a regular guy who's stuck. Join the millions!'

They ordered a glass of wine each, chatted about past cases, and even shared a tiramisu. Clive settled up, and they strolled back to her flat while it was still just light.

Mavis had already put the blow-up, a blanket and a pillow in a corner. She pointed to them.

'There's your bed. Good luck. I'm turning in, got a busy day tomorrow.'

'Thanks, Mavis. If you don't mind, I'll just get up and go early.

You know my weakness for a greasy spoon breakfast along the way; I'll say good night, goodbye and many thanks.'

Mavis blew him a kiss, touched his arm, gestured a wave and mouthed, "see you".

*

Clive woke early. By 5 am he was up. He quietly folded up the bedding and shut the front door without a sound. An hour later, he was in front of a full English on the M5 and still wondering whether or not Mavis was out of his league.

Twenty-Three

Peter Vernon found that in retirement he had plenty to do that he hadn't done before – in particular, keeping the garden ship-shape in the summer which had always been something that Barbara did. It was therapeutic working together in the garden, and it gave him time to ruminate on the two subjects which had pre-occupied his working life, both of which filled the files in his study. Officer Drewett had been grateful for the Faulks papers, which rather spurred him on to do more. He didn't share these activities with either Nigel or Alison, or even Barbara, as he felt they would either tell him what to do or, more likely, what not to do; or they would muscle in and take over. He didn't want or need either; it was now his paperwork hobby.

Today he would revisit a bulging box file called 'Audit Committee'. In fact, there were several box files called 'Audit Committee' spanning the whole of his time with the bank. Endless minutes of meetings with nothing ever appearing to get done, papers submitted invariably on the 'New Accounting Regulations' but also on racy subjects like 'Relationship with External Auditors' and 'Depreciation – Rates & Replacement', which could sound almost exotic in other circumstances. He soon found that he was back on familiar territory: references to Mr Geoffrey Faulks in a different context from before. Faulks had asked for a short-term loan of a sizeable amount 'pending his receipt of a much larger sum out of which he would repay the loan'. The Committee was not impressed but questioned what security he could put up, knowing full well that the value of any shares he might put up would be worthless. To their surprise, he offered a charge on a house in Cardiff. It was his sister's, previously their parents', and was unencumbered. There was a valuation and the bank found itself in a position that was difficult to decline. A loan was made and, following the documentation through, to the surprise of the Committee was actually repaid. Late, of course, but it was repaid with accrued interest to the date of repayment. He put these papers to one side as of possible interest to Officer Drewett.

Next was a note from himself, submitting a request to the bank for payment of a private detective's bill 'for services rendered'. These services were not itemized and the Committee declined to authorize on the grounds that it was personal and not part of the bank's conduct of business. He had withdrawn his request and requested that it was not minuted, but the request and refusal remained baldly stated. Peter recalled this event all too easily and had hand-written a note to himself at his annoyance of both its being declined and for submitting it in the first place. He dwelt on the background and wanted to keep his thoughts to himself. He could hardly re-approach this private dick now he was retired, but maybe Drewett could and extract something instead of him; after all, Drewett could use his official position to grind Faulks down.

Twenty-Four

Mavis also found herself reflecting on the surprise visit by Clive and their evening together. He seemed genuinely pleased to see her, even keen, but perhaps that was because he had dispensed with the demanding Amy. Mavis invented a personal rule on the spot: never make demands or agree to demands. She could see consequences good and bad arising from this, but there would always be a get-out clause. It was very pleasant to meet up with Clive again. She thought he was easy to rub along with.

She must phone Philip …

*

Back at her desk the following morning, some new information had come through.

The enhanced image of the 4x4 dumping the body in the harbour revealed the make of the vehicle, a degree of its shade (given it was a black-and-white image), and four of the letters and numbers of the registration plate. Adrian said straight out that Celia was on to it like a hungry hyena, adding that he didn't want that expression repeated.

The polythene report showed three purchases of the size, type and date range specified; two in Swindon and one in Bristol. Mavis asked Adrian to follow up these three and get more background, including CCTV on the dates of purchase.

Mavis knocked on Robertson's door.

'Is it convenient, Sir?'

'Always for you, Smith. What have you got?'

She outlined progress on the body being dumped, the timing, the vehicle, with further corroboration to be gleaned from Fred and Betty.

'What I'm hoping for, Sir, is to be able to triangulate the few possibilities of each strand of evidence to home in on the target, if that's not mangling my English.'

'Got you, Mavis, yes, I do understand. But still no one has come forward who is missing the deceased. Surely by now someone somewhere must be missing or noticing his non-appearance?'

'I don't get it either, Sir. Please stress this at the Press briefing maybe? A wider circulation?'

'Let's fix it for tomorrow mid-morning. I'll see Brandon now and you see what more you can get from the evidence. I'll want you to present the main thrust of where we are.'

'Thank you, Sir.' She left his office and called Adrian over.

'We need Fred and Betty to look at the images from the Hyde recording. Are they nearby? Can you ask them to drop in this afternoon or evening?'

'On it.' Adrian was back in a few moments. 'They are shopping here at the moment and can be with us in half an hour.'

'"That's good. Robertson's calling a Press briefing tomorrow morning and he wants me to present where we are.'

'You'll be fine, Miss. I'll get the video set up so we can go straight to it.'

*

True to their words, Fred and Betty arrived, somewhat loaded with shopping.'

'You're lucky to have caught us in town; the baby came early, and Julie is in a whirl about everything. We said we'd do all the shopping so she could concentrate on the baby. It's her first so everything is new to her, but thankfully she's feeding well and sleeping well which takes the pressure off.'

'We're so glad to hear your good news. Let's get you both a cup of tea so you can look at some images we've got for you.'

Mavis did a semaphore over the office floor to mean two teas and then showed them into a side room where Adrian had fixed up the recording device.

'Now, we can run this through as many times as you like, but watch carefully. The time is 3.48 in the morning. We also have the images from the CCTV that you looked at last time for comparison.'

Fred and Betty watched the recording through three times, looked at the stills from before, and then leant back.

'Do you think that is the vehicle you followed?' Mavis asked. 'Please be as straight as you can – *yes* or *no* or *uncertain*; there's no point in misleading either yourselves or us.'

Fred and Betty looked at each other, and Betty nodded to Fred to continue.

'I can't guarantee it of course but I'm virtually certain it is. It's the same make and shade, and from what I can make out, the readable bits of the reg plate seem to click with me. The CCTV is 3.55 which, given that time of day, is virtually confirmation in itself.'

Celia appeared with tea and ginger nuts.

'Thank you both. I agree with your logic and that will give us renewed confidence to home in on that vehicle. Thank you.'

They chatted a while longer with more baby talk before they were shown out.

'Adrian, Celia, I think this means full steam ahead on fully identifying the 4x4. There can only be a few missing combinations that match the type of vehicle.'

'I'm on it, Miss. I think I know which one it is already,' Celia said.

'Then we can now follow it through to address and owner details. Perhaps you can get the ball rolling on that, Celia?'

Twenty-Five

The Press briefing did not go well. The journalists present saw all too quickly that nothing much had happened. They recognized the progress on the 4x4 but with no details disclosed, it wasn't much of a story. Mavis said that they would have more shortly. She did a workman-like job in presenting without much excitement until Robertson pitched in.

'Look, we police this country by consent and, despite our occasional lapses, policing is a two-way street. I'm being straight now – we do not know who the deceased is, so please help us. We have issued details to every police station in the country; he's on our files as an unknown. I ask you sincerely to show the photo of this man and his description in your papers and on your broadcasts because that will help further progress, and I promise we will keep you informed along the way.'

There were murmurings in the audience and a question from the back.

'Have you got the best team on the job? I can see that it seems to be a woman of colour plus a couple of juniors. Surely you've got some better staff to sort this one out?'

'Stay right there - my staff are right now getting your name and that of your paper. You will never be invited to another Press briefing or reception of any kind here while I'm around. Disgraceful – uniform, please remove him immediately.'

The murmurings got louder; Brandon stood up and concluded the briefing. He beckoned to Robertson and Mavis to come to his office.

'Well said, Alec, sorry it had to come to that. The Press will now report on that interjection more than the substance of the case, I'm afraid.'

'Sirs, I'm so embarrassed. If you think I should stand down, I will, of course, straightaway. SIO Robertson and Adrian can continue, and I'll go low profile.'

'Mavis, that'll do now. I do the promotions and demotions round here and you will stay in post. However, perhaps the real message is the absence of progress in this case. So, DS Smith, if you want a message, it's this. Redouble your efforts and get a result. That is how to silence that idiot out there. Alec?'

'Totally agree, Sir. I have confidence in DS Smith and I want that to continue. Getting a result on the case is the best way of getting a result on attitudes like that. I trust I didn't misfire in my response.'

Both Brandon and Mavis warmly agreed not, the latter gratefully, and nodded that it had had to be said.

Back at her desk, Mavis called Adrian and Celia over.

'You've no doubt heard the kerfuffle and I'm sorry you're in the slipstream. The message from Brandon and Robertson is quite clear: redouble our efforts and get a result. Now, what have you been able to get on this 4x4?'

'The shade, the make, the letters and numbers we've got coincide solely with one vehicle – it's this one. It is owned by a rental company based in Birmingham. They claim it was returned on time and in good condition. The renter insisted on paying in cash and, as my further enquiries have shown, he gave a false name and address and mobile number. I think that proves it was the car.'

'Well done, Celia. I want Forensics all over that car for the slightest speck of anything.'

''Tis done; they are on their way now. But any number of people could have used that car, even since.'

'Maybe, but they would not have disturbed the blood and DNA of our unknown body. Get the number of miles driven, too.'

Celia left and Mavis asked Adrian for any ideas he'd got.

'It's normally a case of someone reporting a missing person and they turn up a few days later, or they go missing for twenty years.

Here, we've got a body but no name or anyone claiming him. Can we do photo-fit on all driving licences or passports? Teeth have got us nowhere. I wondered about making the artist's depiction of the photo of the guy look younger so someone could recognize him from the past. The fact that no one has come forward rather suggests that he has been living alone or is a recluse. He's just about young enough to have a parent or parents alive, and they might recognize a younger John Doe.'

'I like it very much, Adrian, good one. The younger version could be used for the driving licence scan. Good thinking. You and Celia go out for supper on me, please, but keep quiet about it. I need rescuing on this one, and you've both been excellent.'

'Thanks, Miss, will do. Friday evening. Mum's the word.'

Mavis thought she must be getting soft or old or both. She phoned the artist photographer who did the original piece of work on the newly named John Doe. She also phone Clive.

Twenty-Six

Clive had given further thought to Mavis's comment that Faulks would likely not have slipped on the coastal path. It was true that the weather conditions were fair and the path dry, which was inconsistent with what his sister had been told. If it wasn't an accident, that left an unfortunate and barely credible outcome that he was pushed, i.e. attempted murder. It was a few years ago now and there was no way of getting any more evidence unless Faulks could be found. Faulks was merely an isolated case; no money involved, and one of the easiest cases to file away as a missing person. That left any trail from Vernon's files, and the follow-up on Corinthian Catering and Winning Wines. He was re-reading Peter's notes, looking for any further suspicions Peter had, when Janet brought over the post from Vernon.

'More on Faulks from Vernon.'

'More is good, and thanks. Would you send him our acknowledgement and thanks? I'll sign it.'

Clive delved straight in to the two items that Peter had sent. Why would Faulks go to the bank where he was regarded as suspicious, and was the private detective in any way connected to it? He had a professional regard for Peter's thinking; he did everything for a reason.

Clive phoned the private detective – Benny – at his Know Secrets agency, and after introductions, got down to it.

'My reason for calling is a request made many years ago now by a Peter Vernon, a bank official. He approached you in a private capacity, but it is clear to us that it was in connection with the bank's business. He thought the bank would pay your bill but they refused, much to his annoyance. I'm asking what he asked of you and what was the outcome?'

'One thing I do have is a good old-fashioned filing system. Let me get to the Vs in the bottom drawer.'

There were background noises of filing cabinet drawers going in and out.

'Yes, got it; not many Vs. Yes, you're right, it is a few years ago now. Mr Vernon wanted to know more about why a Mr Geoffrey Faulks was about to receive a large payment and where it would come from. The bank had a charge on some property for his loan, but Vernon was clearly suspicious of anything to do with Faulks. So, an incoming large sum was also deemed suspicious.'

'That accords with our understanding. And?'

'It was cash, and the only name I got out of it was Norton. I remember the case now; I followed Faulks each day because I had been told the payment was short-term and imminent. I never thought it was going to be a cheque through the post or a bank transfer. Faulks met someone in a south London park, had a sociable but brief cup of coffee, and the other guy handed over a brown envelope. They shook hands and left. I followed said guy who went in a zig zag path to the local shops where he bought a few things. Then I lost him. My notes from that time show I went to two of the shops and asked about him, and one of the assistants claimed he was a regular and known as a Mr Villiers. My searches on Villiers came to nothing.'

'Description?'

'My notes say ordinary, medium height, brown hair, inconspicuous bearing and clothing. I fed this back to Vernon who was disappointed I hadn't got more. He clearly thought the payment was suspicious and hardly seemed to be for services rendered or goods provided.'

'Thanks, Benny; good to talk. I may get back to you.'

Clive scratched his head and had a moment. It's got to be blackmail. It fits with Faulks; just the sort of thing he would resort to given a chance. But if it were blackmail, it does rather strengthen the argument for attempted murder on a Welsh cliff, which would have been much later and about five years ago. This is where Mavis and I always did so well together.

His mobile rang. It was Mavis.

'Why, hello, I was just thinking of you. Had one of my leaps of judgment and need you to put some perspective on it.'

'Glad I have my uses, Clive. Share?'

'Sorry, not yet. How can I help?'

'My murder case looks like the body was dumped from a 4x4 rental from Brum. Our Forensics are pouring over it. Could I be cheeky and ask you to go and poke your nose in as a friendly cooperative copper? You can say you know me.'

'I hope so. Yep, can do if it's fairly local – then I can justify the trip. It'll cost you.'

'I know you, Drewett, you'll want blood. Well, you'll have to wait,'

'I'm patient.'

'I know and thanks a lot.' She gave the location and rang off.

Clive thought that life had suddenly got a whole lot more interesting.

Twenty-Seven

Mavis was more than pleased with Adrian's suggestions of a younger face for recognition. She liked the concept and the thinking behind it. The artist/photographer had done a really good job of making the photo younger. Mavis had said five to ten years younger, and the artist had made a creditable attempt. In fact, she produced three versions, and Mavis, Adrian and Celia marvelled at her work. Each of the attempts had tackled a different part of the face as well as the general age shift. One had a trimmed beard, the others clean shaven. Celia was dispatched to attempt a photo-fit with DVLA, and Adrian to do the revised circular to the Press and all police stations as a potential missing person.

Next, the two people in the 4x4. Fred and Betty were convinced there was only one driver and no passenger. The Hyde video was definite – one drove off, the other sloped off round the corner. Why split up? The car was a rental so perhaps they had brought their own car and left it nearby within walking distance. They would need time to clean the rental of any evidence and the mileage from Birmingham would help determine distance. It was not discernible whether they were two men or two women or one of each; but it made sense they were the perpetrators because the bundle was fairly obviously a body, and not a suitable package to contract out.

Forensics, and maybe Clive, would be back in a day or two; ditto the photo-fit result. For these, and for the general public, DS Smith would have to wait and she was more hopeful this time of something turning up.

Twenty-Eight

Clive had convinced himself that Faulks was blackmailing somebody. Proving it was going to be difficult. Faulks had ended up penniless and depressed in Wales, and then disappeared. He knocked on CI Bolton's door and went in.

'Sir, Faulks update.'

'Excellent, what've you got?'

Clive gave a complete debrief, including his thoughts that perhaps Faulks was a blackmailer and may have been pushed over a cliff edge to shut him up.

'Plausible but speculative, Drewett. Just check whether there was anything that came out of the closing down of Corinthian and the Wine one. It sounds like he wriggled out of those and buried himself in Wales. Glad we rounded off the case and thank you for your part. But I reckon it's time to close the file now and move on. We'll know if he turns up somewhere.'

'Would you object to my doing a little more on the blackmailing – er – in my own time, Sir?'

'Own time, fine; let me know if anything crawls out of the woodwork.'

Clive hand-wrote a message on Janet's thank you note to Peter Vernon to say that if anything else popped up out of his notes, to let him know; what he had done was invaluable.

He went along to the forensic examination of the 4x4 as instructed by Mavis. The person in charge was studying the rental schedule around the time of the dumping.

'Hello, I'm Clive Drewett from West Midlands. In all honesty, I've been asked to nose around by DS Smith who's running this case.'

'Hugh Cranston.' They shook hands. 'Young Mavis wanted you involved, did she? Good woman, if persistent.'

'I've worked with her before; I know what you're going through. She did actually brief me on the case and as I was nearby, she asked me to drop by. I won't interfere but mind if I take a look?'

'You've already contradicted yourself. No problem, but don't disturb my people. I did the forensics where the car off-loaded the body in Bristol. He was dead before he went in the water and had been carefully wrapped up in polythene beforehand; there were some stones added but not enough to keep a body sunk. I would say it was amateurishly done, not by experienced criminals.'

'How long was the rental for?'

'Five days. Two before and two after. It's looking like they steam cleaned everything, but we'll find something; we always do.'

'And the rented mileage?'

'Two hundred and twenty-three. That's enough for there and back, and a little local extra to get the car hidden and cleaned.'

Clive went over to the vehicle. With the rear seating down, there was ample room to store and cover a body that would not be observable from outside. It also did not smell right. He mentioned to one of the forensic staff that perhaps they should record the cleansing materials used to clean up the car. The woman nodded and carried on. He went back to Hugh Cranston.

'Please would you mind checking the air nozzles on the tyres and the top to the windscreen water container for prints and DNA? They've been so careful with everything that they might have wanted to be careful that the journey itself didn't let them down, so they might have topped up the air in the tyres or filled up windscreen wash.'

'Not bad, Drewett; she taught you well that Smith. Yes, of course we will and as I say, not bad. You two – er –?'

'In my dreams, Hugh, in my dreams.'

'Aye.'

He made his exit and drove back to the station.

He thought he had taught Mavis all she knew.

Twenty-Nine

A few days later, it all kicked in at Bristol Police HQ first thing.

The DVLA found six possible face matches.

Fifteen people responded to the Press campaign and said they recognized the man in the photograph.

Five people responded to the missing persons files in police stations up and down the country.

Mavis gave the six face matches to Celia to check out as she had done all the running with the DVLA.

Adrian took the Press campaign fifteen; Mavis took the five from police stations; they arranged to meet for updates later at four o'clock.

Mavis had it easy as three out of her five claimed the photo was of themselves and they had been reunited with their families recently but had forgotten to report it to the police. The other two were genuine and she phoned both stations. One said it was her missing father but the age profile didn't work allowing for the ageing. The other one was a woman with a missing brother. Mavis asked her to send in any photos she had of her brother and his last known whereabouts. This was a possible.

At four o'clock, Adrian and Celia marched in, both grinning from ear to ear.

'Okay, looks good, which of you goes first?'

Celia plunged forward.

'Let me get the ball rolling. First up, great idea, Adi, for pre-ageing the pics. The DVLA were soooo cooperative and they sort of entered into the spirit of the thing. These six are the very best of what could have been two hundred near misses. They look serious contenders, and obvs we've got all the info that's on their driving licence cards. Ages and addresses. Please may I follow them up, Miss?'

'Most certainly, and it's Mavis in the office, by the way; work with Adrian for the line to take as we don't want to lose the real one. Adrian?'

'My fifteen were a mixed bunch. Two were females, strangely, and three were well outside the age range. For the ten remaining, I've got or am getting phone numbers so will do more in-depth interviews now; in fact, I've already started them.'

'For both of you, and me, I am thinking some of the key questions or facts are: (a) why hadn't he been missed before and why did no one come forward? (b) lifestyle; this man was captured and beaten and killed before being dumped; how might he have got involved in all that? and (c) what was his money situation? Finally, apart from all that, don't cause unnecessary distress because all but one of these folks are probably alive somewhere. Right, let's reconvene once we have contacted these seventeen.'

They left. Mavis recognized herself five years younger in them – hard working, fun-seeking, no worries. She didn't have many worries even now, she reminded herself, yet she was a DS. Must phone Philip. She looked at her incoming papers and Shirley's three polythene buyers stared up at her. All three were cash purchases in Bristol. The CCTV pictures attached showed two males and one female, each dressed for DIY work and each on their own. Sadly, no faces but it was possible to gauge height against the surrounds. She phoned Shirley.

'Shirley, hi, it's Mavis from the police station. Thanks for the polythene purchases info and the CCTV images; could I ask you for the height of the check-out structure? Just want to gauge height of the folk against it.'

'Give me two seconds.' Slight pause and she returned, stating the height in mm.

'Thanks, really helpful, bye,' but Shirley was already gone. Mavis thought that if you needed help in any situation, Shirley was the one.

She phoned Philip.

'Hi Phil, been inundated, sorry not to have been in touch. How's things?'

'Hi stranger. Me too; suddenly got a lot of house clearances. When can we meet up?'

'Would you mind coming down here? I'm full on Monday to Friday, and some of the weekend. I'm not sure yet. Saturday morning to Sunday evening would work well for both of us I reckon.'

'I know and that's okay, we rarely work weekends, and Friday drifts to a halt after lunchtime. Shall I come down this Friday?'

'Great, yes. Stop at a service station just north of Bristol and give me a ring then we can fine-tune your arrival and whether we meet in town or at mine. See you then, looking forward to it.'

Philip sent a kiss down the phone to finish the call. Mavis sighed and went over to Adrian for him to compare heights from the polythene purchase with the dumping of the body and the CCTV car images with Fred and Betty. Geometry was more exact than life.

Thirty

'Mavis, it's Clive.'

'Hi, get back okay?'

'Thanks, yes. Went along to the forensics examination of the 4x4. Cranston was fairly complimentary about you.'

'Fairly? I thought we got on.'

'Of course you do; he thinks you're good, if persistent. I mentioned three things – the cleaning agent the perps used to do the car over, the tyre nozzles and the windscreen washer water for any traces.'

'I'm sure he appreciated you telling him his job.'

'Yes, funny that, he had a way of twisting it back on me. Oh, by the way, the rental had done 223 miles, which is not that much more than Brum to Bristol and back. Anyway, his report will be in soon – no doubt covering those items. I've officially concluded the Faulks case to Bolton's begrudging satisfaction though I'm going to pursue it in my own time, with his blessing, because there's got to be something more to it – and not just your theories about non-accidental slippages. Got plans?'

'Philip's coming down from Nottingham later this afternoon. It's always a plus and a minus with Philip. You?'

'Oh, quiet, maybe see the badminton crowd, plus some paperwork and reading up more on the Faulks case. Enjoy your weekend.'

Clive rung off and Mavis started winding down and preparing for Philip. He texted her to say that he was on his way. She replied with the postcode of a wine bar overlooking the Avon Gorge and the Clifton suspension bridge where she'd meet him in about an hour. She queried with herself whether the time was right to talk practicalities with Philip. Her conclusion, for no particular reason, was not just yet. She had time to get back to her flat, dress more casually, and stroll over to the wine bar a few minutes after Philip had parked and arrived. They hugged and social-kissed.

'Philip, you look really well. And tanned! You'll be catching me up.'

'I've been doing lots of house clearances out of the office. Catch up means many things. You look great; promotion suits you.'

'At least I can dish out orders now I've got some helpers. It's good down here. What are we drinking?'

'How does a chilled light rosé sound?'

'Now you're trying to impress. Brilliant.'

They chatted about work and life outside work over the wine, and then Philip turned to property.

'Now you're more settled in Bristol and you've had a promotion, I was wondering how you felt about us buying a flat or something, you know, to get a toehold on the property market? I could do the groundwork. It would be very economical as we'd share the bills.'

Mavis gulped and said she had to go to the loo. Once in there, she had to have an urgent dialogue with herself. Why did he have to bring that up when we've only just met? How can I say 'no' or 'not yet' without upsetting him? He must have been hatching this over the last few days or even weeks. He's rushing matters that I can't begin to approach yet. She calmed herself and went back upstairs.

'Philip, it's such a lovely evening so I don't want to spoil it or our weekend with chat about domestic life. There's plenty of time for that but not now, please.'

Mavis thought she had got as close to a no without saying it. Philip thought she was saying a yes but not yet.

'My career is just beginning and frankly I could be drafted anywhere in the UK and I don't want an albatross of a potentially unsellable flat in Bristol round my neck when I could end up in Sunderland or Swansea. Let's enjoy this evening.'

'Okay, I can see I spoke too soon and out of turn, sorry.'

'It's okay, and sweet of you to think like that but the timing's not right. Let's move on.'

They did. They picked up a ready meal on the way back to her flat, made a salad with it, opened two bottles of beer, watched some light TV and crashed out in bed.

Thirty-One

Peter Vernon was at his desk in his study looking at the morning paper. There had been a robbery at a bank branch somewhere in the UK. He leant back, closed his eyes and recalled the events of maybe more than twenty-five years earlier: there really had been a robbery at his bank. He recalled one of the senior executives addressing a full staff meeting one Friday afternoon …

'Thank you for your attendance this afternoon before we close for the weekend. There appears to have been some irregularity in the movement of monies between yesterday morning and today's reconciliations. I have to be straight with you here. On the one hand, we do not have any specific details, on the other hand, it does appear to be an inside job as we are not prepared to accept the possibility that the security van leaving last night was waylaid en route. At the present, there will be an internal investigation and at some point the police may be involved. We have already notified them and because of the nature of what may be an internal matter, they are content for the moment for us to conduct the preliminary investigations. The bank, of course, is taking this very seriously, and Personnel will maintain a database of all existing employees and new starters working here from the beginning of this week until further notice. We shall also include visitors and customers. Internal Audit and others will be interviewing every member of staff and management over the next few days. If anyone is taking a holiday next week, you need to see Personnel to give them your whereabouts. Of course, I understand that the majority of you here this afternoon are entirely innocent and I regret that you have been caught up in this ugly incident which goes right to the heart of the bank's creed of total trust and honesty in dealing and handling our customers' funds. I'm not taking questions. You will all be kept informed, and you'll be invited for interview in the next few days.'

He left quickly, and the general office was quiet and subdued. People did not know what to say to each other. One or more of their colleagues had stolen money from the bank.

Peter and his boss had been summoned to the Chief's room. There was only one subject this could be about – the loss or theft of bank funds some time on Thursday. He remembered the discussion all too well.

'I'm shocked that this sort of thing could happen at our bank. Clearly our controls have been found wanting. We are going to have to make solid progress on this matter to keep the police and the Press out of it. It will leak, of course, but if we're on top of the whole event and investigation, we should be able to control external spillage and reputational damage. The police are regarding this as an internal job for the present. I want the drains up on this one, and I think Peter's the man for it.'

Peter's immediate boss had no problem with that. He could park Peter with the investigation and keep him occupied for a few weeks at the very least, which would also keep him from asking awkward questions about other suspect areas of the bank's business.

'Couldn't agree more, Sir, right up Peter's street, and we're right behind him with support. Peter, how do you see it?'

'The controls worry me. This shouldn't have been able to happen. The sharp-minded will always seek out any weakness. I suppose that's my job. Please may I be given total authority to go where I please, even with our esteemed colleagues?'

'You have my word on that but if in the very unlikely event you need to speak to the Board, then go through me please. I've spoken to the chairman, and he is onside at the moment and is fully supportive of our best investigating audit staff being given the task. Peter, you fit that admirably.'

'Thank you, Sir. I'll press on with that exclusively if you agree.'

They both nodded, and Peter returned to his office. Skulduggery and petty theft were an expected part of the seedy side of commercial organizations, but this apparently had been a planned theft and carried out in broad daylight. He needed facts and a timeline. And he would start right now with the reconciliations clerks in the accounts department.

They were a small team but it soon became clear that the one who had spotted the error knew the most. He was Malcolm and he said that he had been doing this check every day for the last four and a half years. Peter asked him how he had spotted it.

'The used notes were bagged up Wednesday evening and ledger entries done for the amount outgoing at close of play Wednesday. So, in accounting terms, the money had gone from here. The bags of notes are sealed and secured in the safe overnight. The following morning, Thursday, the bags are taken out of the safe and placed in a secure dispatch area before being loaded into a security van later. There is CCTV over the whole area and the tapes kept for a week. The security van departs before close of play and the van is unloaded at its destination that night. First thing the following day, the receiving branch or office acknowledges receipt of the previous afternoon's delivery. In this case, two bags were not received and the error was raised.'

'Thanks, Malcolm. So, the boundaries of the theft, let's call it that for the moment to help dialogue, are late Wednesday to earlier today, is that correct?' Peter couldn't believe he was saying this.

'At the limits, yes, but I would hope we could rule out overnight Wednesday and overnight Thursday. My view is daytime Thursday.'

'Your view may be right but we can't solve this by views. Okay, that'll do for now.'

He phoned Security and asked for all the tapes from the internal cameras that surrounded any areas involving the physical movement of the money bags. They would be available to him first thing Monday morning.

Yes, he remembered it all too well. It had remained a blemish on his career, even now.

Thirty-Two

Mavis, Adrian and Celia reconvened. They had each exhausted enquiries by phone, plus other enquiries, and by eliminating age differences and finally getting confirmation that the person was actually missing, they had one each.

Mavis had David Williams, a possible missing brother, and an old photograph that could just plausibly be a match. He was from Wales and a travelling salesman who could be anywhere at any one time. His sister had said Bristol was possible, but he was more usually around the South East, quote, 'At least part of every day he was on the M25, he said'. She said she hadn't heard from him for three weeks which was longer than usual. They agreed he remained a possible.

Adrian had Edward Vine from the Press campaign. This came via the *Sheffield Star* which had promoted a local campaign to help. Mr Vine had been missing for a month and the family were beside themselves with worry. His absence was unusual and his mobile had been left behind. His girlfriend's photos were of them at parties dancing around and were not conclusive. He was a programmer in an IT department which sent staff round the country. Edward had always requested local jobs but his most recent posting had been to Peterborough.

Celia had Frank Underwood from DVLA. The photo was some years ago now and could be an even younger version of the artist's impression. Her follow-up to the address on the driving licence yielded him as a single man in Chester, clean licence, and phone calls with the neighbours established him as an interior designer for refurbishments around the Chester area. Not really any local connections and generally kept himself to himself; not been around lately, but there was nothing unusual in that.

'So, these might be the three favourites but it's not definite. To use an overworked police phrase, we have to eliminate at least two of them from our enquiries. These three are itinerant, each used to spells away from home, no connection with Bristol, and may have fallen in with undesirables. Celia, please could you organize a representative of each of these three to come to Bristol and, potentially, and I do mean potentially, identify the deceased from the artist's impression of him as he is now? Thank you, moving on. Now Adrian, what have you got from the detail of these local Hyde recordings from the block of flats overlooking the harbour?'

'Well, Miss, they are a man and a woman. He's average height and she's the same height as him. So, I reckon that makes her tall. The DIY store CCTV will be a help if we were to have the couple to compare. Oh, and I think they are a couple.'

'Why?'

'They appear to be about the same age, stay quite close together and he is shepherding her along with a friendly arm.'

'Okay; and anything from the receipt?'

'Cash, no personal information.'

'Okay, try them again for CCTV of the outside car park to see if we can get something on their own car and maybe get a reg number.'

They both left, Mavis noticing that they moved physically quite close together. She got a machine tea and went over the weekend in her mind. Saturday had been a prolonged version of Friday evening, and neither of them mentioned property or changes in their accommodation. They had an extended walk along the Avon Gorge and back, and went to a pub in the evening where there was live music and plenty of local atmosphere. Mavis did relax a little and apologised to Philip for being a bit uptight the previous evening. Sunday morning, they lounged around in bed and then took brunch round the corner. When Philip suggested that perhaps he ought to be making a move, Mavis meekly nodded. In truth, she wanted to get back to her case which was just starting to yield results. She was going to crack it.

Thirty-Three

Peter Vernon was enjoying his first summer in retirement. There were frequent niceties, and golf and bridge of course helped him to keep his marbles. There was also the huge number of files in his study, and Barbara persisting in asking when they were going to be cleared out. He had made progress – one filing cabinet had been completely cleared and Nigel would take it next time they were over. There was his desk – so him! Oak and strong and sturdy; almost attractive. It would have to stay, and he and Barbara would have to make something of it when it was no longer in use, which Peter thought and hoped would be many years away. The other filing cabinet was next on his list. He would start at the top and work his way down.

There was nothing to the top drawer – yet more 'away days' and conferences on 'Depreciation and Accruals for Tax Purposes'. Why did he keep thinking of Jonathan Swift? Second drawer was better and all of a piece about the theft all those years ago. His memory of that painful personal time was always going to be good.

He recalled again the apparent theft of a substantial number of used notes, suspected of being an inside job. It was very serious and, having been put in charge of the case, he had been determined to solve it. He had even felt at the time that he was the only person at the bank capable of solving it. He could see now that was a touch arrogant but it was humbling too, because he hadn't solved it. But he had kept copies of his papers all this time because, again arrogantly, he thought he might still be able to crack it, maybe with some help this time.

The theft had been on a Thursday and the thieves had spotted a gap, both physical and in time, between parting with the used notes and the accounting for them from leaving the bank and arriving at their destination. He looked through his written notes on all the interviews; they were brief and limited to what mattered to Peter. Some of the hard-bitten, longer-serving employees had implied they wished the perpetrator, or perpetrators, good luck, and hoped they had a better time than they'd had at the bank. Some were outraged; some didn't have a clue about very much at all; others were actually helpful in pointing out failures in the bank's approach to controls and an unfortunate mix of paper and computer records. He'd never told Barbara about the theft. He grimly remembered that they didn't find any of the stolen notes and the internal outcome was a report of what was thought to have happened, plus a list of Peter's recommendations. All such had been accepted and the bank subsequently brought in significant tightening of controls throughout. The business climate improved, the bank moved on and enjoyed a successful and profitable time. The theft was written off in the accounts as sundry losses at a time when it was a mere fraction of bigger profits.

It nevertheless remained as unfinished business in Peter's mind. Someone, somewhere, probably from the bank, had got away with it. It was not the sort of problem to burden Officer Drewett with, but he would be someone who would help if more information was needed or indeed cropped up as new evidence. He leant back in his chair and remembered that time all too clearly. One of his first interviewees had been Damon, the security guy on duty that day with the cameras …

'Come in, Damon, sit yourself down, there's water on the side.' Peter's stern voice was trying to be friendly but official. Damon sheepishly sat down and folded his arms.

'This investigation is down to me, and within these four walls you can be as forthcoming as you like and as much as I would like you to be. You are in Security and last Thursday you were manning the controls of the CCTV, correct?'

'Yes.'

'Was that Thursday in any way different from any other Thursday, or indeed any other day of the week when you were working in that capacity?'

'No.'

'Have you subsequently been able to put any ideas or thoughts together that might lead to helping the bank track down the culprit?'

'Not really.'

'That sounds as though you might.'

'Well, there's the incident which I'm sure you're going to come on to when my camera wandered for a few moments. But nothing else happened and it was all over in a trice.'

'Indeed, the distraction of a young lady, whom I shall be talking to very shortly. Do you know her?'

'No, but I know she's in the netball team and some of us go and watch them. She's very good.'

'That may be so, but your angle was rather more basic, wasn't it? Why did you shift the camera over to her?'

'Well, time can drag monitoring the CCTV all day, and she's known to be an attractive girl and I am a normal guy. You do understand that, Sir.'

'I do; I was your age once but that is beside the point. Did you not once think that this was a stunt, intended to be a distraction for some other activity?'

'I've gone over the tapes and nothing else happened, I'm sure of it. I even understand why she got changed there, in the corridor. The Ladies' toilets, and the Men's for that matter, are really manky. She used her noddle to get some privacy and I was – sorry to put it like this – being natural and taking a peep.'

'It's not very gentlemanly, I would add, and it's not part of your job.'

'No, Sir.'

'I may want to follow up this discussion later. You may go.'

Damon left and Peter sighed. Damon had done what probably well over ninety-five per cent of boys and men of that age would have done, especially given the mundane job. He phoned his assistant to ask Penny to come in.

'Come in, Penny, sit yourself down. There's water on the side.'

'Thank you, Mr Vernon.' Penny sat down and smoothed her dress.

'You know that this is to do with the investigation and you've probably guessed what I'm going to concentrate on. Why did you get changed into your games kit there? It's on CCTV now so it's no secret.'

'I didn't know about the CCTV and, if you please, Sir, would it be possible to have the CCTV tape wiped clean? I don't want all sorts of people to be having a giggle at my expense.'

'Of course I understand that and I'll see what I can do. Assume it will be wiped clean. Carry on.'

'Thank you, Sir. The reason is that there's nowhere else. The Ladies is disgusting and there are no facilities at the ground, and just to be humorous for a moment, have you ever tried changing in a small car?'

'Penny, I understand, I do really, and that is a separate point that I will make to the management. The real issue is whether you were part of an elaborate scheme to distract others while one or more of your colleagues robbed this bank, your employer?'

'No, Sir, I'm not and I wasn't.'

'If you were and you have just lied, your crime would be more serious.'

'I got changed in a stupid place, went down to my car and drove off to netball practice. What could be more innocent than that?'

'Precisely. That strengthens both our arguments. Your posing as an innocent bystander works well for the argument that you were a diversion.'

'If I was, then I'm unaware of it. It was a spur of the moment thing to get changed in that corridor rather than slumming it in the Ladies.'

'You have a boyfriend?'

'Yes, Ricky, he works here, on the third floor.'

'Do you live together? Do you share the car?'

'Sort of. The living together is now and then and at weekends. We also both live at home at each of our folk's place. The car is for whichever one of us needs it.'

'You come to work here in your car together?'

'Some of the time. Like last Thursday I went to netball practice in the car and drove back after we had finished and done a bit of socializing. Ricky had returned to the flat earlier and was watching TV when I got back.'

'Thank you, Penny. I may want a follow up discussion with you later, but feel free to go.'

Penny put her glass of water back on the side and left. Peter was not convinced. He thought it was an act. Obviously an attractive girl like her would always be a massive distraction that others could utilize. He didn't think that she would be unaware if others were using her as a diversion. He phoned his assistant to ask Ricky on the third floor to come in.

'Come in, Ricky, sit yourself down. There's water on the side.'

'Thank you, Mr Vernon.' Ricky sat down and straightened his tie.

'You know that this is to do with the investigation and I'm interviewing all staff on behalf of our Chief Executive. My principal questions to you relate to your girlfriend, Penny.'

'Sir?'

'I don't know whether she's told you but she decided to change for netball in a niche off the corridor, close to dispatches exit. Her nubile frame, I trust I can share that with you, caught the attention of one of our CCTV operators who understandably but ill-advisedly zoned the camera in upon your beloved.'

'The pervert! I'll find out which one and he'll have to answer to me on that! And can he be fired? People have been for less.'

'I share your feelings but it raises a rather more important point. It looks to me as though it was a stunt designed to divert attention while someone robbed the bank. It could be you. Is it you, Ricky? Did you rob the bank?'

'No, Mr Vernon, I swear I didn't. This happened last Thursday, according to the gossip round the office. I was all over the place, settling up queries between our department and others. And, no, Penny's not said a word about this to me. She must be gobsmacked and embarrassed, and feel awkward.'

'She does. I've promised her that the offending tape will be wiped clean, although I will retain a copy in my own internal audit safe in the possible event of you and she being guilty. If you've lied to me, your crime would be even more serious.'

'Yes it would, but I didn't do it.'

'Please go through your movements last Thursday from the moment you arrived at the office.'

Ricky struggled his way through the day, trying to remember as many people as possible that he spoke to for any confirmation that Vernon would no doubt get from interviewing other members of staff. Peter let him go and moved on to interview others. It would take at least a couple of days to wade through the rest of the staff.

*

Peter stirred in his comfortable chair. Remembering all that all these years later had been hard work and yet it seemed like only yesterday – which it certainly wasn't. One of the comments from one member of staff was that the only thing different on that day was that one of the young women had decided to change into her games kit in a dark corridor at the back of the bank. It jarred with him now. He should have followed that up at the time like a terrier.

'Perhaps I will send copies of my theft notes to Drewett; can't do any harm, he seems to like cold cases.'

Thirty-Four

Celia had arranged for the three representatives to come in on the same morning to view the current photograph of the deceased in more detail and to account for the disappearance.

The first to arrive was Owen Williams, brother of David Williams. Mavis didn't want this parade to drag out with family sagas until there was some hope of identification. She produced the deceased's jacket and showed Owen the artist's up-to-date portrait. He took a long time over both and emerged with a smile.

'No, that's definitely not my brother though there is a likeness. It gives me hope that he's still alive somewhere.' Mavis thanked him and told Celia to reimburse his expenses.

Next to arrive was Wendy Vine, daughter of Edward Vine, the missing programmer from Sheffield. She had come down by train and took no time at all over identification. She was ready to leave after a few minutes.

'That's not my dad by a long shot. Sorry not to have been more help.' Mavis motioned her towards Celia for expenses.

Finally, Elizabeth Finlay, next-door neighbour to Frank Underwood in Chester, came in. She seemed about the same age as the deceased and plainly dressed. She also took a long time and kept switching between the artist's two portraits and fingering the jacket.

'Yes, it's him, no doubt at all. I ought to know; I've lived next door to him for years and sorted out a few of his problems. He was a dear man and in some ways a dear friend, though he could drive you round the bend. He invited me to his fiftieth birthday party and made a joke about maybe not reaching sixty. Sadly, he didn't.'

Mavis asked Adrian to escort Miss Finlay to a separate room and take a full statement from her. Mavis emphasised the word "everything" to Adrian, and if there were not enough time, she could stop over at a B&B. Adrian and Miss Finlay left; Mavis spoke to Celia.

'Great, we've got a name and our methods worked! Celia, can you now start the ball rolling and get everything on Frank Underwood? *Everything*. We have to find any family first for procedure, including a forensic search of his house. Robertson will want a Press Release and briefing. You okay on that?'

'Yes, Miss. I'm so thrilled it's worked; Adi and I feel we've made something happen that really matters. I'll find his family if it kills me. Back soonest.'

'Celia, it's Mavis in the office, by the way, but can I say that you've both really come on these last few weeks and I know it won't be the last time that you make something happen.'

Celia left feeling ten foot tall; Mavis went up to Robertson's office.

'Convenient, Sir?'

'Always for you, Mavis, come in.'

'We've identified the victim, though details are sketchy. We're taking a full statement from the identifier, and trying to locate the victim's family and carry out a search of his home through formal procedures. Then, would it be okay to broadcast this?'

'Absolutely, but you are quite correct, DS Smith, family first. There may not be any. We need family at the Press briefing. You've done okay, how long has it been now, two months? Brandon will be pleased to hear progress. Next step?'

'It's the CCTV from the DIY store that sold the polythene. We've got the timing and, if we can link the two purchasers to a car in the car park and get the reg, we'll nearly have them. It won't be the 4x4 because the poly purchase is a week or two before, presumably in their own car. The Forensics report on the rented 4x4 is due any day now.'

'Keep showing me you're on top of things.'

Mavis left with a wave and went round to interrupt the Finlay debrief.

'Sorry to butt in; just a question in case it doesn't come up – we'd be interested in any contacts that Mr Underwood had. Like regular contacts outside business or strange contacts that wouldn't be his normal social group, okay? Also, and I'm sure you've covered this Adrian, but what had he been up to in the few weeks before his death. Right, I'm off, catch up with you later. If you need anything, Miss Finlay, please ask.'

It was the middle of the day and Mavis thought she would take a stroll to order matters in her mind and clear her head. This took her to Munch'n'Mange for her salad and a mango smoothie. She sat on a bench in the city centre. She felt the case was coming together; they had the component parts and each seemed to be coming to resolution. There was still no reason why somebody would want to kill Underwood and then dump him in the harbour. She continued this internal thinking – where's the money, as Clive would have said. Funny, thinking of Clive; this was the first case where he'd not been actively involved. Okay, I'm growing up and can handle it, but I miss him in a weird way. He's always looked out for me and never anything more than a kiss. Good one, though. And now I'm with Philip, who I'm not sure whether I miss or not; funny that. Enjoy his company when he's around and forget him when he's not. That's not a nice thing to say. I'll go down to see Mum and Dad this weekend; I need her cooking; and she will always ask about men because she has a grandchild deficit. I can't imagine children at the moment; they are a few years away yet. She smiled at a young boy walking past who smiled back.

*

Back at the office, Adrian was just bidding Miss Finlay farewell. Mavis joined in, thanking her for her help.

'How did it go, Adrian?'

'Hard going but I persevered knowing you wouldn't accept nothing. Thanks for giving me my first statement on my own. By the way, I took "everything" to mean everything.'

'I know I'll see the formal version. Did she sign?'

'Of course.'

'Then let's have a little chat about it. I've brought you a BLT – here.'

'Thanks, Miss. Here goes. Frank Underwood has lived in Chester for at least ten years, all of it working in interior design which he does in a back room in his house. He also visits his employer in the centre of Chester most weeks. He goes out to houses with designs, makes a presentation, and hopes for a sale. His main whinge in life appears to have been that clients would take his designs to a fitter or even a DIY store who would say they could do it, and for less. The money side didn't work: if he asked for the money up front, he didn't get the assignment, and if the design was not accepted or found fault with, clients were reluctant to pay. I wondered why his business model and contract couldn't be tightened up a bit with his employer, and Miss Finlay said she had said exactly the same thing to Frank many times. He claimed to be on a salary plus commission, but she thought it was a struggle getting the commissions.'

'Were they in a relationship?'

'Not according to her, just friendly neighbours, but what did come out later is that neither Frank nor Elizabeth is or were in a relationship with anyone else.'

'Okay, there's nothing wrong there.'

'He lived on his own, cooked for himself or brought a takeaway back, rarely any friends visiting and no sign of family visiting so she assumed he visited them. He was often away. Nothing out of the ordinary apart from the reclusive lifestyle he lived. Your question about recent undesirables struck no chord at all. He saw hardly anyone at his home, so if he did liaise with undesirables, it would be elsewhere. She did notice that the postman was more frequent to his house than to others which might indicate contact.'

'How has his house been since he was killed?'

'Elizabeth now knows when he died and she thought long and hard about anything unusual that might have happened since that date. Nothing came to mind and the post frequency went right down, which I think is interesting.' Adrian stopped to munch.

'Agreed. It suggests to me that the postal communications related to him personally.' At that moment, Celia burst in, yelling,

'Got 'em! I've found the Underwoods. It's the West Midlands and the Isle of Wight.'

'It can't be both.'

'Mum and Dad are old and live in the West Midlands, and have not been aware much of their son over the years; younger sister is in the Isle of Wight and doesn't follow media much as she's tied up doing cream teas on the coast. When I said come to Bristol, there was nothing except "what for?" and extreme reluctance. I don't think any of them would be much use at a Press briefing; it's like his death has removed a problem, and thank God. Some people.'

'Any other relatives? Uncles, cousins?'

'There's a cousin in Swindon, they might come. What do I do next, Miss?'

'Thanks, Celia, give me the three phone numbers and I'll call them to inform them of the gravity of the situation; that's about all we can do but I think we need their blessing to proceed with making this public. Really well done, both of you.'

Adrian punched Celia's arm.

Mavis phoned her mum.

Thirty-Five

Clive was intrigued to receive Vernon's internal notes on the possible theft at the bank. It should have been taken up by the police at the time but it clearly had not been, and they had been content for it to have been handled internally. Peter equally clearly had suspects in mind but no evidence to go on other than coincidence and circumstance. He dropped a line to Poole with the dates and brief summary to see if there had been any follow-up to the bank theft after it had been reported, adding that it was unlikely. As Vernon's notes were in front of him, he referred back to his other main preoccupation – Geoffrey Faulks. And lo! There it was in black and white in the private detective's report: "The subject met a young male, subsequently identified as Damon Head, for coffee in Tottenham Court Road London" and nothing further. Clive quickly and briefly added another note to Neil Poole, asking to search a Damon Head, a former employee of the bank. Clive also mentioned another darts competition at the TAle & TWine.

A response came back within minutes: "Yes to darts at T&T, will have info on Head then, this Saturday, okay?" It was.

Thirty-Six

Mavis realized she needed a break while she was driving down to Devon to see her mum and dad on Saturday morning. The Press briefing had some interest but without any members of the family present for a human interest story, it fell rather flat. Her attempts to cajole the parents and the sister to come to Bristol failed despite bribes of expenses and accommodation. Robertson had alluded to "contacts have been made with the family but appear to have no bearing on the case". The Press were eager for progress and detail which Robertson and Mavis were reluctant to release, even any information whatsoever on the deceased. They did not want Press intrusion at the house in Chester, nor any badgering of the relatives or the helpful Elizabeth Finlay. Forensics were doing the house over on Monday, with a report by Wednesday at the latest.

Mavis had left early to avoid any holiday traffic and phoned Philip en route to say where she was. He glumly replied that he was off to badminton and that maybe next weekend might be better. She signed off with a cheery, 'See ya.' By late morning she was pulling up outside her parents' house just outside Torquay.

'Mavvy my darling girl, lovely to see you! It's been such a long time.' Her mother's torrent of greetings was followed by being swept up in her arms before plonking next to her on the sofa.

'Give your dad a hug, too.' Her father was more restrained but his eyes showed signs of filling up.

'I'm so glad to be here; it's been hectic at work and I hadn't realized how run down I was until I was well on the way here. How are you both? You're looking good; retirement and Devon must suit you.'

They chatted on over family catch-up, had a tour of the garden and the newly decorated bedroom that Mavis would be sleeping in. Her dad brought her a large steaming mug of coffee.

'Just how you like it, and I ground the beans myself.' Not to be outdone, her mum offered a large slice of a coconut-and-cream sponge cake, adding,

'And just how you like it, too.'

After lunch they walked down to the sea front and did the usual, expected things. Supper was her favourite mix of Anglo-Caribbean dishes after which the sea air took its toll and Mavis apologized profusely for crashing out for the longest uninterrupted sleep she'd had for months. It wasn't until late Sunday morning that the inevitable question popped out of her mum's mouth.

'And have you a young man?'

Although Mavis was prepared for this from mother and, indeed, she had superficially prepared how she might actually respond in person, the enquiring tone overcame her.

'Oh, Mum, I'm generally decisive at work but when it comes to that side of life, I'm hopeless.'

'No, you're not, it's called life and we have to think, we have to see, and then eventually light dawns and there's a way forward. Tell me what you want to tell me.'

Mavis hugged her mother and started a stream of what was bottled up in her mind.

'Yes, I do have a few male friends and we enjoy sociable times together and it's nothing serious in the way you mean. There are two who are closer – one who I see about every other weekend and you might say we are girlfriend and boyfriend. We actually are. He's a really nice guy and he thinks I'm a lot more than his girlfriend and keeps talking about moving down to the West Country and why don't we look at a few properties together. I think of him as a good guy but struggle to see him as a close boyfriend and I feel guilty about not wanting to see properties together; I just can't visualize taking it further, to living together.'

'Do you miss him?'

'Not badly; I look forward to seeing him when we meet up each time, but not much in between.'

'Does he miss you?'

'I suspect he does and he shows it; it's quite stressful. It's not a nice thing to say but it's not a reciprocal relationship, Mum.'

'I can see that. You said two.'

'I did and that's certainly not a reciprocal relationship or even a relationship at all. He's a former work colleague; we get in touch only rarely. He has his own life. It's just that we click, always have done, and I can tell that we enjoy each other's company. He kissed me once some time ago and I know it sounds soppy and pathetic, but there really was and maybe is something between us.'

'He will think you have your own life the way you've just said it. Describe him.'

'He's not bad looking; he's sincere and genuine, looks at things straightforwardly and then turns things upside down and looks at things differently. He'll never be head honcho but anyone who has ever had dealings with him has great respect for his humanity and humility.'

'Sounds far too worthy; is he boring?'

'No, never, it's nothing like that at all. He's always alive and brings something to the gathering.'

Mavis's dad had been hovering around, putting glasses away and listening in to this fascinating chat; he gently inserted himself into the conversation.

'Okay, let's consider you from his point of view. You're younger, with a degree, promoted relatively quickly for the police. For all his experience and seniority and, picking on your word *humility*, he probably thinks you're a talented bright young thing who would be looking for someone like *you*. I'm guessing that as a mere male he would never think of being able to have someone like you for himself. That's quite apart from the colour of your skin.'

'Dad, stop it. He would never have any prejudice against me on account of my colour. I think he finds it attractive.' She smiled, rekindling some memories. 'You and Mum are perfect for each other; it's nothing to do with that.'

'Your mother and I fell in love a long time ago; our minds clicked; our interests clicked; our lives clicked and our bodies clicked.' He chuckled.

'Dad! Far too much information. Sis and I have been so lucky to have such loving parents. Okay, I get it; I'll try to spend more time with this guy and see if we in the *mot-du-jour* "click". Better to find out than never know.'

'I think he may be thinking the same thing but not have a clue how to go about it with this brash, strong-minded, forceful, career-minded tiger of the opposite sex.' Another Dad chuckle.

'I'm not mowing the lawn for that!' And she threw a cushion at him.

They enjoyed a leisurely Sunday roast, after which Mavis phoned her sister in the Caribbean on speaker phone, and then said she must be leaving them. Hugs all round before she drove back up to Bristol, getting in just after eleven.

Driving time was thinking time, and she found herself going round in circles in her mind, weighing up Philip and Clive, guessing that the latter was probably not giving her a second thought.

Thirty-Seven

Clive's first and second thoughts were that a 19, plus a double 13 would clinch the 45 needed to win the leg. He chose this combination because he had a good strike rate getting a 19. It didn't work, and Neil finished the game off.

Clive had taken the weekend off and he'd driven down to north London to meet up with Neil for a little work on the side, the usual sharing of an old friendship and some serious socializing with drink, food and darts. He noticed that some of the same crowd were there from last time, including Wilf, which could be useful.

'So, Neil, Damon Head – what have you got?'

They found a table, ordered burgers, fries and some beer.

'Not as much as you would like, Mr Demanding, but more than a little. Been mentioned in files and records but nothing stands out. Likes to associate with folk we think of as undesirables; think of him as a hanger-on or a go-for. Used to be in security for a bank for a few years and then left as part of a redundancy slim down.'

'Can I butt in, Neil?'

'You usually do.'

'Vernon at the bank put a private dick on Faulks – as it turned out, at his own expense and without any result – but it did reveal that Faulks met Head for coffee in Tottenham Court Road; it has to be the same person. Now, why would those two meet? And more, it turns out Head was monitoring the CCTV in the bank at the time of the theft. Vernon reported that Head got distracted by the screen when it showed a young woman changing into her games kit – understandable but what a coincidence. Vernon's notes make it pretty clear that he didn't think it was a coincidence, and the distraction was intended.'

'It doesn't mean that Head had done anything wrong – apart from a temporary lapse in monitoring.'

'It's too much: the distraction, the theft, the timing, the screens monitoring the exit doors for used notes. Vernon's questioning could have led Head to realize that the distraction was intentional and the robbery took place right under his nose. He could never admit that to Vernon but he could surmise that the young woman's boyfriend at the bank took the opportunity to steal the bags. But how and what links Head to Faulks?'

'Money; always is. How the two met is curious – we just know that they did. Once they met, you can build a nice little story of Head talking about an inside job at the bank and Faulks would be onto blackmail before you could say two burgers and fries. Here they are.'

They munched and thought. Clive, naturally cautious, wondered if this ruminating was getting a stretch too far ahead of itself. He continued.

'It doesn't matter if they carried out the theft or not. All it needed was for Head to believe it had happened and for Faulks, who we know was in financial trouble, to go along with him. If the blackmail worked, the two would be guilty and Faulks would take a share of the cash. If it didn't, no proof and nothing lost. We've just got to find these two and see if Faulks was blackmailing them. Slight problem: we don't know them apart from Vernon interviewing them as a Penny and a Ricky, and Faulks has disappeared off the face of the earth.'

'They may have tried to bump him off if he was blackmailing them.'

'That's years later on a Welsh hillside and it supports one of my theories. Mavis thinks he was pushed.'

'I'll come on to her later but I rest my case, milud. Look, there's Wilf looking lost; let's ask him if he remembers a lad called Damon.'

Clive bought Wilf a drink and asked him whether, back in the days when Geoffrey was winning at darts, if there was ever a young lad going round with him.

'He might have been called Damon, normal sort of chap.'

Wilf ran the back of his hand over five days' worth of stubble.

'Thanks for the drink, mister. Yeah, I think you're right. Right little squirt he was, always offering to do whatever Geoff wanted – like he was being paid for it if you get my drift. Show me a photo of him sometime. I'd recognize him straight off with his crooked smile.'

They thanked him and moved away.

'We need to throw a few darts. Okay, next steps: you find Head, I'll re-interpret Vernon's notes on the identity of the two at the bank who are "Penny" and "Ricky" at the moment.'

'Okay, Sir, now you tell me all about Mavis.'

Thirty-Eight

Mavis felt she was really beginning to be in charge of the case. Results were in. The polythene report was back; the rented car report was back; and Underwood's house report was back.

The CCTV pictures of the DIY store carpark showed a couple carrying a roll of polythene, like a rolled up length of carpet. Their appearance from top down was some sort of headgear like a beanie, an anorak and jeans. Faces not fully revealed but, from the general gait, they would appear to be a middle-aged couple; they did not carry the roll of polythene lightly. An enhanced view of the 4x4 into which they loaded the polythene showed the model of the vehicle and some, but not all, of the letters and numbers of the registration number plate clearly enough. Mavis hardly needed to ask Celia to retrieve a full listing for that model with the clear numbers and letters in the right format.

The forensics from the rented 4x4 were not as helpful in comparison. As requested, they had taken fingerprints from the tyre valves and fuel cap, adding whatever they could lift from the internal controls, the door and boot handles, and the top of the windscreen washer container. All of these were incomplete or smudged but collectively it was possible to match up a few of them. Forensics' view was that these prints would be supportive but not conclusive. Much more fortuitous was the retrieval of a disposable coffee cup from a side pocket. The rental company confirmed it was from the customers at that time – they had retained it when they cleared out the car in view of the suspicious nature of the rental. Forensics remarked that this showed rare prescience. The cup was sent off for DNA testing.

The report on Frank Underwood's house in Chester confirmed Frank's solitary lifestyle as observed by Elizabeth Finlay. What Mavis wanted was files, papers and correspondence. These were requested, all bagged up and couriered to Bristol. She had thought there might be a single box file full but five was more like it. She put Adrian and Celia onto going through all of them. Underwood had a car but it was not at his address, nor had it been reported as found in the Bristol area. A search was put out.

Robertson was pleased to see a smiling Mavis appear round his door.

'I'm taking there's progress?'

'Indeed, Sir.' And she gave an account of the three outcomes.

'Nearly, but not quite, would be my assessment; but progress in the right direction nevertheless.'

'Correct, Sir. We now have plenty to follow up and I'm hoping we can cross-check from each of the leads to full identification.'

'Again, nearly but not quite; I think you need a breakthrough killer fact to pin it on them. And, of course, to find them.'

'I know, Sir. It's KBO, isn't it?'

'You've got it; it is, as ever.'

She went home and phoned Clive who was getting changed into his badminton kit.

'Hi Clive, thought I'd give you a ring to see how you were.'

'Thanks, all fine here though I wish I was playing badminton with you this evening. Do you remember those games, eh? I was always on the losing side and you were always on the winning side even when you were lumbered with me. How's the case?'

'Not *lumbered* with, Clive. Colleagues, even friends I hope. Yes, it's going well, got a lot of material now to follow up on. The stuff from Brum helped enormously, so thanks for whatever you did. It might all fall into place but the boss says I need a killer breakthrough.'

'We always did and it happens if you keep looking. You can't see if you don't look.'

'Your PhD is in the post, Dr Drewett. How's your cold case?'

'Remarkable … it's amazing what turns up. I've got blackmail, private dicks, perverted CCTV screens, darts cups, the lot. Would make a novel.'

'Good luck; hope we can meet sometime and share some of that.'

'Me too; sorry, gotta dash.'

Clive drove off to the local leisure centre. He spoke out loud: 'Mavis phoned me!'

Thirty-Nine

It was not until late in the evening two days after his trip to London that Clive was able to go over Vernon's notes and records again. He knew he was in speculative territory with blackmail but there seemed no other simple compelling reason why someone like Faulks would have met someone like Head. They weren't exactly low-lifes, but each had the characteristic of wanting a deal of something for nothing. Head would have been able to tell a strong tale to Faulks about a couple he suspected had stolen used notes from the bank. Faulks would then be on to it straight away. He would want their names, where they lived, and reluctantly would have had to give Head a cut of the blackmail. He and Neil had been right: nothing to lose by trying. If they'd paid, they were guilty and ripe for picking. If they'd told him to get lost, so be it. Clive scoured Vernon's notes on the theft but, after introducing them as Penny and Ricky, he had thereafter referred to them as P and R. Interestingly, Vernon had never suspected Head as being in on the theft, just a bystander who had a lapse. Head could have been in on the theft but three is a tricky number and, if he were, he would not have gone to meet Faulks. Clive thought he saw a simpler explanation: Head was convinced Penny and Ricky had stolen the notes but did not know how to go about using the information. Through a bit of research at the bank, he had found a client who he reckoned had sailed close to the wind and would inevitably be interested in a deal on the side. Using the bank's records, he would have been able to trace Faulks and meet him, though unfortunately for him this coincided with Vernon's private detective searches. Or they might have merely have met up for darts at the pub. Clive phoned Neil.

'Hi Neil, sorry to disturb. Had any thoughts on how to find Head? I think we need him to find out the full names of this Penny and Ricky. Or we go back to the bank and ask for a search. Vernon can't remember, and they are merely P and R in his notes.'

'Not yet. I am on it but I have to fit it in between other work or at the end of the day. Give me a few more days for enquiries to come through. Thanks for coming down by the way; a good evening. And, my man, don't forget about that Mavis.'

'Bye, Neil.'

No, he thought, I'll never forget Mavis; but is it reciprocated?

Forty

Mavis, Adrian and Celia were reviewing the boxes of papers and letters, and the laptop sent down from Frank Underwood's house. Most of them were able to be discarded such as endless quotations and their follow-ups, domestic bills and correspondence. He kept well compartmentalized tidy records which helped.

Celia had analysed the bank statements for unusual items. Most of them were routine, modest amounts; she could see his monthly salary and then quarterly there were his highly variable commission payments; but there were one or two others much more sizeable than commission and not really in keeping with his allegedly modest lifestyle. One, the larger one, was a few weeks before his death, the other nine months earlier.

Adrian wanted to find his car. There was a car file and sure enough he found the number plate and had put in a DVLA request. The mileage shown in the annual returns and insurance showed excessive mileage not accounted for merely doing fifty miles a day around Chester. This guy was out and about, current whereabouts unknown.

Mavis was looking for nuggets. Frank's mobile had presumably been taken by his murderers and trashed, but a mobile number in the records would enable them to access his texts and other phone records. Number having been found, she submitted her request. After Adrian had accessed the laptop, Mavis was straight into emails. There were many, but most, as above, were routine and could be discarded. But there was a series of emails of a different nature – secretive, furtive, and not related to either business or friends. Who was this Geoffrey Faulks referred to way back, and then, more latterly, Damon Head? The other frequent descriptions were: "the target" and "success". She submitted searches on those two guys as well. Oh dear, she thought. Philip!

She phoned him after work.

'Hello, stranger.'

'Hello, stranger.'

'Sorry Philip, I've been up to my eyes in work on this case, and other things as well. How are you doing?'

'I'm fine thanks, and thanks for asking. It's been a little while … I wondered if you were still around.'

'Well, of course I am. Being 150 miles apart doesn't make for casual meetings and I'm generally worn out in the evening. Sorry, I should have called you before.'

'And me too, sorry. I've been doing some thinking and I can't see this working out in the long term, and I don't want to opt out after a few years of a long distance relationship.'

'Philip, are you dumping me? I get what you're saying, but we haven't talked about it before.'

'I don't know what I'm saying. "Dumping" is such a dramatic word but I didn't get a warm response from you about me moving down there and us getting a place together.'

'I know that, dear Philip, I just felt those were mighty big steps and we weren't exactly ready for them.'

'Well, I was.'

'Well, I wasn't, sorry.'

'That leaves me thinking where do we go from here? I have other options of course, and I get to play badminton with a Veronica.'

'Well, you do just that. You go off with your Vera Knickers and see what happens.'

Mavis rang off. Dear me, I didn't handle that very well, she reprimanded herself. A DS ought to behave better. A text came through: "Sorry you feel like that. Talk in a few days' time. Phil x."

She walked back to her flat feeling a bit sorry for herself until the rationalizing process kicked in. No, long distance relationships don't work. No, I was not and am not ready to move into a place with him. No, he would not get an automatic replacement job down here. No, I've got a really good job here, enjoying the challenge of it. Two glasses of wine and a pork pie back at her flat brought her back to normal. She would be totally composed when Philip phoned next time.

Forty-One

Philip phoned Mavis a few days later in the evening.

'Hi Philip, I'm really sorry I was rude to you about your friend. It was wrong on a personal level, obviously, and wrong on every other level I can think of, professionally for one.'

'That's okay, I wasn't exactly Prince Charming myself. How are you?'

'I'm really fine. I'm actually enjoying the work and the responsibility. It's taking up time but that's what you have to do, isn't it, to build a career? How are you?'

'I'm really fine too. My work isn't like yours but it's varied, gets me out and about, and then I crash out with friends at weekends and midweek. Are you seeing anybody?'

'No, I'm not unless you mean you. I too crash out with friends down here but it's the usual superficial social thing. And how's Veronica?'

'She's fine and we rub along well at badminton and with friends. We're not a couple, we're not together, whatever the current jargon is.'

'Philip, I'll probably regret saying this, but if you and Veronica are just fine and you want to make a go of it, then do. Life's too short for agonizing. You and I have had really good times together and you really helped me on that case up there where we all got in a muddle. Can I be straight and say that although we're good friends, of course very close friends, I'm not sure we're pining for each other. Let's give ourselves a break and see what happens. I might even come up and bash your door down. Sorry, joke.'

'I understand all that and you're the one with the brain power so you're probably right. I shall miss you in a very special way but there's no way we can make it work given where we are geographically and career-wise.'

'Now you're showing the wisdom, young man. I will keep in touch with you because that's how I'm made but I'm not going to interfere in your love life. Good luck, by the way.'

'Good luck to you too. Bye, lovely Mavis, you're still part of my life.'

'And you mine. Bye Philip.'

She poured another large glass of wine, sighed, and eventually fell asleep on the sofa.

Forty-Two

Chief Inspector Bolton beckoned Clive into his office. He asked if there were any further progress on the Faulks case. Clive gave an account of his out-of-hours trip to London based on information gleaned from Vernon's records from the bank, generously copied to him. The current state of play was that Faulks and a security lad called Damon had probably been blackmailing the two employees who were Vernon's favourites for who had stolen the used notes. The theft had been internally investigated but never formally handed over to the police to avoid adverse publicity.

'We know that Faulks met with a bad accident in Wales, which we now think may be suspect, and Neil Poole, a colleague whom I've worked with in the past whenever London is involved, is trying to track down this Damon Head. We also need the names of the two internal suspects, at the moment they are P and R, Penny and Ricky.

Damon Head and/or the bank could give us them, but Head wouldn't if he is involved and the bank may not want to open up unless we force them to.'

'Okay, Drewett, that's progress, but not real progress, is it?'

'I know what you mean, Sir, but we are getting into some deep detail now.'

'Maybe, but others are ahead of you. Janet knows my interest in Faulks and that absolutely anything that is thrown up on him nationwide is directed to me.'

'Yes, Sir.'

'This morning she brought a request for info on Faulks and Head from a station in Bristol.'

'Sir.'

'Indeed. A body floating in the harbour has been identified as a Frank Underwood, and in his papers and emails there are some rather opaque references to Head and Faulks. Any comment?'

'It's a massive breakthrough, Sir, and would not appear to contradict our blackmail theory. The targets appear to have taken on the blackmailers. He may be a crook but I suspect Head's life is at risk.'

'Mmm. I don't want to lose this case, Drewett; it's mine and we are going to solve it. I don't want Bristol trampling over it and grandstanding its solution.'

'Appreciated, Sir, but Faulks has been missing for some years now and can hardly be held responsible for Underwood's demise.'

'Faulks will be the cause of it, I'll be bound. I like your blackmail idea; check it out as it's just the sort of stunt Faulks would pull. Robertson's the man in Bristol, though the legwork has been done by a DS Smith – know her?'

'Vaguely, Sir; we worked together once a few years back when she was a rooky.'

'Well, follow it up, keep on top of the case, and report back to me at frequent intervals, understood?'

'Understood, Sir, and will do.'

Clive went back to his desk in a state of utter astonishment. He called Janet over.

'Hi Janet, just been told about the Faulks request from Bristol. Could I see the exact request, please?'

'It's here, Clive, quite short in fact. It's a normal request for info anywhere in the UK but you know that CI Bolton has directed all such requests to him, which is why it's here.'

'He's quite touchy about it – am I right there?'

'You don't know the half of it, Clive. It was a big one with the insolvencies and corruption going on. It was never resolved, and CI Bolton took it personally and has done ever since.'

'I know the DS dealing with this down in Bristol a little. We've worked with her before, very thorough. Mavis Smith.'

'You've mentioned her name before, Clive. I did wonder …'

'No, no, nothing like that.' Clive cut her short. 'Let's just say we worked together very amicably.'

'Well, it's a start, Clive. You seem very eligible to me, Sir,' she said with a smile; he smiled back.

'Thanks for these notes, Janet. I'll refresh my own notes and give Mavis a ring. Thanks for your endorsement.'

By this time, it was late morning and he knew from previous workings that Mavis took lunch at her desk or on walkabout in the neighbourhood. He took stock of his current understanding of his discussions with Poole on Head and Faulks and then called Mavis on her mobile.

'Clive! I'm sitting having my healthy lunch out here in the sunshine. Is all okay?'

'I'm glad you're sitting down. Yes, all is okay though I have a bit of surprise for you.'

'Some surprises are good and some are bad. I'm assuming this is bad.'

'It isn't; in some ways it's wonderful.'

'Oh, go on, you old . . . whatever.'

'Not so much of the old, now. We have received a request from the Bristol station asking for any information or background or previous records of (a) Damon Head and (b) Geoffrey Faulks.'

'Okay, yes, I sent those out a couple of days ago in connection with the murdered man floating in Bristol harbour.'

'I have oodles of info on both – they are lead suspects in a potential blackmail case following a bank theft,' he said in his official tone of voice.

'Clive, you're joking me!' Sometimes she couldn't tell if he was serious or not.

'Would I?'

'Yes.'

'Well, this time I am most assuredly not.'

'Do I come to you or you come to me?'

'My CI is extremely sensitive about this case; it's his baby and he wants it seen that *he's* cracked it. Do you mind? It would help us both.'

'That's fine. I'm in charge of the case here on the day to day level, so there's no problem having a work day away. Tomorrow or the day after?'

Clive fixed her up for the following day with a carpark space reserved for her from 10.30. The rest of the day, Janet observed DS Drewett in a good mood with a continuous smile on his face. She nearly asked for a raise.

Mavis, meanwhile, went back to her desk in an officious manner, telling Adrian and Celia that she was following up on Head and Faulks tomorrow in the West Midlands. This was important in more ways than one.

Forty-Three

Many years previously, Damon Head felt he had survived the ordeal of Vernon's inquisition after the theft at the bank. He had been with the bank from straight after school, and he and his folks were pleased he had got a job there. His father often came out with something like,

'Damon's something in the City, you know', as though he were a stockbroker or a securities dealer. In truth, he had started as a messenger and when security monitors and screens were installed, he applied to join the Internal Security Team. He had never seen, or been allowed to see, any cash or notes, and wasn't too much bothered until he had found out that salaries were higher on that side. Gradually, through his experience in the bank and the few friendships he had built up, he realized he had some aspirations. More money meant a car and social acceptability. He kept on the lookout for better pay and he did achieve more as technology became pervasive throughout the whole bank. What had started as just keeping an eye on screens had moved on to monitoring schedules of routine functions in and out of the bank in the service area at the rear of the building. There were the catering supplies, computer back-up material to be retained off-site, the constant movement of monies via a security company and on the days of board or executive meetings there were always one or two who liked to park their motors round the back to save parking charges. He had screens on the front, of course, but that was largely customers and business people entering and leaving, and logged by Cheryl on Reception. He shared his job with Darren and Dave so they could maintain a constant watch from early till late; their hours were either 6.30 to 2.30, or 11.30 to 7.30. They managed the overlap to coordinate lunch and any shopping.

Over his time at the bank, Damon had acquired a depth of knowledge of the comings and goings, and roughly who did what. So, when that netball player got changed in full view of his cameras, it was something completely different and out of the ordinary. Quite apart from the diverting spectacle, it had never happened before, or since, and it made him think. He had worked out that everything he saw on screen happened for a reason, every single coming and going, so it wasn't unreasonable to think that this stripping off had happened for a reason. He knew it wasn't to seduce him because she'd got a bloke and was scurrying off to netball. The reason given that the Ladies toilets were manky might hold up for management but not for him. It had not happened before. Therefore, there was a reason and that reason had to be she'd done it for a distraction. She was attractive for a start, and he didn't think a girl like her would do something like that for no reason. The inquisition on the coincidental theft of used notes that followed clinched it for him. It was obvious.

He knew it, Vernon knew it, but they couldn't prove it, and the bank was too proud to call in the police for a fuller investigation.

When he was able to, he watched the girl and her bloke. Penny and Ricky they were called and you could not imagine two people more goody two-shoes. He avoided eye contact as he did not want to be linked to them when the powers that be found out that they had robbed the bank.

Once or twice a week he dropped in at his local pub after work, especially if he was on a late shift. He usually paired up for darts with Geoff, who was much better than him, and they would take on another couple for a few quid or a round of pints. He'd known Geoff for a few months and they had started chatting after their turns at darts. It just came out, one evening, without him even thinking about it.

'I know a couple who've robbed our bank.'

'What you mean, Damon? You can't just say that.'

'I can. And I know they did. And since then, they've been acting like a couple of goody two-shoes, making every effort not to draw attention to themselves.'

'Have you reported it?'

'No, because I've got no proof. I'm a nobody at the bank, and they wouldn't believe me anyway.'

'But you know?'

'I know, no question.'

'Let me get this right: you know who robbed the bank and you think or even know that they've got away with it? You could say well done to them but it's not fair, you're thinking.'

'Exactly right, Geoff.'

'Well, why don't we hatch a plan? You get their names and address out of the bank and your Uncle Geoffrey will invite them to share some of it with us.'

'Don't mention my name, please. That's blackmail, Geoff.'

'I won't, nor mine either. I'll find a way; they won't report me because they're even bigger criminals. Let's just say it's an opportunity for us to get a bit on the side. I'll go 50-50 with you, okay.'

Forty-Four

Mavis arrived at the West Midlands Station at 10.15 and parked where the notice said "Reserved". She went in and asked for DS Drewett. Janet came round.

'It's Mavis, is that right?'

'Indeed it is. DS Mavis Smith reporting for duty.' They exchanged smiles.

'I've got a side room for you with coffee and biscuits. I'll get Clive.'

She and Clive didn't know how to greet each other and stood looking at each other for a few moments.

'Coincidence or what?' said Clive.

'Never believed in coincidences.'

'Didn't I say that once?'

'Clive, it's really good to see you and from what I've been hearing, we have a lot to share.'

'We do.' He poured her some coffee.

They spent the next hour or two giving each other a full debrief of what they had been up to, Clive coming from the bank and Faulks end, and Mavis from the end of Frank in Bristol Harbour.

'Let's summarize where we each are, what is fact and what is speculation. Is that a good starting point?'

'Exactly, Clive; so, let me kick off. I have a dead body in Bristol Harbour, now officially identified as Frank Underwood. Our evidence is a couple caught on CCTV who dumped him in the water. Means we are in the process of looking for them. The car they used plus other evidence are closing in on them but we do not yet have their names. Frank's papers and records indicate some dealings with guys called Faulks and Head, but the nature of those dealings is unknown. Blackmail is plausible but sheer speculation at this stage. We have no link at all between Faulks and Head and the couple we are trying to identify. How's that?'

'A start; we have Faulks down as a known duplicitous fellow with bankrupt companies who happened to be a good darts player. There's a bank robbery many years ago, the investigation of which was kept internal by the bank and whose senior internal audit accountant had strong suspicions about a couple called Penny and Ricky, and a Damon Head, all of whom worked for the bank. This accountant, who has recently retired, had no time for Faulks and by having him followed by a private detective, found he was to be meeting up with Damon Head. We also know they met in a pub and played darts together. Then Faulks went AWOL and resurfaced a broken man with his sister in Wales, following which he met with a bad accident falling off a coastal cliff. He was treated in hospital, convalesced at his sister's in Cardiff, and then disappeared, leaving a note that effectively said he was disappearing for good. The rest, as you say, including the blackmail, is speculation. But it would all fit like a jigsaw if it were true.'

'OK, Clive, we are where we are. We need a breakthrough to establish the link. We have to track down P and R and Head, and our lot have got to track down the couple's car and, for that matter, Underwood's car. Faulks is not around so Head must have had some link to Underwood.'

'Agreed. I'll keep pursuing P and R and Head with Neil Poole – remember him? You complete the car ID and anything else that pops up out of Underwood's background. If there's blackmail, there'll be payments and if there are payments, then there are recipients. Banks have records. Look at the time – fancy a late lunch, early supper?'

'Got to get back, Clive, but not just yet; a late lunch would be fine.'

Clive told Janet they were going out for a quick late lunch. She smiled back at him.

'No hurry, I'm holding the fort.'

They went to a Balti house round the corner and enjoyed a reunion lunch, raking over the past a little and dwelling on the present. They each also discovered that the other was currently unattached because work was so busy.

They walked back to her car.

'Clive, I need a hug.' They hugged.

Mavis drove back down the M5. It was good to see Clive again, she ruminated. I've missed him in a way; just a bit different from other jokers in the force and the sort of guy you looked forward to meeting again. No, don't go there.

Meanwhile, Clive back at his desk had to face Janet.

'Well?'

'Well, what?'

'You know.'

'You know what?'

'How did it go?'

'It went well, Janet. Can you get Neil Poole for me please?' He was unavailable but would ring back tomorrow. Later, back at his flat, he reminded himself how good it was to work with Mavis. We get on with things; but do we get on?

Forty-Five

Mavis called Adrian and Celia over to her desk and briefed them on the additional findings from the West Midlands Station. She differentiated between fact and speculation, but tried to bring out a fairly reasonable deduction that blackmail was behind the murder on account of a possible inside bank theft job. Adrian said,

'But no proof. How do we get proof?'

'By pursuing what leads we've got. A colleague in London is pursuing the bank for the full names of Penny and Ricky, and any connection with Damon Head. We've made big progress on the car reg, and those big payments into Underwood's bank account must have come from somewhere. Celia, can you pin down the car reg and Adrian, please chase Underwood's bank for who made those big payments. I'll chase West Midlands and London for Head and P and R, as we have to call them for the moment. Meet first thing tomorrow.'

Mavis's phone went; it was Clive.

'Hello, stranger, how's tricks?' she asked.

'Not great. Damon Head died under suspicious circumstances

three months ago. I'm getting the file for any connection to Faulks and Underwood, plus any reference to P and R. Neil's coming back to me later on progress with the bank. Mavis, it's humming.'

'Here too; so, all three connections with the infamous P and R have been dealt with in one way or another. They could at least be double murderers, Clive.'

'Agreed, but as we said yesterday – no proof; nice to see you, by the way.'

'Ditto. You must come and see the delights of Bristol again sometime. More evidence would help.'

'Yep. Keep in touch with our respective investigations. Bye.'

Formal as ever, thought Mavis. He needs to lighten up. Maybe I do too.

Forty-Six

Neil Poole had an appointment to see the bank's HR Director. He had got prior clearance from his boss and from Clive, via Bolton, as someone on the case to push until he got what he wanted about the apparent bank robbery many years back. There was also at least one suspicious death connected to the case. He was shown into the Director's office where Helena Dickinson was studying two computer screens with a coffee and a Danish pastry on the side. She was younger than he had anticipated, like most company officials these days, he thought.

'Officer Poole, thank you for coming in. How can I help?' She waved him to an easy chair.

'Thank you. We are investigating at least two potential murder cases, and our investigations have thrown up potential links to three former employees of the bank. I have to say their employment was many years ago now but I am able to disclose that they were the subject of an internal investigation here into an inside job – the theft of used bank notes. The crime was notified to the police at the time and it appears that the bank got away with saying that it would be dealt with by an internal investigation. As there are indications of links to murder and blackmail, it now becomes a police matter. Your cooperation is therefore of some importance. There is a couple known so far only as Penny and Ricky and, before you say impossible, I must advise you that your former senior internal auditor, one Peter Vernon, had them and a Mr Damon Head under suspicion for a number of years. Mr Vernon has recently retired but he could also be a source of further information, which we will cross-check. I would be grateful if you would search your records for their full names and National Insurance numbers.'

Neil had kept a serious sober face throughout his discourse.

'Well, I thank you for your address, Officer Poole, but we can't be expected to drop everything and search for a couple of first names just like that.'

'I and the police in the West Midlands and Bristol now require this information and we would appreciate your instructing a search even as we speak. May I reiterate there are two murders and suspected violence implicated, plus blackmail, plus the knowledge that the bank only informally reported the bank theft, a criminal act, at the time. I could return with some fierce documents but at this stage, we seek your cooperation. I can wait.'

'Give me a moment, Sir. There's coffee in the pot; please help yourself.'

Ms Dickinson left the room and Neil could hear her telling someone to get the staff records in some date order and with full names. She returned, trying her hardest to not show that she was flustered.

'This was before my time here, you understand, and there may well be a good number of staff with those initials.'

'Understood, of course, but an important connection or link is that we know that Vernon had the three of them in his sights. We have reference to his files and paperwork which are in note form – they would have meant something to him but not necessarily to anyone else. I'm sure the internal theft would have been well-known and investigated at the time and I'm also sure their personnel files would have had some reference to it. Do you have staff here now who were working some years ago?'

'Yes, that's possible. There's Margaret, of course.' She phoned

Margaret on the internal line and asked her to come up.

It took Margaret only a few minutes to come knocking at the door and entering Dickinson's office. Neil knew he'd got a winner; all companies have at least one Margaret. Ms Dickinson briefly outlined Neil's request. Margaret nodded.

'Yes, that's right, can remember it just like yesterday. Bit of a local scandal, actually. Peter rarely got excited but he did on this one; he took it personally. He's such a nice man and is badly missed, I might say. Yes, the chief suspects were either the van driver who drove off with the notes for himself, and the three of them – Damon, Penny and Ricky. Caused a bit of amusement at the time because we all guessed Penny changed into her netball kit in the corridor just to distract the security cameras. That's why the three of them remained under suspicion for some time. Got away with it, though, and that was that.'

Neil affected polite applause.

'Well done, Margaret, you should join the force. Perhaps, Ms Dickinson, we could have Penny and Ricky's surnames and their NI numbers?'

She went outside again which gave Neil the opportunity to thank Margaret properly. She added that the couple were boyfriend and girlfriend at that time.

Ms Dickinson returned with the information on a piece of paper. Neil read the names Penny Norton and Ricky Villiers, and their NI numbers.

'Thank you, ladies, your cooperation is appreciated. We may be coming back to you again about the robbery. I'll see myself out.'

Margaret comforted Helena.

Forty-Seven

Mavis felt that the noose was tightening. She had briefed Robertson on the link-up with the West Midlands, trying as subtly as possible to imply that CI Bolton was very much in charge of things from there. He wafted that aside but asked to be kept briefed more frequently from now on.

Frank Underwood's mobile records came in, showing calls and texts with Faulks and Head. Mavis put these aside to study later. She called her team over for a progress report.

'Celia, car reg?'

'Yes, this is the car that collected the polythene at the DIY store. Different angles and some zooming in on it do actually narrow it down to three possibilities. I've chased all three at DVLA and it is obvious which one is theirs. The other two were up north somewhere. The lead one is not far from here and is listed under a Mr Villiers, with a village address in Gloucestershire. Can Adi and I go and follow this up, Miss?'

'Let me think on that one. Adrian, the big payments?'

'They were paid in cash directly into Frank's account. The signature is unreadable, with a fake name underneath.'

'Such as?'

'Henry Cooper, Bobby Moore, Fred Truman, you get the gist.'

'Not really, are you having a laugh?'

'No, Miss, but they are. They're sporting heroes from way back.'

'Thank you for that; I suppose that supports the theory that they were blackmail payments. West Midlands has sent through the names of Penny Norton and Richard Villiers, and their NI numbers. Here they are – please follow up, Celia. Do a very full morning tomorrow and you may investigate a certain Gloucestershire village in the afternoon.'

The two of them scuttled off; Mavis called Clive.

'Hi Clive. Thanks for Neil's update. I'm following up on the names as well, not poaching. The car reg has been identified and we're looking into it tomorrow. The large payments into Underwood's account were in cash, and source hidden. Got anything?'

'Thanks, no worries, getting info on Damon Head's death. Strange one; made to look like a ghastly accident, i.e. potentially no perpetrator, just like Faulks's accident, but not very convincing. I'm going to reopen these given what we now know. I've got it into my head that Penny and Ricky attempted all three.'

'Me too. But what did a colleague of mine once say down in

Sussex? We need proof.'

'You are right and I was correct. I was wondering about a trip to Bristol; not been since, well, when I dropped in on the way back from Wales, and the time before that I was in short trousers.'

'That would be really nice. Do you mean it?'

'When have I ever lied?'

'How long have you got? Not this weekend, but the following one is good. Okay?'

They fixed it up and Clive said he'd find a B&B close by. Mavis nearly suggested something else but decided not to.

Forty-Eight

Previously

Geoffrey Faulks had become used to the seamy side of business in his failed attempts to keep first Corinthian Catering and then Winning Wines going. It was pressure from all sides, coupled with orders drying up. One had to resort to approximations to reality, ambiguous language, some mild inventions, even some game-playing. In truth, his deviousness only delayed the inevitable for a few weeks and did not help his reputation, either. Young Damon had painted a scenario that was familiar to him – how to tell a convincing lie that persuaded others to act differently. He would begin with an innocent letter or email:

> *My colleagues and I don't work for the bank so don't imagine that your venture can be contained in the bank; it can't. We are perfectly prepared to remain silent which helps you, of course, but there has to be a small price to pay for our silence. Our idea of a small price is at the foot of this letter. Used notes always work, don't you think, and we enclose a key to a locker at Waterloo Station for your deposit. Don't involve anyone else to watch this locker because we are watching it too. Any interference could get very ugly indeed. The deposit should be made within ten minutes either side of 2 pm next Monday. Please lock the locker after use and retain the key. Thank you.*

Geoff wasn't that sure about using Waterloo Station but hadn't thought of a better solution yet. So, he took the locker and had a duplicate key made. He sent the letter and key to the address Damon had got from the bank.

The following Monday afternoon, Geoff went to the station and opened the locker. There was an envelope with some notes in and a letter. Geoff locked the door again and disappeared to a café in Southwark. He read the letter:

Dear No-Gooder, I don't know who you are or what you think you are up to or even what you and your colleagues are suggesting. Of course we have done nothing wrong and your presumption is outrageous. I don't know if you are a down-and-out but you are certainly pretty low down the food chain. But if you are hard up, I sympathize and make a small contribution to your welfare. Please do not bother me again.

Notes to the value of half the sum requested were enclosed.

Geoff recognized this as a success, much more than a score draw, and a project that could be worked on in a few weeks. At darts that evening, Geoff gave Damon half of the proceeds, slightly rounded down to allow for his own undoubted expenses. Damon was thrilled with the cash.

'You didn't mention my name or anything did you?' he asked nervously.

'Of course not, nor mine either, don't worry. I'll go back for more when I feel the time is right.'

They played a few legs and took a few quid off the local youth.

Forty-Nine

Adrian and Celia were now happy to be called a couple or an item. Despite the long hours and often tiresome work, they did actually enjoy their jobs and working together. They had finished their morning duties as laid down by Mavis, bought two sandwiches and some takeaway coffee, and set off for Gloucestershire, home of the car with the registration number.

'She's all right, isn't she, our Mavis?'

'Yeah, I like the way she brings us in on the big picture stuff. You sort of know what's going on.'

'Have you ever got on the wrong side of her?'

'Some stern words sometimes but it's mainly The Look.'

'Whad'ya mean?'

'The evil eye – she gives you a look as if to say I could really have a good go at you for not doing something the way I want it done, so don't make me start.'

'Oh, I know that one! She brings herself up to full height with a tight mouth.'

'That's the one; best avoided. She's okay, though. I think she's got a bloke, but not here. She used to be in Nottingham but I think the bloke might be in the West Midlands.'

'Private.'

'Quite; we're lucky.' Adrian gave Celia a hand.

'To business then. We're checking an address which is where the car that was used to pick up the polythene is registered.'

'It's in the name of Villiers. Shall we have a snoop round first to see what's there?'

'I reckon. This is the first time out unsupervised so I think Madam will see this as a test.'

They ate and drank, Celia helping to feed the driver along the way. They pulled up short of the address in the rural Gloucestershire village. They walked round the house and gardens as much as they were able to, noticing a number of people who didn't seem to mind what they were up to. There was no sign of the car they were seeking, and at the front door there were a number of bell pushes. They rang the lowest one. The sounds inside eventually led to the front door being opened by an elderly lady with a brisk manner.

'Good afternoon. Can I help?'

'Good afternoon. We're from Bristol Police and we were hoping to see Mr Villiers. Is he around or available?'

'Ah, yes, I'm afraid Mr Villiers is no longer with us.'

'Do you have a forwarding address or phone number?'

'Not in this world, sadly. Mr Villiers died some years ago. This property was sold up and converted into flats as you can see.'

'We have evidence of a car registered to a Mr Villiers at this address. Could that possibly be a son or brother or other relation?' They showed her the registration number.

'Not that I am aware of. Yes, there was a son but he disappeared as soon as the property was sold. No car with that registration is here.'

'Is anyone else here more likely to know the son or where he is?'

'No, you've come to the right person. I would know if anyone does.'

'Thank you. Could I have your name and contact number please?'

'Hammond, Virginia, Miss, and here's my number.' She wrote it down quickly. 'Goodbye.'

They were left on the doorstep. Adrian reckoned they should have another snoop around. At the back was a kitchen garden leading to a small thicket of trees, with a signpost saying "To the Spinney". They left that and went round to some outbuildings at the back. There were some cars but none with the registration number that Celia had. A gardener was drinking tea so they went over to him.

'Hello, Sir, we're sorry to bother you, but who looks after the cars round here?'

'Mostly the residents themselves, Officer, but the estate manager in the office in that stable yonder might be able to help.'

The estate manager turned out to be an ex-military man, happy to be known as an ex-military man. He was sympathetic to their request, particularly about "another Mr Villiers".

'Yes, that's right, he phones up every year to renew the licence and the insurance, sends the cash over, plus my admin fee, and it all works like clockwork.'

'Would this be the registration number?' Celia showed him.

'That's correct.'

'Do you have any further info on him, like an address or phone number?'

'Sorry, no. It just happens; I'm not sure who I'm dealing with but he or she or they assure me the car is real and in full working order.'

'And all the DVLA stuff is at this address?'

'Correct. I'm assured it's legal.'

'Maybe. Thank you, Mr …?'

'Colonel Martin – here's my card.'

They thanked him and left. They stopped at a pub half-way back, still in uniform. Adrian was at pains to reassure the publican that they were off-duty and were trying to relax.

'Our Mr Villiers isn't going to satisfy Madam.'

'Nope. A waste of a day but it had to be done.'

'Not quite a waste, I'd say. I think we've proved that the other Mr Villiers does not want to be found and, from the CCTV of his car, he and maybe she are involved in Underwood's murder.'

'You're right, Adi, but we never seem to get positive proof. He may not be the guy, we haven't seen him, and he might be, well, private.'

'Okay, I get that but when are you going to move in with me?'

'It's a ho ho from me. I don't want to rush things and regret it later. We're really good together so let's not ruin something good.'

'That Mavis is having some influence on you.'

Fifty

Clive reopened the file on Geoffrey Faulks' accident. He had also received Neil's report on Damon Head's death. He absorbed himself in both. Faulks had taken himself off to South Wales as a retreat from the lifestyle he had enjoyed elsewhere at a time of life when he was free to do whatever he liked. Okay, he did want to get away from the fallout of Corinthian Catering and Winning Wines, and the beady eye of Vernon at the bank; but he could have done that by re-entering the spirit of his existing way of life anywhere in the country. If he were still involved in blackmail, his behaviour suggested he wanted to hide himself away under the cover of his sister's house; or, conversely, he was blackmailing somebody else, or was on the receiving end of it. Then there was the report on his accident. He slipped and fell off a cliff path. In all his years, Clive had not met that format as a type of death, neither in police circles nor as a private citizen. He sided with Mavis's view. People took care on cliff paths, especially on their own. Accidents may happen with a group or in a proven case of murder. The coroner's report stated that the weather conditions were favourable and the paths in that area were no more slippery than usual. Telling his sister that conditions were slippery must have been to ease the message. No cliff-top deaths had been recorded there for decades. Clive's conclusion was that Geoffrey was shoved off the cliff but it could never be proved. It would be plausible if there were a link to Damon Head or this new case in Bristol, Frank Underwood. If he had been shoved off the cliff, then the perpetrator's intention was to kill him. He or she did not hang around, and they were unlucky; something must have cushioned Geoffrey's fall and thus he lived. His subsequent disappearance after convalescing had to mean that he remained, or thought he remained, under threat of a further attempt. There was no information of his whereabouts afterwards or currently.

He turned next to Neil's report on Damon's death. His account was made up of extracts from police and other official records. He was killed a few years ago in his back garden. The death was recorded as a severe blow to the head, severe enough to cause instant death. The perpetrator or perpetrators had let themselves in through the gate at the back of the garden and left without trace. Neil had questioned any forensics surrounding the back gate and any CCTV, but there was no evidence to go on. Neighbours had been unaware that anything had happened. The report was clear that the killing took place in the garden, and the body not moved. Damon had lived by himself and his body wasn't discovered for a few days. Police requests for any witnesses or strange movements produced nothing. Damon's papers, mobile and laptop had been scrupulously searched, yielding nothing but a mundane life. His bank account showed routine items with bigger amounts being credited about every eighteen months. Texts and emails revealed some inexplicable or cryptic messages to untraceable accounts. Clive replied to Neil to ask that a more thorough search of these latter accounts be made by an IT expert.

Clive was beginning to see or imagine a ghastly bigger picture. Crudely put, Geoffrey, Damon and maybe Frank had been blackmailing a person or persons who had robbed the bank, who in turn had attacked or killed each of them over the years up to now. There was a connection between Damon and Geoffrey through darts, Damon had worked at the bank, Geoffrey had had problems with the bank and would be well-disposed to get one over on them. And now, Mavis at Bristol had found a connection between Frank Underwood and Faulks and Head. The couple at the bank were Norton and Villiers, who seemed to not exist or at least were untraceable.

'I have my hypothesis; now I, or we, will have to prove it,' he said this out loud.

He phoned Neil and outlined all of the above to him.

'Sounds plausible, Clive, but evidence or proof would be nigh on impossible.'

'At least try a mobile and laptop expert on Head's devices.'

'It's underway as we speak. There's a search on for the car with the reg from Bristol and ditto for finding Norton and Villiers. It's called good old-fashioned police work; we'll get them.'

'Like your optimism; talk soon.'

Clive returned to his flat and put a few things in a small suitcase. A weekend in Bristol with a young old friend might help.

Fifty-One

Previously

Geoffrey Faulks and Damon Head continued their stunt about every eighteen months or so. They kept it low key and to low amounts. Geoffrey did all the communications and collections, and it all appeared to work like clockwork. Then Damon observed that Geoffrey was not his usual self. He confided in Damon at their last darts meeting in the pub.

'We've got to stop for a while. I think they are on to me; maybe they've been watching me collect from the locker at Waterloo. I've decided to close the locker and think of another method. Any ideas, you let me know. I'm moving to my sister's in South Wales, but we can keep in touch.'

'Let me take over now, Geoff. I'll keep to our bargain and send you half the takings. I've got the wording. I'll say there's been a change of management but the project continues as before, unchanged.'

Geoffrey reluctantly agreed but in the strongest possible terms asked that the next request not be made for a year at least. Damon had to agree and asked him for his South Wales address.

Somewhat later, Damon became aware that he had lost contact with Geoffrey; they hadn't spoken for weeks. He phoned his sister's number; she answered in tears. She said that Geoffrey had slipped and fallen off a cliff on his daily walk.

'He wasn't himself these last few weeks and he must have just missed his step. The police file stated that he must have slipped on the path and fallen down the cliff. He's been in hospital, broken bones, but he eventually recovered enough to come home. Then, when he felt more mobile, he just upped and went off, and disappeared. He left me a note but I haven't heard from him since. He's now classed as a missing person.'

Damon wasn't that convinced and reckoned that Ricky and Penny had got to him and tried to shove him over. There would be no trace of any involvement on the couple's part; they would have just driven off. Yes, he would leave further requests for some time. Meanwhile, as he was known to the couple, he'd need to find someone to replace Geoff to front the venture, someone he could trust.

He went through his contact lists, his Christmas card list, and his old address book. This eventually produced Frank, his best old buddy at school. Not the sharpest tool in the box but he was a reliable best mate all the same. He rang what he knew would be an old number. After three passings on and re-directions, a familiar voice answered the phone.

'Frank here, how can I help?'

'Frank, it's Damon, remember? From school days? And the great pocket money swindle?'

'It's been a while, Damon, me old mucker! What are you up to?'

They swapped career progression, if one could call it that. Damon said that he looked at screens all day, and Frank said he looked at kitchen plans all day.

'Frank, I've got an idea I'd like to discuss. Can we meet?'

They agreed to meet halfway at a pub that Frank knew near Lichfield for a Sunday roast that weekend.

They greeted each other as close old friends, which they once had been. They were well into second pints and the roast before Damon outlined his plan and how it had gone hitherto. He did not mention Geoffrey and gave the impression that his proposition had been passed on to him to develop with a colleague. Frank was obviously sceptical at first.

'It's blackmail, Damon, it's criminal, it's as simple as that.'

'Maybe, but I know that they are criminals too and we've always got the option to turn them in. I know they are guilty. I know from the bank that the file on the theft is still open.'

'Do we have to disclose identity?'

'Of course not, no way. The trick is to find somewhere to collect or a different means of collecting.'

'I've retained a disused company bank account with an old address. Would that do?'

'Excellent. Maybe change the address to a PO Box number.'

'And deduct the cost from the proceeds before sharing, yes?'

'Frank, you're ahead of me. Let's enjoy the STP and custard, and then decide the date of the next venture.'

After several coffees, they each drove back home in high spirits.

Fifty-Two

Clive arrived at his B&B in Bristol at 6.30 pm on Friday, dumped his stuff and left the car, then walked to Mavis's flat. It was autumn now, but there was still some warmth in the evening sun and it was still light when he rang the bell to her flat. Mavis came down.

'Clive, you made it!' They hugged.

'And why wouldn't I? It's good to see you again. Promotion suits you.'

'Clive, stop it! I've said that before. Come in. Tea, coffee or drink?'

'Tea, please. You remember?'

'No sugar, little milk, darker than me.'

'Now, now, stop it! I've said that before.'

They reminisced and caught up with their career progressions, more hers than his, and what life was like.

'I'm so busy, Clive – this case and its ramifications, and running my small team. Philip and I were never going to work and sadly he got quite upset about it though we've had a nice chat since.'

'I bet he did but I wouldn't be a mastermind if I said that I think he was more into you than vice versa.'

'Perceptive, DS Drewett, as ever. What about you, Romeo?'

'Nothing really. I was glad to escape from my previous. Busy too, both on this Faulks and Head case for the boss, and the day job as well. Still do badminton now and again but I'm no good.'

'We could do a stint in the morning, you know, for old time's sake.'

'No! That's in the past for me; let's walk the length and breadth of Bristol, the suspension bridge, the docks, and maybe a pub or two and a restaurant. The more we walk, the hungrier we'll be.'

'Let's go then. I've booked the Italian up the road.'

They enjoyed their evening, deciding that they would discuss a certain mutual case the next day. Three courses, two bottles of wine and two coffees later they walked back to Mavis's flat. She linked his arm and found herself somewhat mellow.

'Clive, I was wondering …'

'So was I, but we're not.'

'So masterful.'

'Not really; but sensible.'

'If you say so.'

She turned round to face him and they kissed.

'I remember that time before; you kissed me and said it was your way of saying yes, agreeing to my refusal to start a close relationship. And I said you must say yes more often, Mr Smoothy.'

'Ah, yes, I remember it well. I really do, and it was well said at the time.'

'And now?'

'Now is different and I've got to get back to my digs. What time in the morning? Shall we meet for coffee and croissants at that place in the square we passed?'

'Great idea, 9.30 am, and I won't ask if you've had a full English. Night.'

Clive walked back to his B&B in something of a daze. He'd always liked Mavis, obviously, but thought she was way out of his league. Her promotion had made her a more mature person, even more normal, but maybe he had grown up some more as well.

Under the duvet, Mavis thought Clive wasn't quite so boring after all.

*

Clive was at the café in the square well before 9.30, admittedly after a sneaky bacon butty and black pudding at the B&B. He ordered coffee and a croissant, and got his notebook out to review what business was relevant to the cases. He thought he knew what had happened in reality, but had absolutely no proof, so he hoped the Bristol end of things would have something that helped. Mavis turned up in walking gear at 9.35 and greeted Clive, saying she would have what he was having. Clive started getting official.

'I thought we could review where we'd each got to and see if and where we could fill in each other's gaps, yes?'

'Let's enjoy this autumn sunshine and warmth. It may not last. I've got a walk planned and you can lecture me while we are on the hoof. Also, I haven't had breakfast and I bet you have.'

'I don't lecture.'

'Only occasionally.'

'Well, this isn't one of those occasions. I agree with your agenda.'

'Do you mean what a lovely idea for a relaxing weekend in Bristol?'

'That is true.' He smiled. They chatted over breakfast and then started their walk. Over the course of the day, they covered the suspension bridge, the Cabot tower, the SS Great Britain, the harbour and art galleries, the shops and Saturday markets, Clifton village, and Brunel's railway shed. Included in this tramp were various coffee shops and pubs, then finally back to Mavis's flat to decide on the evening.

They had compared notes on the two murders. Clive wanted to know whether there was any progress in finding the car, its owners and their whereabouts, and also what the search of Underwood's house had revealed about his contact with Faulks and Head.

'The car is under the name Villiers, as is one of the suspects from the bank. The dad is dead, but his son, Richard Villiers, has outsourced all his car admin to a Colonel Martin, at what was his dad's property. Martin deals with the DVLA stuff and doesn't seem to be aware of anything untoward. But on the other hand, he is maintaining confidentiality.'

'That's got to be breakable, Mavis. I suggest we apply gross police pressure on Martin to reveal what contact he does have. There has to be something.'

'Okay, agreed, I'll send in the heavy boys.' She could not imagine Adrian and Celia applying pressure to an ex-Army guy.

'And Frank Underwood?'

'Infrequent larger cash payments paid into a side account. Signatures were old sporting heroes; you would know them.' He did.

'They stopped sometime before his death, which could suggest he had just made a demand and they decided the time had come.'

'How did he communicate with them?'

'Dunno. Nothing on text or email; must have been by letter.'

'Which he would not have kept copies of, obviously. What's the angle? How can we unravel this?'

'They know he's dead, because they killed him. But they don't know if he had a colleague in with him.'

'It was Head, but they got rid of him some time ago. You're right, they don't know if he had a new partner or not, but they did resort to extreme methods to deal with Frank. Perhaps it was a lesson to anyone else thinking of going down the same path – don't mess with us.'

'It doesn't mean a partner doesn't, or didn't exist, though.'

'Have you had a look at Frank's environment, who he hung out with, someone he would have to trust?'

'No, not really. It's up in Cheshire; we can liaise with them and see what turns up.'

'Too vague. You've got his family contacts?'

'Aged parents in the West Midlands, younger sister in the Isle of Wight, cousin in Swindon.'

'They all need leaning on for who his old trusted friends were.'

'Clive, you have a muscular way of conducting police work.'

'There's valuable info in people's heads. How else do you get it out? Lean on doesn't mean beating them up.'

'Okay, but can you help with some of these, please?'

'I'll do Swindon on the way back, and the West Midlands parents this coming week. Then can I persuade you to spend a weekend in the Isle of Wight?'

'Clive, are you trying to be romantic? It's not exactly Majorca.'

'It's where sis lives and she will know him best out of all the family. They grew up together. It's mild down there, you know, a micro climate.'

'Yes, done, but we go halves.'

'Of course. Now, this evening – what do you suggest?'

They went to a recommended gastropub and on the way back, again in mellow mood, they had exactly the same conversation as on the previous evening.

Clive, back at his B&B, reflected on the happy day they had had. He found Mavis's company as natural as grass being green and sky being blue.

Under the duvet, Mavis wondered if Sir Clive was playing hard to get, or pretending to play hard to get, or simply just not interested.

*

The next morning, they enjoyed a brunch in a harbour-side hostelry and then said their goodbyes. Hugs and a social kiss and they were each on their separate ways. Clive dropped in on Frank's cousin in Swindon. To no avail; there had been no contact with Frank for years and they had not mixed growing up. Nor did he know anything about Frank's life. It was either the parents in the West Midlands, or the Isle of Wight; some choice.

Fifty-Three

Mavis had given Robertson a full update of where her team had got to and the outcome of further discussions with the West Midlands Constabulary.

'So, you want heavies to prise information out of Colonel Martin? Your Midlands colleague is going to pursue Underwood's aged parents because they live round there; plus a freebie to the Isle of Wight to quiz the sister. Is this all strictly necessary?'

'The highly coincidental circumstantial evidence of the deaths and the disappearance points to this couple being the only suspects, and it is three for the price of one. They have been clever enough to avoid any sort of evidence that would satisfy a court or even, may I say it, you, Sir. They've fooled the DVLA.'

'Quite. Carry on.'

'We've got the car, the names, some technical evidence and the photos. CI Bolton is determined to find Faulks guilty of some old fraud cases, even though it seems he has disappeared of the face of the Earth. I'm sure we can split any expense with West Midlands. Let me say, if we get this info, we will solve the three cases and get the criminals sent down. Guilty as charged.'

'You're putting your head on the line, Smith. Not always the right career move, you know. You don't want to be stuck in a corner on Traffic and be known as the person who thought she was right but it didn't quite work out like that. Also, let me say, I want Bristol to get credit for solving these cases, not anyone else.'

'So, you agree, Sir?'

'Run along, keep me informed. You might get most of the credit if it works but remember I'll get the blame if it doesn't.'

'Thank you, Sir.'

She went back to her desk and started to develop a plan for the next few steps. Celia sidled up to her.

'Got a minute, Miss?'

'Celia, it's Mavis in the office, right?'

'Yes, thank you. May I ask a hypothetical question?'

'As long as you are prepared for a hypothetical answer.'

'I was just wondering, you know, that if, for example, me and Adrian or anyone, were to get hitched, would I have to change my name?'

Mavis smiled. 'I hope you're not two-timing Adrian given where you two are. Relax, Celia, of course you don't. It's very normal these days for women to keep their birth name for professional work. It's continuity for a start and avoids that dreadful title "Mrs". I'm happy to be Smith, everyone knows how to spell it and it will follow me all my days however many husbands I may have or don't have. No, you stay as you are and we won't let Adrian know we had this chat.'

'Are you going to get married?'

'Ho ho, I've no idea. Romance isn't dead and life is full of surprises. No, Celia, no current plans.' They both laughed and Celia went back to her desk.

A lightbulb went on in Mavis's brain. Of course, it's obvious, or could be. They've changed their names. She texted Clive:

"Clive, thank you for the weekend, lovely. Had a brainwave (or not) – Norton and Villiers aren't their names now. They've changed them. That's why we can't find them. Agreed? M"

A few minutes later, a reply pinged in:

"Possibly spot on, old girl. Agreed. How to unravel change of name? C"

"Not old, not girl, M"

"Agreed, C"

Mavis called Adrian in and asked him to find out how you would trace someone who's changed their name when you only know their previous name. She winked at Celia.

Her next job was to deal with those who Robertson had described as the heavies. Her gentle enquiries round the office made the choice easy – everyone agreed that Roy and Rob were who she needed. She went down to a lower floor to brief them. They were sitting at their desks facing each other. Mavis was reminded of the rugby matches she had watched on TV.

'You lovely boys have been specially recommended to me.'

'Not 'alf as lovely as you, girl. What's in it for us?'

'Let's say just one pint of West Country bitter. Each, okay?'

'And another for success, okay? You coming to the Christmas social?'

'Yes, and we'll have to see in that order. Now, there's a Colonel Martin up in Gloucestershire and we want some information out of him which he says is confidential between him and his client. We have the right to this information as it is in connection with, er, certain police enquiries, but we'd rather he didn't know that because he could pass it on to his client. You get my drift?'

'Perfectly, darlin'. You said Colonel, so he's ex-Army?'

'Well, he's not Army now so he must be or he's a fake.'

'Lucky Roy and me did a stint in the Army so we know what's what. It'll be a doddle. Tell us the information you want and no more; it helps us if we don't know the ins and outs so he doesn't try wriggling out of things. Fancy a cuppa?'

Mavis was direct in making it very clear exactly what she wanted out of the Colonel. They promised to report back in two or three days. She said she was looking forward to it and left after receiving an unwelcome pat on the bum. She gestured back in response.

Finally, she phoned Frank's sister on the Isle of Wight and arranged a day for her and Clive to meet her.

Fifty-Four

Clive easily located Mr and Mrs Underwood in a quiet cul-de-sac off a main road just out of Birmingham leading to Worcester. He phoned mid-afternoon and invited himself to coffee the following morning. It was understood to be in connection with Frank's death.

They lived in a bungalow set in a tidy garden where a gardener was tidying up various beds and perennials. Mr Underwood answered the door and invited Clive in.

Mrs Underwood had already prepared a tray of three cups of coffee and a few digestive biscuits. She led the conversation.

'How can we help, Officer? Are you any nearer to finding the culprits, or I should say murderers?'

'You should, and I am pleased to report that the net is getting tighter day by day. We are working closely with Bristol Police and they seem to be well-advanced identifying the cars used on at least two occasions, and we have lead suspects. To charge them, we have to be confident that we have enough proof, and that is somewhat elusive at the present. Today, I would like to focus on Frank's friends; not work colleagues, but mates he would have known and trusted over many years, probably since school days. I'll take any names and whereabouts now but it might be more productive if you take some time to dwell on Frank's life when I've gone and let me know your thoughts in a day or two. Does that make sense?'

'Perfectly, Officer,' said Mr Underwood. 'I see what you want and we've done little else but focus on dear Frank's life since his murder. I can think of one or two that he kept in touch with for many years, you know, Christmas and birthday cards and the like. The trouble is he led a very private life; came to see us fairly regularly and chatted quite generally about what he got up to, but the rest of it was private, especially more recently. He did not particularly open up about his private life. What do you say, dear?'

'The same as you, yes. I can think of a few now and obviously we'll let you have anyone else who we come up with. What is your angle, Officer?'

'We think Frank was working with someone on a matter that you could say indirectly led to his murder.' Clive stuck to the word "murder" as they had used it, and it seemed to help the gravity of the discussion. 'Also, we wondered if his sister, your daughter, might have been a confidante of Frank?'

'Oh, Emily and Frank were always so close, only eighteen months between them, you know. Same school, a year apart, and they shared a flat originally, but work and their careers took him to Chester and Emily to Shanklin in the Isle of Wight. Lovely place, we've been down there many times, haven't we, dear?'

'Yes, of course. They are – or were – always so busy with their jobs, but they usually come here for Christmas and we visit each of them in the summer. They give the impression of being in constant touch with each other; you may find Emily more helpful than we might be. Sadly, no more visits from both of them together.'

'Neither you nor her were able to come to the police appeal in Bristol?'

'The timing was wrong, Officer, and Emily is very much tied up in the business in the summer months. We didn't think it would make much difference whether we were there or not. Those appeals on the TV, they look so staged and teary.'

'I understand but it makes a big difference to the local people and the local Press; it's their territory. But never mind that; let me record what names and whereabouts come to mind now, and perhaps I could call you in a couple of days for any more.'

Clive left twenty minutes later, thinking of his own parents and hoping they were slightly more attached to him. He should phone home tonight. He sent Mavis a text saying he'd seen the Underwoods and his report would follow tomorrow. He thanked her for organising the Isle of Wight date and said he would book somewhere to stay.

Fifty-Five

Adrian was struggling to find anything useful about changes of name. If one knew the current name, it seemed easier to look up any previous names; finding whether a previously named John Smith, for example, had changed his name years ago to Isambard Kingdom

Brown was altogether different. Celia came up and looked over his shoulder. She touched his arm.

'Can I say something simple? I won't say *obvious* because you'd have already thought of it.'

'And I won't say anything about simple, either. What are we doing tonight?'

'You're coming to mine and staying over. No, seriously, if these two are criminals, and we think they are, they'll have moved house or flat and called themselves something different, right? All the official stuff will be in their birth names provided they have got someone to front for them in a different place. Locally and with new friends they would be known by their new names; but for stuff like tax and the DVLA they won't have changed names, just used a cover. Like his dad or this Colonel Martin.'

'Who's a clever girl then. *Obviously* we search Villiers and Norton and see what comes up.'

'You said *obviously*.'

'I know I did and I meant it. I better let Mavis know so she can brief R and R that there's more to dig out. She and that Clive in West Midlands – anything I should know about?'

'No, not for you, but she is showing signs of being quite guarded about any intrusion in her private life. See you.'

Adrian returned to his police searches. He knew he had the right to search anywhere in connection with an actual case, but having the right did not mean it was easy. After two hours, he got confirmation that the car was in the dad's name, care of Colonel Martin, tax was their own names, care of Colonel Martin's address, Council Tax was as yet untraceable as the address was not known and nothing under Norton or Villiers. He went over to Mavis's desk.

'We think they are using aliases; Celia's idea actually, but I agree. There's more stuff connected with his dad's address, with or without Colonel Martin's name attached.'

'Very good, both. You want me to let Roy and Rob know that there's more to get out of him? I hope he survives.'

She went downstairs where R and R were tackling bacon

sandwiches.

'We've found out that Colonel Martin and his address is a cover for our suspects. Top of the agenda is getting their new address; names would be good, as well as anything else you can find out. Are you okay about this?'

'Never more so, lovely lady. We've also been busy, like tracking down his service record. He's not the Duke of Wellington, though actually he also had his bad side. Turns out he was dismissed from service for deliberately falsifying records for his own benefit – should make our job easier if he doesn't want the locals to know. We also don't reckon he can or should retain his courtesy title. Looking forward to it; want a ringside seat, my dear?'

'Perhaps another time. Thank you boys. I look forward to your return.'

She went back upstairs and read an incoming email from Clive:

"Booked hotel in Ventnor, 3 miles from Shanklin, B&B, separate bedrooms. C."

She wondered why he needed to mention specifically the separate bedrooms ... She hoped it was because they weren't at that stage yet and he was being a gentleman, rather than keeping his distance. She replied that it would be fun, as well as doing some serious work.

Fifty-Six

As well as fun and work, it was also logistics. Mavis was to get the train down to Portsmouth; Clive was to drive there and pick her up for the ferry over Spithead to Fishbourne on the Isle of Wight; then a thirty minute drive over to Shanklin and Ventnor on the east coast. They discussed how they might tackle Emily, Clive giving his preference for both that afternoon and the following morning, 'so she can think about things overnight'. Mavis agreed and said that they would know more after the first session which she then arranged.

Lunch had been a baguette and coffee on the ferry; then they drove straight over to Shanklin and parked up. A short walk into the town brought them to "Kosy Kaff – All Home Made!", a welcoming small café with two assistants and an obvious Emily in charge. They ordered tea, and Emily ushered them into a tiny back office.

Mavis could see a likeness to her brother Frank despite his injuries, and Clive recognized similarities to her mother. Emily gave every indication of efficiency in her manner, her business and her appearance. It was nevertheless reassuring to see how open and friendly she was with her staff and customers. After routine exchanges of sadness, Clive started exactly as he had with Mr and Mrs Underwood.

'I am pleased to report that the net is getting tighter day by day in encircling the criminals we have under suspicion. We are working closely with the Bristol Police, DS Smith here is heading up your brother's case, and she will come to that in a minute. My involvement has come about because we strongly suspect that the same criminals are very likely to be connected to other crimes we have under investigation. Your mother and father were most helpful. To charge these suspects, we have to be confident that we have proof and that is turning out to be elusive at the present. Today we want to focus on Frank's friends; not necessarily work colleagues but mates he would have known and trusted over many years, probably since school days. We'll take names and whereabouts today but it might also be helpful if you could dwell on Frank's life and let us know, say tomorrow, when we hope we can drop by again. DS Smith will give a picture of how the Bristol case is progressing.'

'Thanks, Clive, yes. Emily, the case in Bristol is going well: we have positively identified the two cars used in Frank's case. One we suspect is the suspects' own car and the other is a rental used when, er, Frank's body was thrown in Bristol Harbour, and we have some evidence from that. We also have a link from Frank's records of him being connected to another case that Clive has mentioned. How does that all sound?'

'Perfectly, Officers, thank you,' said Emily. 'I see what you want and, although I've been really busy, I've dwelt a lot on dear Frank's life since his murder. He was quite private and I was probably as close to him as anybody over the years because we grew up together for most of our early life. As to any recent close friends, I have no idea as we lived so far apart. He came here, of course, but always on his own, and when I went up to Cheshire, I didn't meet any of his friends there. So that leaves old friends from our childhood, teens and twenties. Let me make some tea and have a think.' She left the room. They looked at each other, their faces indicating all too clearly that it was going nowhere. Emily returned with three teas on a tray.

'I can think of one or two that he kept in touch with for many years. This would be his young man period, you might say. They could be helpful because they probably went to pubs together and tried chasing girls. Let me find a piece of paper to jot them down.'

'Neither you nor your parents were able to come to the police appeal in Bristol?'

'The timing was all wrong, sorry. Summer is so busy here and I didn't think it would make much difference whether we were there or not. We all think those appeals on the TV are so artificial.'

'So your father said; but it makes a big difference to the local people and the local Press; it's their territory. But never mind. Thank you for these few names and locations; perhaps we could drop in for coffee in the morning just in case you've thought of one or two more? We are staying over in Ventnor.'

They thanked her warmly and drove on to Ventnor, a small town set on the slopes down to the sea and on the way to St Catherine's Point, the most southerly point of the island. They checked into a small hotel just up the hillside.

Clive had booked adjacent bedrooms, each en suite, with a sea view over the Channel. Mavis declared her satisfaction and suggested a walk to discuss the case further. They followed a coastal path over to Steep Hill Cove, enjoying the countryside and volumes of fresh air.

'There's one name both the parents and Emily have come up with and that's Damon Head. That's not a new name but it's very reassuring. It strengthens the link of Frank to Damon that you found in Frank's papers and records. Trouble is, Damon's dead so we don't know whether Frank continued the blackmail on his own or with an old chum as his new partner, as it were.'

'Agreed. All three of them speak of Frank as private and keeping himself to himself. Not the characteristics of someone who would trust a mate with sharing ongoing crimes.'

'Maybe; but against that would he have the confidence to carry on by himself? He must have continued because they did him in.'

'Unprofessional language, Clive, however I do think you're right. I don't see Frank going solo. We have to do a check on the names from the Underwoods and from Emily. Maybe one or two more; she seems a thoughtful lady and memories do need a jog, which I hope we've given her. Look at that cruise ship.'

A large, multi-layered ship cruised from left to right as they looked out to sea.

'A few thousand people escaping the daily grind but locked up in a superior prison and let out a day at a time in foreign parts.'

'That's a touch cynical, Mr Know-it-all. Ever been on a cruise?'

'No, but I've heard about them. They're marmite or binary or chalk and cheese; you either love 'em or avoid them.'

'I think it's romantic and it's up to each person to make something of it; meeting people, visiting different places every day or two, plus wining and dining and the floor shows.'

'So, if I invited you, you'd come?'

'In a nano-second.' And she changed the subject. 'Shall we dine together this evening or do you have plans, mister?'

'I've made a tentative booking for dinner at a local restaurant. Would you care to join me?'

'I've not got a posh frock as I'm travelling light but I'll try to make an effort. When we're back, give me a timescale and I'll be ready. I'm also going to give these names from Emily to Adrian back at the ranch to make a start on finding them.'

They walked back to the hotel via the sea front and watched some children messing about in the wavelets of the incoming tide.

In his room, Clive wondered whether Mavis was enjoying this break. She hadn't mentioned leaving early – yet.

In her room, Mavis wondered what on earth to wear. She hadn't been out to dinner since Philip and, because of the train journey, had travelled spectacularly lightly. It had to be trousers, a top and a casual jacket. Plus, accessories.

He texted her: "See you in the bar downstairs at 7. C." She replied:

"OK. M."

Clive was down at the bar first at ten to seven, and ordered a pint. At ten past seven, Mavis arrived. She'd fixed her hair, found some earrings, a necklace, a bracelet and a gold effect belt. Some lipstick and perfume completed the transformation. Clive didn't know what to say and the look on his face was bovine.

'Well?' she said. 'Any chance of a glass of wine?'

'Er, red or white or fizz?' He took her hand and kissed the back of it, then let go quickly.

'Chilled dry white would be just right.'

'Mavis, you look, er, well, gorgeous.'

'Not so bad yourself; at least you've changed your shirt.'

He ordered a sauvignon and motioned to the easy chairs.

'Supper is round the corner in half an hour so there's time to enjoy our drinks.'

'Are we talking business or pleasure this evening? Don't mind, either is good.'

'Shall we wind down from the case and have an evening off as it were? We're both more than a hundred miles from home.'

'That makes it sound like what happens in the Isle of Wight stays in the Isle of Wight.'

'I don't want to report this evening back in the West Midlands. Maybe something like "We spent the evening comparing notes on the interconnected cases, setting out a plan for further work tomorrow and back at the station in the coming days", and being very careful about which expenses to claim.'

'Like half a pint of bitter and a burger and fries.'

'You've got the picture; this evening's on me, by the way. We've worked together or in tandem for far too long for me not to treat you and to thank you for always being around somewhere to lend a hand.'

'Clive, that's really touching, thank you.'

They chatted over drinks and then walked round to the nearby restaurant. They had a table by the window, and enjoyed local fare including fresh fish followed by sticky puddings. Clive indulged his limited wine knowledge and Mavis equally indulged him in drinking his selection. They did some reminiscing of their two previous joint cases and some of the interesting people their careers had bumped into. They strolled back to the hotel in the mild autumn evening with the sound of the sea shore audible. She took his arm and suggested she get him a nightcap at the bar.

'Might that be a single malt?'

'Your wish is my command. Sorry not to be more original; that was a lovely supper, thank you.'

She ordered one of the well-known whiskies for Clive while she had a sparkling water, and they relaxed in the hotel lounge for a while before dragging themselves upstairs. Just as they were getting their room keys out, Mavis said:

'It's still early and my room's better than yours. Thank you for that, by the way. Why don't you change into something comfortable and come in here for a chat?'

He did, and when he went into her room, Mavis was half-way into bed and watching a crime drama on the television.

'Is this work or pleasure? It's always obvious who did it. It's the all-too-innocent, goody-two-shoes big sister.'

'You're probably right, as ever. Just snuggle in here and leave work behind. I want a hug.'

He gently crept into bed, keeping well apart. She turned the light off and gave him a big hug.

'Thank you for today; one of my best days.'

'Mine too – and an improving finale. You don't wear much in bed, do you?'

'And you are wearing far too much, Mister Detective. Let me get you organized.'

They struggled for a few minutes and then relaxed in each other's arms. It had been a long day.

Fifty-Seven

Roy and Rob had worked and played together for many years after they had first met each other in the Army. Both happily married in an old-fashioned sort of way that gave them plenty of time for sport, evenings in pubs, working on assignments together, and now and again going out with their wives as a foursome.

Mavis had been totally clear what she wanted them to get out of Colonel Martin and they in response had turned up what information they could find on the Colonel and had briefed this back to Mavis.

They were in uniform and kitted out accordingly for the drive up to Gloucestershire. They stopped for coffee on the way and agreed a good cop/bad cop approach to unsettle the Colonel.

They drove up to the outhouses of the big house and knocked on the door.

'Won't be a minute, just putting a jacket on … Oh, good morning, Officers.'

'Colonel Martin?'

'Tis me. How can I help?'

'We hope you can. We're following up a routine visit by two of our colleagues from Bristol Constabulary in connection with a certain Mr Villiers.'

'Oh, them, yes, I did try to be as helpful as I could but, as I explained to them quite clearly, these matters are confidential.'

'May I remind you, Colonel, that this is an ongoing police investigation and as a member of the public, nay a former member of the armed services, that your full cooperation is being asked for, and it is your duty to co-operate.'

'I do understand, Officers, I really do and I know you have your job to do, but I fail to see how disclosure of a client relationship would assist in any way to progress your investigations.'

'So, Colonel, not only are you suggesting that you know more than we do about our ongoing investigations, but you are also impeding, indeed frustrating, the course of justice in these green and pleasant lands. Let me ask you formally: are you going to give us the name and address of your supposed client, known as, or formerly known as, Mr Villiers, son of the Mr Villiers now deceased and previously of the address here where you carry out your supposed confidential duties?'

'I'm sorry, Officers, but part of my employment here is to carry out certain duties confidentially, and strictly nothing more. I have not broken the law and I have my rights, you know. I would like to help you as much as I can, but in these matters I have to retain confidentiality. I know it sounds pompous and unhelpful, but it is my duty.'

'It is your duty to cooperate with the police in any ongoing investigations into matters that may or may not be criminal. You've cooperated with the authorities before, haven't you, Colonel, when it suited you to save your neck?'

'I take it you mean those silly trumped up charges of a small misleading accounting error? It was never proven, you know.'

'We know that it amounted to a few grand in your favour. The case was withdrawn as prosecution was never going to be possible or desirable. It was hushed up so as not to cause the Army any embarrassment. These people we're talking about, your colleagues here and the folks in the village – they won't know anything about this aspect of your past life, will they?'

'I have a clean record and no one to answer to.'

'But the Army withdrew your rank and, only by concession, allowed you to join civvy street with a courtesy title. How did you get them to agree to that?'

'I left the Army voluntarily with a clean record.'

'We know that you were forced to resign on suspicion of graft and profiteering.'

'I've made my position clear; so farewell, gentlemen.'

'Not so fast, sunshine.' Rob pinned him to the outside wall of the stables and Roy stood in the doorway. 'Either you tell us the name and address we're asking for, or all your sordid history will be plastered over the local Press and beyond. Plus, there'll be a court summons to account for.'

'How dare you! Take your filthy hands off me, and your evil minds away from here. I repeat, I have a clean record and I do not have to answer to you at all.'

'Colonel Martin, I'm going to read you your rights and take you into custody for withholding information in connection with multiple serious crimes being investigated elsewhere.'

While Rob continued, Roy slipped a pair of handcuffs over his wrists and frog-marched him to their car, shoving him into the back seat and locking the door.

'Leave him there for five minutes and see if he has anything else to say for himself.'

They chatted and smoked a little way away from their car, returning eventually and making to drive off.

'Look, I say, you chaps, perhaps I was a bit pompous and standing on ceremony back there. Can I make a suggestion?'

Ten minutes later, Roy and Rob drove off, leaving Colonel Martin behind with his pride and his dignity hurt, but no bruises. Mission accomplished.

Fifty-Eight

Clive woke up at half-past five, worked out where he was, gathered up some clothing and slipped into his own bed next door. What had he been thinking? They must have had just a little too much to drink. What he remembered made him smile but he wondered what he might not have remembered. Words like "consent" and "entitlement" and "work colleague" went round and round his head. He fell asleep and was woken up three hours later by a dressing-gowned Mavis offering a cup of tea and sitting on the edge of his bed.

'Where did you get to, my knight in shining armour?'

'Mavis, I'm so sorry. I don't know what came over me and I humbly apologise.'

'Silly boy – what for? First of all, we're both grown up and single; and secondly, Mr Gentleman, nothing happened.'

'Are you sure?'

'I think I'd know. It's not exactly flattering to be left like that; I did think you had some feelings for me, but now I'm not so sure. You're a fine man, Clive.'

'Mavis, I ... I ... I ...' She clamped her hand over his mouth.

'Save it for later. Up we get, showered and downstairs for what you guys call a full English. See you downstairs in twenty minutes.' She left the room.

Clive was downstairs first, and when Mavis came into the dining room, he stood up and held a chair out for her.

'Can I get you anything?'

'It's one of those self-service breakfasts but tea would be good and some fruit juice. Clive, relax.'

They chatted over breakfast which did include the said full English. The chat was polite and respectful, and then Clive suggested they had a walk along the front before they went to see Emily again. The day was fresh with an offshore breeze coming in; little waves lapped the rough sandy beach. Clive started.

'I won't say I'm sorry again because it's not true. I, and I hope you, had a wonderful evening and everything, and I mean everything, could not have been better. I hope you don't think less of me for over-stepping the mark, particularly as you're a work colleague.'

'Clive, dear, stop all this political correctness. It was a wonderful evening and to hug you at the end of it was a treat which could have gone further. I have feelings for you and I think, or did think, that these were reciprocated, but now I'm not quite so sure. You absolutely did not take advantage of me and I at least thank you for the respect.'

'I've had feelings, strong feelings, for you for some time now. Let's not go all Jane Austen with each other, but I would like to continue our friendship as closely and as deeply as you want, or *we* want.'

'And slowly. We've come a long way in a few hours. We know each other very well, of course, but not like that. I'm relieved to find that the reason you didn't stay in my bedroom this morning wasn't because you didn't want to.'

'Can I make a suggestion?'

'You usually do.'

'It's Saturday morning; let's stay another night at this place.'

She gave him an enormous smile. 'Okay.'

It was easier to find Emily's place second time round. They ordered coffee and, when she had a gap serving or supervising, motioned them into her little office.

'Thank you for bringing me up to date on so many things to do with Frank. He may have done wrong but he's always been a good brother to me. You asked me about former long-standing, trustworthy friends. Damon Head dates from school days but after that Frank joined a rambling group and the name Stan kept popping up in conversations: Stan this, Stan that, Stan thinks this, Stan thinks that, et cetera, so I wonder about Stan. I think they were both at school together as well. They both lived in Chester and I think he was single too.'

'A surname would be good.'

'It starts with either a B or an M because it sounds like one of the two famous Stanleys – Baldwin and Matthews. That's how I remembered, it sounds like one of them. Sorry, Officers, it's a cryptic clue.'

'No worries, we'll search.' Mavis straightaway sent a text to Celia mentioning Stanley, Chester, surname sounds roughly like Baldwin or Matthews, Underwood's age.

Clive asked that if there was anything, absolutely anything, she could remember about Frank, please would she get in touch.

'Best walks round here?'

'Coastal path either direction, can't go wrong, and pubs en route. Going back today?'

'We're liking it so much, we've decided to stop tonight as well.'

They left the car in Shanklin and walked north through Sandown then up and over the top to Bembridge for a late pub lunch and all the way back, returning to their hotel at six.

'What or where do you fancy eating this evening, special one?'

'Not yet, too early. How about we have some tea or a drink now, then a takeaway later?'

And it was so. A Chinese takeaway in Mavis's bedroom with some wine and a double bed led to all that they imagined or might have imagined the previous evening.

Fifty-Nine

Monday morning was all action at the Bristol station. Celia had taken on board Mavis's cryptic clue.

'Nice weekend, Mavis?'

'Not bad at all. And you?'

'Great. The Chester Stanleys got me going. I've got Stanley Bawden, Borden, or Ball for the Bs and Mitchell, Mason, Matheson or Madden for the Ms – all within a few years of Frank's age.'

'Good; need to refine it further. Hiking clubs, maybe darts, maybe slightly dodgy, and single.'

Then Roy and Rob sidled up to her desk.

'You owe us; and you're coming to the Christmas Social.'

'I didn't promise you that but the beer is on if you've got something interesting to say.'

'Of course we have; fair exchange. The Red Lion 6 pm after work.'

'I have plans.'

'So have we, darlin'. See you there.'

Mavis decided that she would take Adrian and Celia, just in case, you never knew. They were pleased, Celia especially, as she wanted to probe more into DS Smith's private life.

Celia had also in fact narrowed the choice down to Stanley Matheson, mostly by elimination, but Matheson, being the secretary of the CHAPs, Cheshire Hikes and Pubs, clinched it. Mavis asked Chester for a formal online interview with Matheson, if the Chester police could get hold of him and bring him in.

At 6 pm, the three of them strolled round to The Red Lion. Roy and Rob were well into their first pints and cheered the arrival of Mavis to set up their second.

'I'll get these, boys. Roy, Rob, Adrian, Celia, okay? But the information first.'

'We trust you to keep to a deal.' Rob handed over an envelope. Mavis opened it and read two names and one address.

'Is this information correct?'

'Gold-plated, copper-bottomed, safe as the Bank of England correct. Plus, our own personal guarantees. Do you want to sit between us?'

Mavis got the round of drinks in and sat between Roy and Adrian. After some office chat and gossip, Roy and Rob moved off to join some mates at the other end of the bar, though Roy did mention that he would be coming back for more given the success of their mission. Mavis gave him a thumbs up sign. Celia could wait no longer, particularly as Adrian had also wandered off to see a colleague.

'Was the weekend as positive as expected?'

'Yes, it was Celia. Was yours?'

'Very much. I think Adrian and I have found a place.' The two of them smiled at each other.

'That's wonderful. Moving in soon?'

'Hope so; it's a rental with a six-month break clause. We're hoping to buy something together eventually.'

'That's a big commitment; you've discussed all the pros and cons between yourselves, I hope.'

'Adrian's very sound. Are you working on any commitments, Miss?'

'Celia, Mavis is okay socially. Let's just say the future looks more promising that it did.'

'So, you've got a bloke?'

'And the future is more *interesting* than it was.'

'Is he that one from the West Midlands?'

'You're very good, Celia. Now here's a note or two for you both to enjoy another drink and please get another pint for Roy and Rob. I'm off now, bye.'

Mavis got back to her flat and phoned Clive.

'Missed you.'

'Missed you.'

'We think Emily's Stanley is Matheson, of Chester: single and secretary of a walking group. Doing an online interview with him shortly to see how much involved he was with Underwood.'

'Good. How are we going to manage our weekends?'

Sixty

Stanley Matheson had been brought into the Chester police station for questioning. He was not under arrest, but he had been told that the interview was in connection with broadening their understanding of an ongoing police matter. They asked for and took down all his personal details, which DS Smith was listening in to, and then she was connected up with the interview room by video. She could now hear him and see him, but he couldn't see her. The formalities of introductions were dealt with, and Mavis started.

'Good morning, Mr Matheson, just to repeat, I'm DS Mavis Smith from Bristol. Can you hear me okay?'

Matheson nodded. 'It's fine.'

'What is the nature of your relationship with Frank Underwood?'

'We've been good mates forever from childhood and through school. In fact, I've known him all my life. We were also in the same form at school and had the same interests, same things we didn't like, and we got on.'

'What were those interests and things you both didn't like?'

'We were both good at maths and working things out; liked doing the experiments in chemistry and doing maps in geography. We didn't care much for games or PE, and neither of us got on well with French.'

'What about the social side of life?'

'We hung around coffee bars together, and when we were in our late teens, we hung around the sort of pubs that kept asking your age.'

'What about clubs, drama, things of that sort?'

'No, there was nothing like that. We went to the cinema about once a month and had a Chinese afterwards. Where's all this going, by the way?'

'I want to build up a picture of you and Frank. Are you aware that Frank is dead?'

'Of course I am, and I'm very sorry to hear that. I did wonder where he'd got to because his house seemed to have been empty for some weeks and he wasn't answering his phone. He normally gets in touch with me, if you see what I mean.'

'And he approached you either late last year or earlier this year, didn't he, and suggested you met up, after a long gap?'

'Yes, he did; it had been more than a few months since our last contact, and we met and talked.'

'And what exactly did you two talk about, Mr Matheson, after such a break?'

'To start with, it was all catch-up. You know. What each of us were doing, any recent changes; we both seemed to have been in the same jobs and in the same position as the last time we talked.'

'And then?'

'Then he talked about some venture he'd got on the side, work that he was involved with and he wanted to bring me in on it. I felt at the time that he didn't have the means or the courage or even the inclination to carry on with it, but that he needed to financially, or that it was difficult to get out of.'

'What happened next?'

'I agreed to meet him, actually for a Chinese for old times' sake, but he never turned up, and I've not heard from him since.'

'Didn't you get in touch with him to ask him to explain why he stood you up?'

'It was never like that with Frank; there was always a certain vagueness about him. I just took it that he'd changed his mind.'

'Thank you, Mr Matheson. I'll say goodbye for now and have a word with one of the officers with you.' She signed off the audio and separately spoke to one of the local police.

'Stanley can go for the moment. I'm not sure yet if he wasn't involved in the blackmail activities that led to Frank's death. Please tell him that we will probably need to speak to him again and he should stay in the area. Strange, he never asked about how Frank died. That could be a mistake.'

'Okay, Miss. He has had some minor scrapes with us in the past, so your line of thinking could be right. Talk soon, whenever you want.'

They said their farewells, and Mavis called Adrian and Celia in for debriefing.

'After Head contacted Underwood, the two of them continued the blackmailing process. Then Head dies, or is killed, and Frank is all alone in the venture which he sees as an income stream but is not sure enough or confident enough to do it on his own, so he wants to haul in an old mate that he can trust. Sound plausible?'

'Very. It's whether the Underwood/Matheson partnership got going in full, or Underwood was killed before it even started.'

'Until we find the culprits, we won't know that. Our Stanley sounds like he's going to stick firmly to his story because Frank can't say anything now. I better see Robertson.'

She put her head round his door.

'Good time, Sir?'

'Always for you, Smith. What's the latest?'

She filled him in on Matheson's answers.

'He can stick to that line forever. Thought you'd got the names of the suspects?'

'Yes, we have, and I need to do some work on that. They don't seem to exist at the minute.'

'You have an address. If you want to keep your powder dry, how about having an undercover snoop around with the locals for gossip?'

'I was wondering about something like that. Is that okay with you, Sir?'

'Yes, of course. Proceed with gusto, Smith.'

Mavis went back to her desk. Modestly, she thought she would be too conspicuous in Gloucestershire. It had to be Clive, and maybe he should take Adrian to help out. She phoned Clive.

Sixty-One

'So, you fancy yet another away day – in sunny Gloucestershire this time, Drewett?'

Clive had gone in to see CI Bolton about a strong follow-up lead on the Faulks case. He had been both pleased and irritated that Mavis had phoned. It was great to be involved, and Faulks was his case, of course, but he was mildly put out that it was presumed he could and would go. Mavis had asked nicely and sweetly and, in all honesty, had said why she couldn't do it. Stick out … sore … thumb. He agreed to go, of course, and thought afterwards that his initial reaction had been wrong. Would he have wanted her asking anyone else? Of course not.

'We're closing in on the murderers of the Bristol case,' he said to Bolton, 'and the suspected blackmail that Faulks must have had a hand in; I know your interest in the case, Sir, and I've been asked if I could do some local snooping.'

'Report back afterwards, and make sure you get something.'

'Thank you, Sir.'

He arranged to pick up Adrian at Cheltenham early, but not so early that Clive couldn't have a greasy spoon en route beforehand. Adrian jumped in and they drove to the village of the address given by Roy and Rob. Clive had suggested they were to be country walkers, him and his young friend, tramping the Gloucestershire footpaths.

'Pity we don't have a dog, they're priceless in situations like this,' Clive said to Adrian.

'What, for sniffing them out?'

'No, no, for having aimless chat with just anybody. Even if they haven't got a dog, you can get near them and say, "Down, Rover, there's a good dog. I'm so sorry but he's just being friendly," and then you're away. You can talk about absolutely anything.'

'Well, we haven't,' chirped Adrian. 'We could however be hopeless hikers, lost our way, is this the path going to take us to …'

Clive agreed.

They found the house, The Old Rectory, with sturdy gates and seemingly impenetrable fences and hedges surrounding the property. They walked all the way round and confirmed it.

'They don't want intruders, for sure. You might say consistent with the criminal mind.'

'Let's go to the village café for coffee, see who's there.'

They went into Christine's Café where Clive ordered two coffees and two scones. They mumbled a low conversation until a friendly middle-aged lady came in with two Scottie dogs, ordered a tea and a bun, and sat at an adjoining table. Clive had to wink at Adrian.

'Aren't they lovely, your two Scotties! Are they related?'

'Yes, they are, thank you for asking, it's lovely they're related. They're brother and sister, Jack and Jill. Keeps me fit, mind you, and it's like feeding a family.'

'They look very well on it. I suppose you know all the paths round here?'

'Every blade of grass. We meet all the dog walkers in the village.'

'That footpath, just past The Old Rectory, does it go anywhere?'

'Down to the river then circles round to the other end of the village. It's a lovely walk.'

'We must try it. We're doing as many paths as we can to work up a thirst for lunch at the local. The Old Rectory – does the vicar live there?'

'Oh no, it was sold off years ago; a couple bought it quite a few years ago now. Keep themselves to themselves, no children, no dogs, so we don't see much of them.'

She wittered away until Adrian said they should be getting on and it was nice to meet her. They decided to walk around in the hope of finding someone in their front garden, preferably near The Old Rectory. They did find a gardener who said he was an odd-job gardener as well. They chatted about what a pretty village it was, ('All down to you, I expect.'), and so forth, and then Clive took the plunge.

'The Old Rectory has a big garden – is that one of yours?'

The gardener, who looked past retirement age, sucked on his pipe and leant on his fork.

'It is and it isn't. They call me in to do a job and when I say the roses need pruning or the shrubs need seeing too, they just shrug and say we'll get back to you. Sometimes they do and sometimes they don't so, no, they're not one of my regulars. Generous payers, mind.'

They moved on. Adrian didn't see how they could get much more when Clive yelped:

'Get your phone out. There's a car coming out.'

They concealed themselves as best they could behind a bus shelter and clicked as much as was humanly possible while the car drove by with a single occupant.

'Get yours and mine over to Mavis, DS Smith, soonest. That was priceless. Our job is done, Adrian. Let's go to the village pub and see if there's any more gossip to glean.'

There wasn't, but there was shepherd's pie for dish of the day and some local real ale. Adrian had a lager.

Sixty-Two

Mavis and Celia devoured the info and data that came back from Clive and Adrian's visit to Gloucestershire. The photos, once blown up and clarified, were virtually the icing on the cake. The male person in the car seemed identical to one of the couple at the DIY store and the dockside where Frank's body was dumped. The car itself matched the car at the DIY store.

'That leaves a slight problem of verifying the names of each of them against the names the boys forced out of Martin. The photos of the house suggest a big leap up from junior bank staff to living in suburban London. Like, where did the money come from?' Mavis could already hear Robertson saying, 'Where's the solid proof?' Then she remembered Clive mentioning the theft of used notes.

'There's always inheritance, or they might be renting and paying cash each month,' said Adrian somewhat gloomily. 'But it was a good day out and I learnt a thing or two from DS Drewett.'

Mavis smiled inside; she was pleased that Clive had entered into the spirit of things with her, and now also his protégé.

Mavis went into Robertson and gave him as full a debrief as she could.

'Nearly done and dusted, Sir, though we need to be totally clear on their current names and also whether the wife/partner now is the same one as before. We've identified him enough, I feel, and it would be nice to get a glimpse of her.'

'Well, she's an active outgoing woman. She's not going to stay indoors all day. Send one of the boys down to hang around until she makes an appearance.'

'It's one of those villages where everybody knows everybody so an outsider would be conspicuous, Sir.'

'Flower delivery, bodycam, come on Smith, you'll find a way. Come back on Monday with the answer.' It was the first time he had been short with her. She scurried back to her desk and got Celia and herself thinking of the best way to get a woman to the front door and not be too bothered about a hidden camera.

Meanwhile, Clive had gone in to report to CI Bolton.

'I believe we've found where they live, at least there *is* verification of the male. Bristol are working on getting a mugshot of the female to check it's the same woman. If so, I believe we can arrest them, take them into custody, house search, DNA, everything, Sir.'

'Well done, Drewett, I knew we'd crack it. So, the plot is these two stole the money from the bank, Faulks found out from Head and they blackmailed them; they tried to bump Faulks off and he disappeared, and Head continued blackmailing with someone unknown and they bumped both of them off as well. I'm not sure we have proof of all that yet, especially the demise of Head a little while ago. The report said he was beaten up and left to die. That could be an entirely separate dispute, especially in London.'

'Correct, Sir, and my contact in London is getting some feedback as to what exactly happened and who told whom to do what.'

'There's more yet, Drewett, so get on with it and remember this is a West Midlands operation.'

Clive went back to his desk and phoned Neil.

'Hi Neil, sorry to interrupt, but what was the back story on Damon Head's death?'

'Yes, hi, thanks for calling. I know I'm due to get back to you on that. To put it bluntly, he was beaten up by a gang, identity unknown, and no one's talking. There is a likely gang in that area, but there's no story coming out. The guess is that they were meant to rough him up but they went too far. I do have another contact, and I'll have to go off-piste and incognito, so give me a few more days. How are you and Mavis getting on?'

'Er, well, thank you, call you soon, bye.' He rang off and gave some thought to just how much Neil had really helped him in life and his career; he must make it up to him sometime.

Sixty-Three

Mavis and Celia were chatting over coffee at Mavis's desk. They didn't think acting as flower delivery people would work in case someone like a cleaning lady answered the door and took them in.

'So, it has to be something to sign for. Our messenger can remark that it just needs a squiggle so he or she can show their supervisor later.'

'I think the messenger should be a man because it's easier for a man's clothing to disguise a bodycam. It is summer and the day could be warm.'

'Some delivery men just wear a T-shirt and denims; he's got to look convincing.'

'What about a summer picnic hamper – it's seasonal, right for the area, and should be very welcomed?'

'Perfect, I like it. Now, who to deliver? Roy or Rob don't quite cut it for drab incognito. Could Adrian carry it off, do you think? You could train him, Celia.'

'He said he did drama at school and college, and I could make sure he looks the part. We'd need to rent a small unmarked van. Are we allowed to do this sort of thing?'

'Robertson said flowers, whatever, get on with it; so, yes.'

Celia said she would whip young Adrian into shape immediately.

Adrian was flattered to be asked but of course went into logistics.

'Who do I say it's from? What if Nosey Parker in the village recognizes me from last time?'

'Well, let's think about that, Adi, and come up with some answers. Prosecco at the pub after work should do it for me.'

They both left on time.

Sixty-Four

Adrian had arranged to rent a small, plain white van. Plain meant absolutely no trade markings or anything to do with the rental company. He put some empty boxes in the back and Celia had got a summer picnic hamper delivered from a well-known prestigious grocery. She was also ransacking Adrian's apology of a clothes cupboard, and decided on trainers, navy blue trousers, not jeans, checked shirt and his fake leather jacket. The jacket had a versatile top pocket, able to accommodate a body cam which would be able to record the whole interaction with the customer.

They practised his routine and then did a dry run-through with Mavis.

'Ding-dong.' (The house bell.)

'Hi, I'm Dexter from Cheltenham Deliveries. Is the lucky lady of the house in?'

'Who the hell are you?'

'Well, I'm Dexter from Cheltenham Deliveries and I'm pleased to say the lucky lady of the house has been awarded one of ten special prizes in the lovely county of Gloucestershire. This one is a top of the range, all you ever wanted summer picnic hamper, champagne included.'

'Who's it from?'

'I can't take it back with me, and I'm not supposed to say who it's from as it's a gift to this address. It should be obvious from the contents that it's a promotional gift, and something to do with one of her ladyship's contacts.'

'I'll give it to her.'

'Er, ha ha, sorry, not so fast there; the lady has to sign. I have to see her take delivery with at least a squiggle – here – and then I can photo the hamper on your doorstep. I can come back tomorrow if it's not convenient. Look at the weather, though! Made for a picnic.'

Mavis smiled. 'I get the picture; it might work, but you'll have to think on your feet. I like the bit about coming back the next day, the last thing they would want. Adrian, are you comfortable about this? I have a couple of cheeky chappies in town who might volunteer.' She wondered if Darren or Charlie might be better, with Adrian as the driver.

'No, I'm fine thank you. Once I get into character, I'll be in it as the delivery boy, no longer an off or on duty policeman.'

'Celia, do you agree? You know him the best.'

'Yes, Miss, er, Mavis. I've seen him in AmDram, and he's surprisingly different. Quite worrying, really.' She pretended to pinch him.

'Okay, off you go. Celia you better go with him. Can you look like some down-trodden girl friend or sister in the passenger seat helping out?'

'Thanks for that.'

'And have a burger on the way back.'

They left the following morning, stopped for coffee on the way over, and drew up just short of the house to adjust the bodycam position and to switch it on. They arrived at the house late morning.

There were two cars in the drive, so they were hopeful the couple was in.

Celia gave him a kiss and told him he was wonderful whatever happened. They put the bodycam recorder on and she watched Adrian from the van. Meanwhile, she took a photo of the two cars.

A man answered the door and Adrian engaged with him. He put the cardboard box down and they were both talking, Adrian waving his hands. There was a pause, and a woman came to the door. Celia could see she was thrilled and touched, though the man was surly throughout. Finally, she did a squiggle and Adrian photographed the cardboard box on the doorstep and made steps back to the van. He also took a photo of the house.

He pretended to do something with the back doors of the van, then quietly drove off.

They stopped two villages further on and went into a café.

'Well, how did it go?'

'No problem. He started talking about it not being a very sensible way of marketing, but if they were stupid enough to dole out hampers then he would fetch his wife. She was thrilled but a bit wary. So, I said the worst thing that could happen was that I either had to return to the depot as a failure, or leave it with the neighbour next door and tell porkies. She signed straight off and I said what a lovely house, mind if I take a photo. Help yourself, he said. Mind you, I don't want to go there again.'

'Adi, you're great, well done. I'm having a whopperburger and fries! What about you?'

*

They returned later that afternoon and reported back to Mavis. She was well pleased, relieved Adrian of the bodycam, and sent it off for processing for sound and picture.

'How did they refer to each other?'

'He said "my wife", and she was wearing appropriate rings. She called him darling. The inside of the house was nothing out of the ordinary. We've got the number plates of the two cars, Celia, please divulge. There was absolutely no way I could get any fingerprints or

DNA, sorry.'

'Don't be; could be tricky if used in the future, anyway. Right, let's wrap up today and we'll look at and hear the bodycam tomorrow. Have a good evening.'

She saw Adrian and Celia slope off, even closer together than before.

She phoned Clive.

Sixty-Five

The next morning, Mavis reviewed the video images and sound recordings from Adrian's bodycam. The sound was fine but the video sequences were jerky. The gist of it was in line with Adrian's debrief, and blown-up stills from the video showed a clear frontal picture of the woman's face; there was even a sidelong profile of the man. Mavis sat back in her chair and sighed deep breaths. Yes, she thought, we've got 'em, and collectively we've cracked a robbery and at least one murder. Phew. She went into Robertson.

'Got a minute, Sir?'

'Always for you, Smith, come in and sit yourself down. I fancy you've something to say.'

She ran through all the recent events, quietly but definitely emphasising the parts played by Adrian and Celia, even a mention of Roy and Rob and a certain DS from the West Midlands.

'You and him have done some work together before, haven't you?'

'Yes, Sir, he taught me all I know down in Sussex a few years back.'

'Mmm. I had heard on the grapevine that you were quite close.'

Mavis blushed but hardly detectably so.

'I've been professional throughout, Sir.'

'I know, I know. I was actually being complimentary because a certain CI Bolton up there has been in touch and speaks highly of him. Bolton is happy to share the credit but he would prefer something in the region of 90:10. I was thinking more the other way round, given the work you've put in.'

'I'm happy it's solved. Maybe we could split the difference, Sir?'

'Very diplomatic; I'm happy to authorize the arrests, but take some support with you. Roy and Rob will be happy to help.' There was even the trace of a smile on his lips.

Mavis was left thinking that Robertson didn't just live in an ivory tower in his corner office, he also put out tentacles every which way.

She went back to her desk, and phoned down to Roy and Rob.

'How are you both placed for a morning arrest just outside Cheltenham? Robertson's authorized them and suggests you both come with me.'

'Now, isn't that nice of him? A real gent, that one. Course we will, my love.'

'I'm not anyone's love, or even yours. It's DS Smith, though it's Mavis in the office.'

'No offence, my, er … We're available and we'll be ready for you outside at 7.30 tomorrow morning.'

'Thank you, Roy, I'll look forward to it. Maybe a bacon butty on the way?'

'You're talking the biz now, my, er … Yes, my kinda nosh. See you.'

Mavis had to smile; these unreconstructed uniforms could be the salt of the earth – if only they would realize it.

She phoned Clive in the evening and ran through it with him. He was pleased for her and glad that she had got a couple of heavies in attendance.

'Maybe we could get together afterwards to celebrate?'

'That's a very good idea; I almost thought of it myself. Yours or mine this weekend?'

Sixty-Six

DS Mavis Smith had written out all the right words on a card and she had memorized them to perfection.

'Penelope Amanda Norton, aka Amanda Wightman, and Richard Anthony Villiers, aka Anthony Ollerton, you are both to be arrested formally for the murder of Frank Underwood and further charges will be made later. Please step this way for the formal charges to be made. We also have a search warrant for your house, the premises and the gardens, and the authority to collect DNA and fingerprints.'

*

They had left Bristol Station promptly at 7.30 am in two vehicles – Mavis, Roy and Rob in one, and the supporting uniforms in the other. Roy and Rob would do the man-handling as required, and the others would encircle and secure the property at the same time. They had reached the village by 8.30 and, as they were all already briefed, drove straight into the property and pulled up outside the front door.

Mavis went up to the front door, knocked and rang the ornate chimes. There was no response.

PART II

Previously

One

Some twenty five years or more earlier, Penelope and Richard were working in a bank. They had been chums since childhood and were known universally as Penny and Ricky. School exams did not reveal any academic skills and, with an aptitude for turning pence into pounds via picking up discarded items from skips and bins, they happened to drift into working for the same local bank branch. Maybe they both had in mind the crime boss who had said that was where the money was. Ricky had always had that side to him. As a teenager, he would take on any challenge for money, even including having a scrap in the school playground as a bet. After leaving school, this confrontational approach had become ingrained in him and he continued to dabble in money-making ventures such as collecting or pinching things, changing or improving them, and then selling various parts for cash. Penny went along with this side of his nature, sometimes venturing to say as much as 'Are you sure about this?', and then joining in the fun afterwards with the cash to spend.

They both made steady progress through parallel departments in the bank and got themselves moved on to a bigger branch. They lunched and socialized together during the week, mainly because they were both still living back home with their respective parents. As time passed with their growing relationship, they moved from being girlfriend and boyfriend to a steady partnership. They were as close as siblings, even twins; very self-contained with each other; independent from other friends, and this quickly built into a solid total trust with and of each other. They could literally talk about anything to each other, with absolute confidence that it would remain private between them. And each knew that whatever they said or did, no offence was given or taken. They were a unit.

Over the next few years, their knowledge of the bank's workings grew enormously. They knew who did what and when; they knew about checks and balances; they were familiar with the flow of cash and cheques, and who reported to whom. More insidiously, they learnt about the personal rivalries, the allegiances and romances. It was like a big village where they had all grown up together and where everybody knew everybody.

About this time, Ricky's adolescent aptitude for turning pence into pounds resurfaced. It had been a while since his last little jape of collecting discarded road signs and traffic cones and passing them on to a stall in the market for cash. They had rented a fixed caravan on the south coast for a few days, away from parents. At two o'clock one morning, Ricky turned over in bed to face Penny.

'Penny, you awake?'

'Am now. What's up?'

'I think I know how to rob the bank and get away with it.'

'What is wrong with you? Have you been drinking? There's no way we wouldn't get caught. Guilty as charged, and then we're in clink. No thank you very much. It's way, way out of our, I mean your, league.'

'Not if we got away with it. We wouldn't get caught and it isn't out of our league.'

'Okay, smarty pants give me a clue about *how*. I'm not going to prison.'

'It's not original, far from it, but it's to do with how they dispatch the used notes. Either to be destroyed or to recycle to other branches or head office.'

'Go on, I'm listening.' She wrapped herself closer to him.

'There's a gap. There's a physical gap when the bank notes are moved on to dispatch, and there's a time lapse between the dispatch and the paperwork doing the reconciliation. Two people can intervene in those gaps.'

'I'm getting it, Ricky, you're actually right, I know what you mean, but that still doesn't mean we'd get away with it, does it?'

'No, agreed. It needs lots more work and thinking and research. Then there's the consequential shifting it when the notes are in our possession, and finally, there's what we do with the cash without getting caught. The Great Train Robbery didn't work out too well. This would be a smaller amount, obviously.'

'Glad to hear it, dearie, but the bank's internal people would be right on it, and on everybody who could have been involved.'

'Not if they didn't realize for a day or two. I'm warming to this.'

'Me too, but only very, very slightly; so, let me be clear, King Richard, this has got to work because you and I are not going to do time. No way. Ever. So, the plan and its execution has to be absolutely flawless, right through to how we spend the money. We've no history of flashing the cash so anything obvious is going to draw attention to us. Don't forget you have a bit of a reputation for odd deals.'

'Spot on. Tell you what, I'll come up with the plan to get the money bags; you work on how we handle the afterwards. Now, come here.'

Two

Despite their wayward thinking, Penny and Ricky were nevertheless highly conscientious in their employed work and, separately, equally so in their private plans. One weekend, a few weeks after Ricky's lightbulb moment, they took a long walk into the country and outlined their respective thoughts to each other. Ricky started.

'The notes are bundled up in large, official looking, stiff, brown paper bags and sealed with a reference number on. A few of us were chatting and I tossed one around with some of the guys. They weigh around five pounds, that's two and a bit kilos. I'd like to pinch two of them but we may have to settle for one. These bags are piled up in a dispatch chute and when it's full, it's released to send them down. The operator can't see the chute but the CCTV is on them. Now, to one side there's a little cosy corner. I was thinking that if you were changing into your netball kit, all innocent like, the operator would turn the CCTV onto you and not the bags.'

'Thanks, and I'm permanently on record getting my kit off.'

'No, because I would go up to him and accuse him of gawping at my girlfriend so he'd better delete it, which he would because he'd want to keep his job.'

'But what will you be doing?'

'While he's distracted, I put two of the bags into one of those bags for getting rid of plastic cups and lunch waste, and move them to the big waste bin. Because the chute would be only half full at that stage, the operator wouldn't be able to assess how many bags should have gone in and would carry on sending the bags down. Meanwhile, I shift the waste bin, lift out the bin liner with the money bags in, take it outside and put it in the boot of our car.'

'Someone will see that you're not in the office; someone will notice you carrying a waste bin bag.'

'Not if I'm helping clear some space in the staff restaurant for the new drinks machine. Then you get in the car and drive off, having told everyone you're off to netball practice.'

'It's neat, but it's not neat enough. More work on that please, Ricky; now to my bit about the aftermath – which is making the enormous assumption that we can carry it off successfully without being caught. First of all, we do absolutely nothing for several weeks. Normal work, normal activities, normal chat at work. There will be massive investigations; they'll be getting the drains up. On what you've just said, the operator will be forced to say something about me changing. I'll be saying I was late for netball practice, I didn't have time to go over to the smelly changing rooms in the Ladies, and I thought it was private until that pervert started filming me. You'll have to cover yourself for the waste bins thing. Then back at the ranch we count the notes, shuffling them in case they are in some sort of order. Depending on the amount, we then have to buy things that can be sold later for money that can go into a bank account. I think it's called money laundering – turning bad money into good. Thoughts at the moment are a car, or cars, if they'll take cash, antiques, about which we know nothing, wine, ditto, buy something sellable off a foreigner who is happy with sterling. If we had a house, we could extend it, paying builders and plumbers cash, and then sell, but that seems a bit extreme. You got any ideas?'

'The trouble with buying something for cash and then selling is that it is bound to be at a significant loss. That's the way the world works. I guess we are going to have to do all of them in small doses so as not to attract attention. Once it's in the banking system, we can buy a flat or something, and have a good holiday. Yep, I like your thinking. You're right – much more work needed from both of us.'

Three

Penny and Ricky mulled over their plans for several weeks more. Mainly because of her confidence in Ricky, Penny was starting to come round to the idea that it might just possibly work. It was too risky for just one of them, both in execution and detection. Penny had got more involved in the bank's netball team to strengthen that part of the operation at least. Also, it clarified the best place to park their car for a clear exit to go to netball practice on D-Day. Ricky made use of his job as a bit of a go-for and made sure to be visible all over the corridors and offices so his appearances anywhere at any time would always been seen as normal. In particular, he wanted to get a handle on the frequencies and timings of the used notes dispatch. It seemed to be Tuesdays and Thursdays, the former from the weekend trading, the latter prior to the weekend trading. There were three operators of the dispatch and they generally kept themselves to themselves. Ricky called them Tom, Dick and Harry. With three of them, and twice a week, that meant a three-weekly cycle. They were all conscientious, they had to be, but in Ricky's judgment Harry was the least sharp and carried out his duties reliably but robotically. Ricky's wanderings also established the best time of day when the chute was roughly half full, and also when there would be minimal people traffic for doing the switch out of the line of sight of the operators. And there had to be a netball practice.

They had found a flat not far from the bank in suburban London where they lived happily together, sharing much of the cost of rent, food and other bills. Over coffee one Sunday morning, they decided to have a review of where they had got to.

'We have to do a pretend run, like a dress rehearsal, to check we've not overlooked something.'

'Agreed. We can hardly do it at the bank so we're going to have to do some sort of simulation here.'

'It's a two-room, K & B flat.'

'Confined is good. Let's configure the main problem areas. I hide from the operator here, you saunter down with your netball kit, have a nervous look round, look suspicious, and start getting changed. The important bit is you change into your sports bra.'

'I know that's the bit you're looking forward to.'

'It is, my darling, because that's when the operator's gaze will be on you. Perhaps do some readjustment with your bra, you know what girls do.'

'Thank you, Mr Pervy, I can dress myself.'

'Then I grab two of the bags, mid-load, put them in the wastebin liner and then into the bigger bin, move it to the general waste area, put the black bin liner in the boot of the car and saunter back to the Credit Department. You apply some finishing touches to yourself and equally saunter down to the car and drive off. The bags will be covered up with a blanket, you can do normal netball and be out as long as you like. Back here, we stuff the bags at the back of the cupboard and live a very normal life at work and home for several weeks. We will count the dosh and decide how we're going to play the laundering bit. But that is in our own time and without any interference from the outside world.'

'I like the idea of buying something off a foreigner who'll be happy with sterling cash.'

'We'll have to spread. We could go to Amsterdam or Hamburg and see what they're selling. I wondered about buying a lock-up garage for the cash and then selling it.'

'And I wondered about putting ponies on ponies! What about just the favourites and second favourites?'

'They would take cash, but we could only hope for half of it back at the very most. Anyway, that thinking is down the track a bit, as it were.'

'Okay, timing: we need to coincide a Tuesday or a Thursday with Harry, and when it's netball practice. Let's look at schedules at work and find a date. Are you really up for this, Penny? Of course I want to do it because I think we can carry it off, but I want you to be committed too.'

'I think I am. Perhaps a bit more thinking time from me; give me a few more days to attempt to cover the risks. Same question to you, Ricky?'

'Yes, and if it makes you more comfortable, if anything isn't quite right on the day, we abort without delay and try another time.'

'Remind me why I'm not getting changed in the Ladies?'

'The corridor has a secluded corner and it's convenient to go straight from there to your car for netball practice. Also, and I'm guessing here, there are some women you'd rather avoid in the Ladies – plenty of unwelcome gossipy asides going round the bank about *that*. Also, maybe you have some misgivings about the state of cleanliness? It's certainly true of the men's. Does that work?'

'You're mostly right, and I can work up a good yarn on that, even mentioning a few names if it gets dirty.'

All was agreed; the next event would be the heist.

Four

Ricky had fine-tuned and double-checked his plans over and over again. Even though he had done some shady deals in the past, none of them was like this. This had to be zero tolerance; if not, he would have let Penny down and that was the last thing he wanted. He had asked her again if she was in. She said, 'Yes I am. Get on with it.' She was his rock. He firmed up the plans.

Yes, it would be Harry, and it would be next Thursday. Yes, it would be netball practice prior to the weekend game. Yes, the car had petrol and the tyres had air. Yes, Penny and he each had car keys.

They did not sleep well Wednesday night. Penny understood her role, which was "merely" to get changed, go down the stairs and drive off. She imagined a police posse right on her tail, forcing her to stop the car, strip searched, and put in gaol for years on end. Ricky imagined his dexterity of placing the money bags into the bin liner going all cack-handed and clumsy, tripping over his feet and spilling the beans – or rather, the notes.

It was now Thursday morning. They dressed inconspicuously. At work, Penny kept a low profile, working studiously at her desk and not drawing attention to anything significant. She chatted to colleagues either side to make sure they remembered her at her desk. She also went away from her desk, mentioning going to another department, to make an absence routine.

Ricky on the other hand was determined to be conspicuous. He made himself visible to most departments, sometimes carrying files or an adding machine, sometimes with bin liners for the paper waste and other stuff.

Their planning and behaviours paid off. It went as swimmingly and as totally according to plan as Ricky had envisaged.

Penny had carried her games kit bag down to the secluded corner, making sure she was able to be seen by the CCTV. Then she did her coy female act to perfection; she could hear the CCTV device whirr round onto her, but did not look up. The sports bra sequence would win an Oscar. Then she picked up her clothes, pretended to look round nervously – not difficult – then casually walked down the stairs, threw her work clothes in the back of the car, and drove off.

Ricky meanwhile had hidden in the adjoining corridor until he could hear Penny starting to get changed; he even heard the same whirr of the CCTV device as Penny had. He nipped round the corner, put two money bags into a black bin liner and scuttled off down the stairs, dumping the bag first into a bigger bin which he wheeled away nearer to the back of their car. He put the bin liner into the boot and spread a blanket over it. He then went round the block to another side door and went back to his desk carrying a cup of the machine coffee. He behaved the rest of the day as he had in the morning, and left for home when most of the other staff did. He took the bus back and waited for Penny.

Netball practice was routine. Penny performed as her usual self and made an effort to neither shine nor fumble. The girls laughed afterwards and suggested a pub which Penny sadly declined. She wasn't sure about that decision as her main thought was how fraught Ricky would be until she got back. Thankfully a few of the other girls also left after the game, citing boyfriend or children or family reasons.

She drove back and parked the car as normal and rushed up to Ricky.

'Did it work? How did we do?'

'Okay I think. There were no noises at the office today; that'll come when accounts do the reckoning. How was netball?'

'Fine. I think I did a good play-act, though I'm not tempted to try drama as a different career. They're in the car. When shall we retrieve?'

'When it might look normal; there are always net curtain twitchers. I suggest we have supper and then take some rubbish down to put in the bins. We can then muddle up any potential witnesses as they'll see bin liners being taken down and brought back up.'

'That's if we get caught. Looks okay so far, darling.'

'Early days. Tomorrow at work will be crucial. We've got to be so normal, do exactly what we normally do the next few days. It'll kick off either midday tomorrow or after the weekend on Monday. What are we eating tonight?'

After a tense supper, Ricky took a black bin down to the communal bins and then back via the car. He retrieved the black bin from the back of the car and, as nonchalantly as possible, returned to the flat. It was now twilight so they could draw the bedroom curtains. They opened the money bags to reveal lots and lots of used notes. They hugged each other very tightly. This was their most daring exploit ever. They had robbed a bank and got away with it. They couldn't get caught now.

Ricky had prepared a cupboard with a bottom drawer that could be covered over with all sorts of domestic stuff. First, they put the notes into two bags, flattening them down and putting photo albums, boxes of games, sundry files and papers on top. Then they disguised the cupboard and drawers with messy blankets and duvets on top of it. The idea was to make the cupboard look as normal as one would expect in any cluttered flat. They opened a bottle of wine and had an early night.

The next day at the bank was as challenging as the previous day, but in a very different way. They decided to be inconspicuous, normal, chatty but not too chatty. At least Penny could discuss the netball before the game the following day. Ricky adopted the same role as the day before but spending a little more time at his desk to gauge any office gossip. There was none until about three o'clock. One of the senior executives had called a staff meeting to make an announcement about a theft of used notes, and said there would be a full internal investigation. Everyone would be interviewed after the weekend.

Penny and Ricky returned to their respective desks and buried themselves in work. Ricky phoned Penny on the internal line.

'Back to the flat separately, you take the car. We have some removals to do.' Penny got it straight away and put the phone down.

They left, not together, two hours later, and didn't meet up until they were both back at their flat.

'I reckon that after the staff interview with Harry, they will pick on you and therefore me sooner rather than later. They will know that we will think that too so we have to move the booty out of here. We have to expect them to get a warrant to search this place and I'd far rather say welcome, search away. This is not a mistake, Penny, it's them doing their job to investigate when something appears to go wrong. We just have to run with the investigation and keep to what we decided to say all along.'

'Yes, I get that, but it will be hot next week. Where do we hide the stuff?'

'A locker at a railway station will be under CCTV. What about your or my folk's place?'

'Far too risky. Got a safe deposit box?'

'No, and anyway that would be too small. We can't trust any friends. It would be safer in our lockers at the bank but that's a touch brazen. I've got a strong, sealed metal box that would be big enough. Where could we bury it?'

'Your dad's Spinney. He never goes down there and it's private, so no one else does.'

'Hello, Dad, we've just come to bury some stolen stuff, don't mind us. How? It's miles away too.'

'We'll drive down there in the morning. I drop you off with said box at the fence where you can get in. I'll drive up to the front door and say your joining us in an hour or so, let's go down to the Hops & Chops, our treat for Saturday lunch. Oh no – I've got a netball match.'

'You can't miss that, far too conspicuous.'

'Yep, we'll have to do our preparation before the game, and then go over to your dad afterwards. Saturday supper, not lunch.'

'Okay but what if it's too late, or he declines, or he says where's Ricky?'

'It'll be fine, I'll phone him.'

Next morning, they stuffed the notes first into black bin liners and then into the strong box. They also wrapped polythene round the strong box and covered it with a blanket in the back of the car, together with an open hamper containing bottles. Ricky dropped Penny off at the ground and decided to watch the match. She impressed him with her game, and after their win, she made her apologies to the team about having to go to a family gathering. They drove back to their flat, and soon after she had showered and changed, they left for the West Country. Penny dropped Ricky at Horseman's Corner, lifting the box over the wall with a fork and spade. Ricky chose a secluded spot and started digging. The ground had not been touched; it was hard work and he had to work quickly. He double-checked that the box was sealed and wrapped up tightly in polythene. He deposited the whole package in the bottom of the small trench he had dug out and covered it over first with plenty of clay and soil, and then more loosely with leaf mould and leaves to give a natural look. He took the fork and spade back to the inside of the wall at Horseman's Corner, climbed over the fence and strolled into the village. He got cleaned up before joining Dad and Penny at their table at the Hops & Chops. They enjoyed their supper together, dropped Dad back, picked up the spade and fork on the way back, and had a quiet, late night drive back to their flat before collapsing into bed.

Five

Monday morning at the bank had to be as natural as possible and they both kept their heads down doing their normal work. Ricky stuck rigidly to his normal demeanour and wandered around with office equipment on trolleys and various bin collections. They were both interviewed separately by Peter Vernon from Internal Audit who told them that he had been put in sole charge of the investigation, pending any police involvement. Penny's sports gear change allowed her to say that she wanted that tape wiped clean, and Vernon gave that undertaking, 'Unless the police take this further'. Ricky's interview was complete ignorance and innocence, venting his outrage that cameras had been trained on his girlfriend. Vernon had been direct about the consequences of lying during the interviews.

Both back at the flat, they compared notes. Ricky thought they were in the frame but the bank had no evidence or proof. Penny was reassured by Vernon's promise to wipe the tape clean; Ricky didn't mention Vernon's caveat. There was a phone message that evening from Security at the bank, requesting they both stay at the flat in the morning for a visit to continue discussions.

Tuesday morning, next day, they remained at the flat, and at 9.15 two men in navy blue overcoats arrived.

'Please, may we come in?'

'Please do. Can I get you gents tea or coffee?' Penny was urbane politeness.

'We're fine, thank you. I'm Brian and this is Alan. We're from Internal Audit at the bank and acting under the authority of Peter Vernon.'

'I think I've seen you around. You're normally buried in files on the fifth floor.'

'Sadly, yes, so this is an away day for us.' The attempt at humour failed on this occasion.

'We'd like to ask you about your situation vis-a-vis each other, and how closely you work together, and maybe take a look around to support what you say. Do you have a garage?'

Ricky thought at this stage that this was a pretty juvenile approach, then caught himself wondering if that was itself an act. It was obvious they had been sent round to see if the money bags were here. Like we'd put them on the mantelpiece! He let Penny do her charm bit.

'Well, we live together some of the time, mostly weekends. We've known each other a good few years now and obviously we're not in any other relationships, if that's what you mean. We get by on two bank salaries in relatively junior positions and we have a normal social life. As well as that, I play for the bank's ladies' netball team which, as you probably know, is doing really well. We practise regularly.'

She didn't say like last Thursday. 'Do have a look around, we generally live quite modestly and, no, we don't have a garage but our little car is out there in the parking place assigned to this flat.'

Ricky was itching to say that they had absolutely no authority or right to search their premises, but chose to bite his tongue. Don't draw attention to yourself. *We want to keep our jobs.*

While Brian continued with the chat, they could hear Alan opening and shutting drawers. Ricky was inwardly fuming. Alan came back into the main room and nodded at Brian.

'Thank you so much for putting up with us; we'll be on our way. If you think of anything relevant to our discussion, do please just pop in to see me on the fifth floor. Goodbye.' And they were gone.

Ricky put his index finger to his lips and waited until they were well out of sight.

'Hardly Knacker of the Yard, eh, but was it an initial probe before more?'

'They have nothing to go on. If they up the ante, we can respond with violation of our rights and civil liberties, and all that crap.'

'Good we moved sharpish on Saturday; I'm sure nobody saw us.'

'Agreed. We need a long period of quiet stability now and we do nothing that draws attention to us or our lifestyle.'

'Also agreed and it gives us time to work out how to exchange the notes for genuine assets or cash, or whatever. It's going to be tricky, Pen.'

'Yes, but we always have the fallback option to dribble the cash out a bit at a time. Worst case scenario is effectively a salary supplement – can't be too bad, can it?'

*

Alan and Brian had reported back to Peter Vernon as soon as they were back at the office.

'No progress with the money as there's no physical place to hide the bags in the flat. They're either one hundred per cent guilty and in league with each other, or entirely innocent and the kit change was an unfortunate coincidence for Penny.'

'Do we actually know that the time of the theft coincided with Penny's change?'

'No, we don't, but it is the only thing that happened that day that was out of the ordinary.'

Six

Penny and Ricky stuck to their plans and laid low. They dutifully carried out their tasks and routines at the bank. There was a further follow-up meeting with Vernon, but nothing came out at it or from it. They avoided the security screens area and had no contact with Harry, who was actually called Damon, and who they knew had been questioned as well. For netball, Penny either got changed in the Ladies or came to work already partly dressed in her games kit. They regularly split up going back to their flat, sharing the car at most once or twice a week. Supper talk continued to be how to get the used notes into other forms of assets. Penny was the more analytical, pointing out that purchases had to be acceptable in cash, no questions asked, and equally had to be capable of being turned back into cash at a later date. This was a given. She also said that they had to assume that filling up their flat with expensive assets would not work as they could not rule out another visit from the bank. They started to read the "Other Assets" section of the investment pages of the financial Press: fine wines, vintage cars, rare stamps, antique furniture, works of art – all very good and wonderful, but not quite for them, plus there was the storage issue.

Penny suggested they look in other weekly periodicals to see what people were actually selling, to get some ideas. She produced an issue she had bought the previous week as this problem had been on her mind. Cars, boats, houses and flats dominated, none of which had much appeal because they'd have to be bought through official channels. Then Ricky finally came to a conclusion.

'It's got to be a property or land out of the way somewhere. Someone who's desperate to sell and will take cash. Something so non-descript that we can maintain it minimally and sell out when we can be free again.'

'It has to be in someone's name.'

'That is a problem. Even if you change your name, there would be a record of that somewhere. Fancy getting pregnant to put it in baby's name?'

'What about abroad? I suppose that means a currency exchange somewhere. What about someone from abroad?'

'How d'you mean?'

'Well, say, let's assume there's someone over here from continental Europe looking for someone in the UK to buy a house, villa, flat, shack, whatever back home that they want to get rid of?'

'How do we find such a person, and even trust them?'

'A small ad in this periodical, for example: "Couple seeking to purchase small property abroad for clean sterling cash, without chain or delay." How does that sound?'

'Brilliant if it works. Let's do it.'

They smartened up the wording and made it fit the size required, placing it for three consecutive issues under a box number.

'Now we wait.'

Seven

They had waited. Three issues had gone and the most recent was now over a fortnight ago.

'Well, it was worth a try,' said Ricky over breakfast on the hoof. In the evening when they got in, there was a letter forwarding a response made to the box number.

'It says, "Am interested. No agents or any intermediaries. Can meet London coffee place. Phone me."'

There was a phone number with the message.

'It's brief and cryptic; it could be us writing it.'

'Quite. What if he's a criminal or a detective?'

'Join the club. We have nothing to lose, and if it's suspicious, we put the phone down. I'll put it on speaker and do the unknown number thing.'

Ricky phoned the number given. After at least six rings, a man answered.

'Hello.'

'Hello, we're responding to your response to our box number advert. Thank you for responding.'

'I have a small house in Belgium, really small, in fact. I can register your name or names as a buyer, providing you are good for the cash.'

'Sounds good. What do we call you? Please could you send photos of the house and the neighbourhood, and give an indication of price? We are happy to forego survey and solicitors, it's just a toe-hold abroad for us.'

'For the moment, call me Mr B, for Belgium. I get your drift. I will call you Mr L for London. Photos no problem; let's meet for coffee in London, shall we say a café near in Piccadilly Circus, and I can describe the property and show you photos, and we will try to agree a price. I do not want anyone else involved and sterling cash is fine. This Saturday morning, Glasshouse Street 11 am, Bye.'

They looked at each other.

'It's either perfect or a complete scam. How do we tell the difference?'

'Dunno. Meet him and see what we think, yes?'

'Absolutely. Did you think he had an accent?'

'Sort of global; sounds a much travelled man. Might be trying to get rid of a love nest or consolidate his wealth or is bankrupt or wants to disappear … or whatever!'

'You did say "we", so he knows I'll be coming too.'

'You'll be perfect, darling.'

Eight

On Saturday morning, Mr B for Belgium strolled into a café in Glasshouse Street at 11.15. Penny and Ricky had got there a few minutes before 11, and they had the feeling that he had watched them arrive in order to get a better feel for them before the meeting. They would then have been instantly recognizable to him.

'Good morning. May I call you Mr and Mrs L?'

'Hi Mr B, we're just Penny and Ricky if you're okay with that.'

'Of course.'

Mr B had the manner of a successful business man, well-groomed, probably in his early fifties but looked younger and clearly a regular at the gym. Penny got up and gave the orders for three coffees, Mr B having a straight black.

'Shall we get straight down to business? Here are some photos, a spec of the building and the small patch of scrub at the side and the back; and a map showing the location marked with a cross. You take your time; it's important.'

They were looking at a small country cottage. Romantic retreat would be far too much of an overstatement; a hovel would be unkind. The map showed it at the edge of a village a few miles from Bruges. The property comprised a reception room and kitchen downstairs, and one bedroom and bathroom upstairs. No loft, and there was a pretence of a lean-to at the rear, and the small patch of scrub at the back amounted to thirty square metres at most, with boundaries of overgrown hedges. They smiled and looked up at him.

'Clearly I will take questions but it might save time if I gave you my take on it. The pluses are that the village is sweet, there's room for a car in the front. It is what it is, and I've been very happy staying there. The minuses are the state of repair and lack of decoration; and the kitchen and bathroom are not exactly mod con.'

'Thanks Mr B. Why are you selling?'

'Right. I bought it ages ago as a place to get out of the rat race, to unwind, like a retreat. Since then, I've been relatively successful in business and I've acquired a couple of other retreats which, shall we say, are much nicer places to live in. I've been late in forming a stable relationship and my partner, shall we say, also prefers my other two places on the continent. My cost of living has increased, and it seems perfectly obvious that as I've no real emotional attachment to this property that I should (a) get rid of it, and (b) get some cash. Now I'm going to do the gentlemanly thing and walk round the block and when I return, I would ask you to be forthright with me one way or the other.' He got up and left.

'Pen, let me say straight off that if he answers our questions to our satisfaction and can smooth the conveyancing and agree a price, we should go for it.'

'Yes, okay, that's three qualifiers. We know our maximum absolutely and we must leave something over for some refurb. But yes, I agree.'

'Shall we find out his asking price first? It might be out of our range.'

'Okay. Here he is. Shall we have another round of coffees, Mr B?'

'Excellent. Now fire away.'

They first asked about the property, the neighbours, the neighbourhood and the general state of repair. Then the conveyancing.

'Mr B, we know nothing about conveyancing in Belgium, or the transfer of ownership, presumably solely yourself, to us. What can you do?'

'I have a local solicitor friend in the village. He drew up my purchase from a local farmer years ago. I trust him to do the same. The Belgian authorities are a closed book to me; he does all of that and my strongest suggestion to you is to let him continue. He's already involved, so any problems there are, he has to sort out. There are taxes and you will need to find a way to pay him from the UK. It worked for me.'

'We like the concept, Mr B, and I think it's going to suit our purposes. That just leaves price and I would mention here it will be sterling cash.'

'I'm going to write a figure on this piece of paper; you write something against it.'

Penny and Ricky looked at his opening offer. They were shocked to see a figure well within their absolute maximum.

'Is the property free from debts and any liabilities or anything external like council demands etc?'

'Nothing at all; I stand by what I said – it is what it is.'

Ricky wrote down a figure several thousand pounds lower.

'Shall we split the difference and shake on it?'

They looked at each other; Penny nodded.

'Let's.'

'Well done, good business; you'll go far and it's nice for me to know that such a lovely couple are taking over. Now, details; I'll brief my solicitor friend to draw everything up. I'm assuming you're happy for him to act for you as well? Good. Here's his phone number, he speaks good English. He'll do the transfer documentation, I'll sign, then you sign to complete and hand over the cash. I'm happy for you to give it to him. You may be lucky; he comes to London now and again so you can complete here.'

'No part of this is anything to do with the UK authorities? He won't lodge details here?'

'Relax, Ricky. I can assure you there's absolutely no chance of that.'

They shook hands again and he was gone, lost in the crowds in seconds.

Penny and Ricky just laughed at each other.

'Are we mad? Yes! I fancy a Chinese and some booze.'

They drifted into Chinatown.

Nine

Penny and Ricky had been busy. At work, they studiously kept to their regime of keeping their heads down, dutifully doing their daily tasks and routines, minimizing the time they spent together or being seen together. They tried to keep negotiations with Mr B or his solicitor, a Monsieur Hector, to the evenings, but occasionally one or the other came through during the day. They claimed each one was a private call during their permitted coffee breaks. Ricky had asked by personal email for a report on the general condition of the property and any outstanding or topical issues raised by the local council. These came through after a couple of weeks and seemed sufficient for their purposes.

'All we need to know is that if and when we choose to sell, we can at least get our money back and preferably a bit more,' said Penny.

The perceived bigger issues were signing the transfer of title to them and the physical handover of cash. Ricky thought a country pub, but Penny thought they should take a room in a quiet hotel somewhere because Monsieur Hector and they themselves would want to count the notes.

They asked Monsieur Hector about his upcoming trips to the UK and he did concede that he could justify a trip in about two months' time. Ricky suggested meeting him off a train from Paddington, near his dad's place. He was agreeable to that, adding that the fare and other extras would be added to his fee, payable at the same time. Penny, who had a logistical side to her brain, piped up that they couldn't just dig the crate up and turn up looking like a couple of urchins.

'We need to stay at your dad's place, send him away for a couple of days so we can have a base there, get cleaned up, count the dosh and appear professional and presentable.'

'Yes, too right, Pen. He loves bridge and I'm sure we can find him a hotel bridge event to attend and maybe take part in. I won't mention two spades.'

'Okay, can you arrange that when we've got the date or dates from Monsieur Hector, and I'll look for a suitably quiet hotel just past Reading out of Paddington for him.'

They had wondered about going over to see the place but decided against it. Going abroad could get back to Vernon and renew his suspicions of them. There were no other internal suspects as far as they knew and the idle gossip at work was turning to the van driver or some contact of his during his journey from the bank. On a personal level, they were aware that Damon Head was avoiding them, and if their paths did cross, there was no eye contact either way. Their perception was that the event was no longer a topic of interest and life had moved on.

Late on a Sunday morning a fortnight later, Monsieur Hector phoned Ricky's newly acquired mobile.

'Good morning, Mr and Mrs L. I trust you are well. I have completed all the documentation to my and Mr B's satisfaction. I will need your full names and address to fill in some blanks and the actual date of completion. I can be in the UK in two weeks' time, so can we agree the date now, please.'

They did, and Penny asked to have a further word.

'Hello, Monsieur Hector, please can you confirm that any and indeed all of the information on the documentation will never be made aware to any UK authorities without our prior permission?'

'You ask a good question, mademoiselle. I can confirm that the sole requirement as the law now stands is that a copy of the documentation will be deposited at the council offices in Bruges. They are available for access by an interested party such as the owners of adjoining properties or by the local police if a local court official has authorized disclosure. Nothing will be notified to anybody in the UK although I have to repeat that the papers are available for access. Why would anyone be interested in this somewhat battered cottage out in the Belgian countryside?'

They agreed and gave Monsieur Hector their full names and the address of Ricky's dad's house, with the stipulation that all contact must be by mobile.

'I understand and I look forward to meeting you. You know the purchase price and I will send my bill shortly before we meet. I am grateful to you for paying my expenses. Goodbye.' And he was gone.

Ricky phoned his dad and offered him a bridge weekend in Harrogate, Stratford-on-Avon, or Bath for his combined birthday and Christmas presents. He was thrilled, even more so when they offered to house-sit for him.

Ten

Penny and Ricky had got themselves and Ricky's father organized. His dad had left for Bath on the Friday morning and they arrived at his house as soon as they could get away from the bank. They did not arrive till gone 8 pm because of Friday evening traffic, and without delay went straight to the Spinney and dug the crate up. There was no damage to the notes except a dampish moist smell which they hoped would be gone by Sunday. They hid all tracks of the ground being disturbed, covering the area with dead leaves, and then carried the crate up to the small attic box room at the top of the house. Penny shoved a pizza in the oven while Ricky counted out the purchase price of the property. When Penny brought the pizza up, Ricky was barely halfway through. He handed her what he'd already counted for her to check. By 11 pm, they had agreed the counting of the purchase price and then sorted the rest of the cash in bundles of £100. They left all the notes out on the floor to get rid of their smell.

Penny had booked them in the following night at The Bell under false names and asked for an extended checkout time as they were stopping on for Sunday lunch. Ricky had arranged to pick up Monsieur Hector at the local station on Sunday at mid-morning, with the plan to complete their transaction before a traditional Sunday roast lunch. As they would be going straight back to their flat later, they tidied up the house before they left and put the notes surplus to the purchase price in a separate suitcase.

Thanks to planning, it all went like clockwork. The nervy part was packing all the notes into two suitcases, plus their overnight things and making it look like a couple staying over for a weekend in the country. Ricky brought Monsieur Hector back to the hotel.

'Our friend is joining us for lunch, so there will be three of us'.

In their bedroom, Monsieur Hector immediately got started on counting the notes. Purchase price agreed, he presented his bill. This was twice what Ricky was expecting, with the explanation that it included some tax, his expenses, and a small recognition of his time away from other professional dealings. Ricky rounded this up to the next £100 and handed over the bundles they had previously counted. Monsieur Hector did not count them.

'Please join us for lunch, Monsieur Hector.'

'Sadly not my friends. I have to return tonight but would like a lift to the station if you please before you Rosbifs enjoy your roast beef. Let's all sign along these dotted lines, a copy for you and a copy for Mr B. I congratulate you on your efficient arrangements.'

Penny wanted to see a signed document of indisputable ownership, and this was handed over complete with Mr B's alleged signature. Monsieur Hector gave them an understanding of what the documentation meant, concluding by saying the property was now theirs. They shook hands and congratulated each other. Monsieur Hector's suitcase easily accommodated the notes and Ricky drove him to the station. When he returned, Penny was at the bar, sipping a glass of champagne. He joined her.

'We'll enjoy lunch, cover our tracks, and pay the total bill in cash. I don't see any CCTV cameras outside or in here, so we were never here. Nor Hector.'

After a late and leisurely lunch, they drove back up to London. They had packed the balance of the cash into a separate case which they could make fit into some cranny at their flat.

Next morning at the bank, a colleague asked what they had got up to at the weekend.

'Oh, quiet, you know, a walk in the park and a takeaway in front of the telly.'

Eleven

Penny and Ricky had kept up their squeaky clean image at the bank for several months now. There were no signs of further internal investigations. Management were nevertheless still showing some signs of caution: Damon Head was moved to a different set of security screens on another side of the building, Penny was moved up two floors into a different department, and Ricky was moved down a floor. There was no obvious admin or social need for any contact between them unless they lunched together in the canteen. Penny and Ricky lunched together once a week and were never seen with or talking to Damon. Separately and without fuss, they each left the bank, several weeks apart. On leaving, each of them told colleagues that they would continue working locally.

In truth, they wanted to create some space between them and the bank, and see what the rundown cottage near Bruges was like. There was plenty of cash left over after the purchase and expenses for them to live on for a while. They had hidden the notes in the flat and in lockers at two London railway stations, so they were being as anonymous as possible.

They took the train to Brussels and a local train to Bruges, followed by a taxi to their property investment. First reactions were better than feared, worse than hoped. However, they easily convinced themselves that it was worth what they had paid for it. Mr B and the particulars had described it fairly. They dumped their luggage and walked into the village and to the nearest hostelry, ordering a beer and a white wine.

'Shall we play curious or admit we've bought the shack?' Penny said.

'It's going to come out eventually, so why not admit it? We might learn something.'

'That we don't like.'

'Better to know now.'

There was a couple at the next table, probably local but who did occasionally lapse into English. Penny said hello and told them they'd just moved in.

'Oh, where?' said the man of the couple in a sociable manner.

'The little cottage up the road, just past the farm.'

'The rundown one?'

''Fraid so. We're going to tackle it as soon as money becomes available.'

'The previous owner, a single man, was there like once every two or three months. What are your plans – to live in, to rent out, or to sell after doing up?'

'Oh no, we want to stay round here as much as we can. We like it, and Bruges is so lovely.'

'Too many tourists eating chocolate but you'll be okay there. I'm a handyman, can do the basic stuff if you like. And Jeanette here,' he presented his friend, 'she's a homemaker and cleaner. We could help you on several fronts.'

'That's so kind. Can we swap phone numbers so we can get in touch as and when we're next over?'

They did, and Ricky ordered a round of drinks for the four of them.

'I don't know if your skills extend to plumbing but would you be able to have a serious and urgent look at the water, both hot and cold, and also the toilet? We're talking about the basics of living.'

Francois, for it was he, said he was okay on basics but not refitting boilers.

'You want like an annual service, right? Is early tomorrow okay?'

It was and they left to do some shopping in the village. After a makeshift supper, they explored the bed and bedding. Penny was clear what the next day's tasks were: sheets, duvets and a microwave. The night passed as no other had done before: character forming came to mind, and they rose early to find Francois waiting outside with a bag of tools. His preliminary findings were that the boiler would need replacing, not his sphere, but he could give it the once over to prolong its life. He replaced some washers and peered into the toilet cistern.

'Same as the boiler; give yourselves a few weeks and then I'll find a proper plumber to replace a few things. Is that okay?'

'Totally, and we're so grateful. Boiler, toilet, maybe one or two other things as winter approaches.' He gave Francois a figure to work to and got a shrug of acceptance.

The summer was coming to an end but the autumn was promising to retain enough warmth for most days. There was a basic open fire and plenty of wood in the back garden which appealed to Ricky's caveman survival instincts; even Penny could see the romantic side to it.

Twelve

Penny and Ricky were by now fully settled into their post-bank lives. The flat in the London suburbs was now where they lived full time; the cottage near Bruges was their holiday home. It worked out quite well: get to Brussels, then take a local train to Bruges, and then either a long walk, bus ride or a taxi to the cottage. Francois and Jeanette had been true to their word and had been an enormous help in getting the place first habitable and then comfortable. They paid them market rates though they found that the French couple always did a bit extra in terms of time and effort. They became good friends as well, and every time Penny and Ricky went over they went out to local restaurants or bars. Bruges was not for them: 'Far too expensive and over-run with tourists from anywhere.' Penny didn't agree and often popped into Bruges to wander around and have a coffee in the main square. Ricky took this time to continue clearing the front and back garden. He knew he would sell sometime to launder the funds and set up some sort of business in the UK. They did not tell anyone about their Belgium investment, not even their parents, and didn't invite friends over. They explained their absences as: 'You know one of those cheap breaks, we couldn't resist – such a bargain!', and were largely believed.

Penny had stayed in the financial world and had a job as a book-keeper. She took to spreadsheets easily and was rewarded with a promotion and better salary. Ricky got a job with a publishing company, with a remit to increase advertising in its periodicals and local newspapers. It was a people business so he soon got into his stride.

They discussed getting married but neither of them saw the point.

'We love each other, don't we, and neither of us wants children so what's the point?' Details like capital gains tax, inheritance tax and joint ownership of a property, or maybe later properties, were not drivers in any shape or form and were just technicalities to get round.

*

Back in London, the arrival of a letter from an unknown person asking for money because they knew about the bank theft brought a juddering jolt to Ricky's life. It included a key to a locker at a train station. He did not show it to Penny, and responded as though it was a bluff from a down-and-out. He responded with a much smaller amount than requested, and thought that would be the end of it. There was no one he could discuss it with. Several months later, another request came. Ricky now fully realized that he would have to do something or it would get out of hand.

Thirteen

Ricky eventually had to tell Penny that he was getting mail asking for small contributions as the price of the blackmailer's silence. She was not pleased and made it absolutely clear that paying blackmail was never the solution.

'Paying is an admission of guilt, and it's probably a shrewd guess with no proof whatsoever. If it went to court, it'd be thrown out. Peter Vernon couldn't prove anything at the bank, and look how many staff he interviewed and repeatedly so. Why would a court be any better?'

'They made a guess and they were right, provable or not. What else can we do?'

'What we have to do is find some way of shutting him up. Let's meet him and get him to realize that if he persists, there will be consequences.'

Ricky said he would try to make contact and have it out with him. A crude disguise would help in case there were further proceedings.

Ricky received the next letter several months later and the amount requested had doubled. He took that to mean that the blackmailer was sure of his case. This time he didn't contribute anything along with his letter in the locker. He simply stated they had to meet and suggested three possible dates, each in a different place in London. On the first two dates, nothing materialized but Ricky suspected he was being watched. On the third occasion, and twenty minutes later than proposed, a man in his early fifties came and sat opposite him.

'It's Ricky, isn't it? I've observed you the two previous times to see if you're a man of your word.'

'I am, but you're not. What do you think you're playing at?'

'Nothing at all, Ricky. I make a suggestion and you respond, thank you.'

'Well, that's the end of your little game. No more letters; no more cash; we each get on with our lives.'

'If you like, we could. Then I and my associates will just have to go and have a little chat with PC Plod and the bank. No matter; I'll be off now.' And he got up to go.

'Hold on a minute, old boy. I and my associates, to use your words, can already go to PC Plod and have a chat. We too have been observing you and you're not Mr Shining Innocence, either.'

'Thank you for the *either*; it sort of confirms your guilt, doesn't it, sunshine?'

'We've done nothing wrong, but you have. You haven't heard the last of this. Any more letters and I will take this further.' Ricky walked off and disappeared into the London crowds.

Penny followed him and caught up with Ricky on his mobile.

'I'm tracking him now and as he doesn't know me, I can get quite close. I'm going to follow him home and keep you informed along the way. Going in the Underground now.'

Ricky went to a tea place in a side street and waited for Penny's text. She rang instead.

'Got him; it's a side street just off Parsons Green, West London. Got the address, saw him put the light on in the upstairs flat. See you back at the flat.'

They met back at home and discussed what to do next.

Fourteen

Penny and Ricky did not conform to being one of those couples who would naturally resort to violence to resolve disputes, but the blackmailer's attitude to continuing his game meant that they had to confront an unfortunate truth. He had to be stopped. Surprisingly, it was Penny's idea that he should be roughed up, and Ricky said he knew some chaps who would help. One of them was an old mate who had moved on to getting things done using his physical skills. He phoned him, giving the address in Parsons Green and also the degree of roughing up required: 'Just this side of not enough for A&E.' The men complied with Ricky's instructions on the target's return home from work the following evening, and reported back that the job was done. Ricky met them later at a pub and handed over a brown envelope.

Several months later, a different communication arrived, but the request was exactly the same wording as previously. Ricky went round to Parsons Green after work and knocked on the door. A woman in her twenties answered.

'Yes?'

'I was looking for the guy who lives here, you know the guy with the dark hair and tiny spectacles? We used to meet up down the pub now and again; been missing him.'

'He left some time ago; went to Wales to live with his sister.'

'Oh, I'm sorry to have bothered you. Do you have his forwarding address or phone number?'

'It's here somewhere, I have to send on his post. Hold on.' She went inside and returned with it written out on a piece of paper, including his name: G. Faulks.

'That's really kind of you, thank you.'

'Shall I let him know you called?'

'No need; I'll get in touch directly with this. Does he come back at all?'

'No, not at all but he does phone to see if any post has come.'

Ricky returned to their flat and recounted the conversation to Penny.

'So, he doesn't want the post office to know his new address but a stranger can give his address to a stranger. Funny, isn't it?'

'She made a mistake. What now?'

'Let's have a mini-break in South Wales; he knows you but he doesn't know me so I can follow him fairly freely. We've got to stop this.'

'Agreed, we do; maybe a final settling up will shut him up.'

'It doesn't usually; but do you even think this recent request is from him?'

'Who else?'

'He could have passed it on to a mate.'

'Too risky.'

*

They took a budget-priced hotel in a South Wales resort and within two days Penny had sorted out where Faulks lived, and his lifestyle. He spent the evening in the pub, and during the day he walked over the cliff path and back.

'It's deserted out there; one small slip should do it.'

'Penny, my love, just what are you suggesting?'

'We may be criminals of sorts but so is he and it could easily happen by accident.'

'It's murder! He'd get a few years if we turned him in.'

'And he would grass on us without any doubt; and we would get far more.'

Ricky shook his head, unable to find the right words.

The next day was fresh with a mild breeze. The cliff path was barely muddy at all, even after a recent light shower. They set off on their walk, then hung back till Faulks had started out, and then followed him some hundred yards behind. At the highest point on the cliff path walk, Ricky silently pitched up behind Faulks and shoved him over. He screamed all the way down, then silence. The two of them turned inland, treading only on tired grass, then through some barbed wire, another field and finally into a residential road of bungalows. They covered their faces with scarves and hastened back to the hotel. They didn't say much but had recovered by next morning.

Fifteen

Another six months had passed. Penny's and Ricky's jobs were proceeding well and they were both surprised and delighted to receive an email from a French estate agent.

Bruges is booming, he wrote, *and the surrounding villages are also receiving the benefit. So much so that a small development of your property is proposed, and the two adjacent ones plus some land at the rear of all three properties. The developer knows the current value of the properties, including yours, and he knows the best sale price of the proposed new development, and it is a proposition he can't let anyone else steal off him.*

A sale price of their property was suggested. They smiled at each other.

'This will get us a decent house in the country with room to spare, no pun intended!'

'How do we get the money here? There are no records here that show that we own property abroad.'

'Transfer to a UK bank account, and we've laundered the cash plus the sizeable extra.'

'What do we say to the bank receiving the transfer from a Belgian bank?'

'Who knows? Who cares? An investment, an inheritance, a lottery win, anything.'

Penny was not so blasé as Ricky.

'I think each of us should get four separate accounts we can pay into and split the proceeds up into eight banks and building societies; and obviously not to include the bank which was our employer. We'll tell the Belgians it's our quaint British ways: children, godchildren, nieces, nephews and so on. I don't want each single payment to be noticeable or out of the ordinary.'

'Even eight ways, it will be sizeable but I accept it will be explainable without it being referred upstairs.' He thought of Peter Vernon at the same time.

They haggled over the price and achieved a small uplift. Much more importantly, they got agreement to split the proceeds eight ways, which they would be charged for, and that there would be no communication to the UK authorities, just eight clean bank transfers.

They phoned Francois and Jeanette, had a chat about the development, which they thought would present some work for them. Penny and Ricky said that they could help themselves to anything in the cottage as they wouldn't be coming over again. There were expressions of how much they would be missed, all four ways.

*

Three months after the property proceeds had come through, another blackmail communication arrived requesting double the previous amount. Ricky, feeling flush with cash, kept this from Penny and made a payment smaller than requested through one of his own banks. He also replied to the email that the game was up and if there were to be any more of this nonsense, he would go straight to the police. He recognized the email address as an old one from the bank, one Damon Head. So that toe-rag had got Faulks involved as a front man and was now taking it up in his own right. Well, we'd have to see about that.

Sixteen

Ricky's first step was to track down Damon Head by following him home from the bank where he still worked. Ricky noted his address for future reference. One never knew. Sure enough, a few months later, another request came in, half as much again as previously. He had to bring Penny in this time, but he did not refer to the previous request.

'This is that Damon from the bank, the one who gawped at you on the screen.'

'We required him to gawp – sorry love.'

'Okay, fair enough. He must have befriended Faulks and, now that Faulks has gone, he's picked up the baton. He must have accepted the official line that Faulks's demise was an unfortunate slip off a cliff path, rather than seeing it as a fatal threat to his existence.'

'You'll have to send in the heavies again.'

'I'll have to think about that. Are you with me on this? I don't want this to come between us.'

'Course I am, absolutely, what else could we have done? And what else can we do?'

'Well, that's a bit of an open question but thanks for saying it.'

Ricky went away and paid the same amount as previously without any uplift, adding that this really was the very last time.

It stayed very quiet for another few months, no messages, and for the first time Ricky was hoping that it was all over. It wasn't. A follow-up request came in, nicely and easily worded, asking for double the previous amount paid. Ricky didn't share this with Penny as he didn't want to upset the rest of their life because it was by then so settled and enjoyable. He didn't reply but got straight onto phoning his contact with the muscle team. He gave them Damon's address with exactly the same instructions and understanding as before with Faulks. A week later, the head heavy phoned Ricky back.

'All done, job complete, slight difference this time.'

'What do you mean – difference?'

'Well, he's a bit of a delicate chap and although we did exactly the same as for the other chap, he didn't come round.'

'Meaning?'

'We gave him a shake and pressed his chest like they do on the telly, but he was finished. Dead as a doornail.'

'You mean you *killed* him?'

'We didn't mean to. No worries, we were all covered up and we took everything away and burned the lot. Nothing is traceable to us but your problem is solved, mate.'

'Any witnesses?'

'Nope, and nobody saw us arrive or leave. We entered quietly at the back, did the business, and exited the same way. Someone will discover the body in a few days' time and they will think it's a revenge job, like the mafia, which it is in a way.'

'I'm not the mafia. Did you check thoroughly when you left?'

'As thorough as Sherlock Holmes, squire; we took our time, you see.'

'I don't know what to say.'

'Then don't; all done. It'll die a natural death, you might say. One thing, though, it'll be a bit extra this time, you know for mopping up the forensics. You need us not to get caught.'

'Too right. Yes, I understand about your, er, fees. Let's meet up in a fortnight, check that the dust has settled and that there are no other consequences. Usual place. See you.'

Ricky put the phone down. *I'm turning into a ruthless criminal,* he thought. He didn't let any of this reach Penny but he did pay particular attention to local radio, television and the Press. Jimmy had been as good as his word. The death was reported as a tragic gang warfare reprisal and the police were calling for witnesses and any information about the deceased. It all died down over a few weeks. Only now, the police were involved.

Seventeen

Several months passed by and Ricky was getting more relaxed about the past. He had done some dreadful things but they were over with now, and they could both concentrate on the present, the here and now. The funds from the Bruges property were established in ordinary deposit accounts, earning some interest, all duly entered in their tax returns. They began a search for a detached house buried in the country somewhere, and after talking with agents, searching the internet and poring over maps, they found exactly the right place in a rural Gloucestershire village, not all that far from Ricky's father. They bought it for cash and moved in. Just for fun and for a fresh start, and without formality or officialdom, they decided to be called by new names locally in the neighbourhood. They both hoped it would be a further superficial layer of disguise from their pasts and give a fresh start to life. Penny decided to be Amanda and Ricky latched on to Anthony, or Tony for short. They became the quiet new couple in the village, naturally respectable as a settled young middle-aged couple in that abstraction called Middle England. They were liked by the few who came into contact with them, and they were known to be generous when needed to be. As a newly reinvented couple, Amanda and Anthony were seen as having been together as a couple forever, enjoying their comfortable life in rural Gloucestershire. He needed to go up to town once a week to report in; and then out and about for two or three days a week visiting hotels and restaurants to do his reviews under a pseudonym for a glossy periodical. She kept the books for a number of small businesses in the Cheltenham area; this meant spreadsheets at home and occasional visits to her contact at each client. There was no pressure in either job so their gentle life was complemented with tennis, golf and holidays home and abroad, both incorporating their ball games. They were not married and, as children had not appeared or desired, there seemed little point in getting married. Amanda ran the household accounts incorporating his and her earnings, which were broadly comparable, but very occasionally she suggested he should treat her to a nice holiday, "just to level up", only partly in jest. Apart from the absence of the patter of tiny feet, one could not imagine a more idyllic existence. For friends, they stuck to people like themselves, and generally kept a low profile in the neighbourhood. Locals would say they seemed a quiet, happy couple who kept themselves to themselves. They went to the parish church at Easter and Christmas for carol singing, and were known to contribute generously.

This was their story: they had lived simply in Norfolk, where they had grown up and went to school. They left Norfolk after school and, after a spell in London, eventually settled down in Gloucestershire in their current house. There was no stress in their lives or their jobs and that was what they wanted above all else.

Ricky, now Tony, was also careful in constructing barriers to communication and rediscovered an old boy contact of his dad's. He called himself Colonel Martin, solid Army straight out of central casting. Ricky's father had fallen ill some months ago and was not in the best of health. Sadly, shortly after they had moved into their new house, he took a bad turn and died some weeks later. They held a small, quiet family funeral in his village, with the undertakers doing everything. They attended the funeral as Penny and Ricky, and went home straight after the funeral, leaving Colonel Martin to secure the house and deal with any intrusiveness; Ricky had made sure that he was well paid for services rendered. Ricky dealt with the solicitors himself over the phone; he was the sole beneficiary of his father's will.

Once the formalities of his father's death were over, calm again returned to their peaceful existence. The rhythm of life was their non-demanding jobs, some trips away, and a state of happiness between them. It was not ardent love but at the very least it was gentle, unquestioned love from having known each other for a long time and actually enjoying each other's company and having total trust in each other. Never for a minute did either of them wonder about ifs and buts, or want to be anywhere else or be with anybody else; it would not even occur to them. Their life and relationship was far deeper than basic contentment and acceptance.

This idyllic state was shattered some months later by the receipt of a fresh request by letter for funds to keep quiet. It could not be either Faulks or Damon; and Ricky, now Tony, didn't think either of them had relatives who would take up the baton. He showed it to Penny, having not previously shared Damon's death with her.

'He's done what Faulks did,' Penny said. 'Faulks needed a partner or someone to share proceeds with for solidarity. Damon's done the same; he's brought in this new one! What's his name?'

'Frank.'

'He brought in Frank, first to get some fellowship because Damon is not the strongest person to tackle this sort of thing, and second, someone to pass on to when he felt the law was getting too close.'

Tony did not comment on Damon's "existence".

'How has he found us?'

'Dunno. Damon knew where we lived before so maybe this Frank followed up on us just as we did on Faulks. Frank's approach is rather naive or juvenile, I would say. I suggest we ignore it as though it never happened, and see if he goes away.'

They agreed and a few more months passed by until a second letter arrived. It was addressed to Penny and Ricky.

Dear Penny and Ricky

You don't know me and I don't know you. What I do know is that you robbed a bank and got away with it. Two people have suffered so far because of you covering up your theft. I'm not associated with anybody apart from a good mate, who can bear witness to any goings on. In order to preserve the status quo, please deposit the sum previously requested into the bank account itemized below.

Frank

'What does he mean, two people have suffered?'

'He means Faulks and Head. Perhaps Frank's involvement is because Damon has stopped being active.'

'Did you have anything to do it?'

'No, I did not, I promise.'

'Okay. Frank doesn't give an address or a meeting place, but he obviously knows where we live. We do nothing, agreed? The worst that can happen is he turns up here and we have to tackle him.'

'Or he goes to the police and turns us in.'

'He won't do that; he's indulging in crime too and we have this letter from him.'

'We need to turn our minds to making security better here, just in case he does turn up. How do you feel about a gun? We are in the country and can take up shooting wildfowl and foxes.'

'That's a good idea, yes, let's.'

*

They called it The Siege. There was no drawbridge or portcullis, and the house was open to visitors, but they did reconstruct the frontage of the property to define a single entry drive. The boundary hedges and fencing around the house were moderately impenetrable to all but the most adventurous. These precautions did not affect their daily lives but it did mean they were constantly on the watch. The day came when Frank drove up, parked outside their front door, got out of his motor and surveyed the scene.

They saw him arrive from an upstairs viewpoint. Tony took the gun out of the locked cabinet and placed it conveniently in the hallway. There was a knock at the door, which Amanda opened.

'Yes?'

'And hello to you too. I'm Frank and I've come for a meaningful discussion.'

'There's nothing to discuss; you're not welcome here; you're a common little blackmailer. You go straight back to where you came from and don't bother us again, else we shall report you to the police.'

'But you haven't so far, have you.' It was not said as a question. 'And that rather says quite a lot about you two, doesn't it?' This too was not said as a question. Tony had by this time sidled up behind Amanda. They could both smell the alcohol on Frank's breath.

'It doesn't say anything. In fact, it shows how generous we were to someone down on their luck and who out of desperation saw a cheap way of funding his failed life. We've done enough to date but now this is the end of the road.'

'I can see that you're losing patience and getting a little exasperated, but I've come to discuss a final offer, a final settling up, you might say – in lieu of any further future bother to you and me.'

'And what is your suggestion? And that does not mean we agree with your idea, as trust is not much in evidence.' Tony had taken up the dialogue.

Frank mentioned a figure in a manner that suggested it was an ordinary amount that would not much trouble the likes of them.

'If you could round it up to a nice round figure, then that would be uncommonly decent of you.' Frank was looking at Amanda as he said this. He did not see Tony pick up the gun by the barrel and swung the lock in a semi-circle which ended side on the back of Frank's head. He went straight down out cold. Tony sprang into action.

'Quick, let's get him down into the cellar and lock him up. Then we'll get rid of the car.'

Amanda was so shocked, she couldn't find words to speak. They lifted Frank up and edged him down the cellar steps, manhandled him to get his jacket off, tied his wrists and ankles together and then locked the door behind them. Tony found the car keys.

'I'll drive his car and hide it in the wood at the back, then we'll have to decide what to do with him and the car later.'

When he got back, Amanda was more composed, but much more troubled.

'What have we done? Where do we go from here?'

'I don't know, love, one step at a time. Put the kettle on for a think.'

They talked erratically over tea, discussing the possibilities. Tony was the first to say that they had to finish him off. Ambulance and hospital could only spiral downwards, and Frank may already be brain-damaged. Amanda said that she couldn't do it, but she would help with all the cleaning up.

The car would have to be driven miles away and dumped in a lake or the sea somewhere. The house would have to be cleaned spotlessly for absolutely no trace of evidence or DNA. Amanda surprised herself and Tony by a blunt comment.

'If we're going to finish him off, it would be better and kinder to do it now, and put the poor guy out of his misery.'

Tony reached for his gun, and unlocked the cellar door. Amanda heard him close the door, walk down the stairs, a brief period of silence, and then the sound of a heavy clout. He came back up a few minutes later, very shaken and with a wobbly voice.

'He was still unconscious, probably dead already, and he wouldn't have known a thing. I hope I never have to do that again.' Amanda gave him a heartless cold hug.

'Let's leave all logistics till tomorrow morning. I'm going to drink a lot and then go to bed.'

The next morning, both of them were in management mode. Tony was against burying the body in their woods because any future successful search for Frank's body would prove them guilty. He preferred a disposal many miles away. Amanda did not contribute much to these discussions.

'Rivers are too shallow, the sea is tidal, the south coast docksides are too busy and have too much CCTV. From my memory, part of the Bristol Floating Harbour is quiet and secluded overnight. I'll go over there and check it out.'

'And can you get lots of plastic wrapping so poor Frank is totally wrapped up? I don't want to handle his body any more than I have to.'

Tony did not comment on her "poor Frank", thinking he was the blackmailer and had brought his death on himself.

'Good point, I'll go tomorrow. If you stay here, don't go down to the cellar.'

'I'll come with you; I don't want to be on my own in the house or round here.'

'We'll be back by two at the latest. We'll be fine, love.'

The rest of the day was quiet, with little conversation. They had an early night, and decided to be off the next morning as early as they could.

Eighteen

Early the next day, Amanda and Tony drove over to Bristol and spied out the harbour and suitable dropping off points. Next, they went round to a large DIY store to purchase swathes of industrial strength polythene. They carried the roll out to the car together. He had agreed with Amanda on the wrapping. They were back by 1.30 pm and decided to have lunch in the village pub and see if there was any gossip. Apparently there was something in the local paper about the proposed route of the new by-pass. Those with houses on the route were not happy; it was nowhere near their own house.

'Until they change the route, of course. Sorry, just saying.'

They chatted with the locals some more, and walked slowly back to the house. Tony said he would remove all belongings in Frank's pockets and any possible items of identification, then roll the body up in the polythene many times.

'Can you look out all the parcel tape we've got? I'll need yards of it to be on the safe side.'

They decided to dump Frank as soon as possible. Tony said they should hire an estate from elsewhere for 48 hours to give themselves some anonymity and time to clean out the car afterwards. He arranged a car rental in cash for 24 hours, saying it was one of those urgent jobs to get the mother-in-law from A to B. The rental firm reluctantly agreed and demanded a much higher refundable deposit, also in cash.

Tony went down to the cellar with the polythene and the parcel tape. He removed Frank's jacket, socks and shoes, labels, watch, everything that would aid identification. He laid the polythene on the cellar floor and firmly rolled Frank and a few stones into it. There was some stiffening of the limbs so there had to be some heavy pressure to get Frank's body aligned. Then, many times rolled up, he finished with yards of parcel tape. The end result was cylindrical, just under six feet long and about two feet wide.

The sequence of events flowed as expected.

Body in back of car; drive to car rental late just before they shut; drop Tony at the car rental to collect it; meet back up a little further on; drive further on to a quiet spot and transfer body; park up their own car; drive to Bristol Harbour, arriving at 2.30 in the morning; dump body over side of harbour; split up but reconvene in side street away from any cameras or people; drive back to own car; both set to and clean the rental car thoroughly in the early morning light; Tony drop rental car back in convoy; meet up with Amanda round the corner; drive back to Gloucestershire; collapse into bed.

They slept in till late.

'Job done,' was the first thing Amanda said as they both surfaced at two in the afternoon.

'Not quite. There's the car and cleaning up the cellar.'

'How do you get rid of a car?'

'Dunno. How about I drive it to somewhere like Newcastle and leave it in a quiet street, then get the train back? It would be miles away from where Frank is now or even has been, and when it's found, it'll be assumed it's been stolen or Frank has driven somewhere round there.'

'Perfect, but first you've got to clean up all evidence of you.'

It was agreed, as was also agreed that, while he was away, Amanda would clean up the cellar.

Three days later, it was as though nothing untoward had happened in their quiet Gloucestershire village.

Until several months later when there was a knock at the door.

PART III

Resolution

One

DS Mavis Smith had got all the right words written out on a card and she had memorized them to perfection:

Penelope Amanda Norton, aka Amanda Wightman, and Richard Anthony Villiers, aka Anthony Ollerton, you are both to be arrested formally for the murder of Frank Underwood, and further charges will be made later. Please step this way for the formal charge to be made. We also have a search warrant for your house, the premises and the gardens, and the authority to collect DNA and fingerprints.

Roy and Rob would do the man-handling and there were other uniforms preparing to encircle the property at the same time. She knocked on the door and rang the ornate bell chimes. There was no reply. There were two cars in the drive so she motioned uniform to go round the back in case of attempted escape.

Nothing.

'We have the right to enforce an entry so go ahead, boys.'

After a few hefty blows, the front door was forced open and swung right back on its hinges. They all drew back and gazed at the shocking sight before them.

In front of them, lying splayed across the hall floor, were Penelope, aka Amanda, and Richard, aka Anthony, both shot in the chest, clearly at close range. It was equally clear that neither one would ever draw breath again.

Mavis knew what to do.

'Search everywhere for the assailants and don't touch anything.

I'm getting Forensics here straight off.' She called Hugh Cranston and her explanation needed only a few sentences.

They assembled in the front drive ten minutes later. Apart from the victims, the house and grounds had been found to be deserted.

'Thanks, everyone. It seems someone was ahead of us. At first glimpse, it looks like a front-door killing, but they did pull the door closed after them. Forensics will be here within the hour. We'll keep the house guarded and do some house-to-house enquiries.'

They split themselves up into pairs while two uniforms kept the property under watch. The local enquiries yielded nothing, and no one in the village shop and café had heard anything. One resident thought he had heard a car come and go "earlyish", but he'd seen nothing as he was still in bed.

Mavis phoned Robertson who was surprised and made a smart remark about being a day or two late. Mavis just said, 'Yes, Sir, we'll follow whatever Forensics come up with.'

She phoned Clive, partly to keep him informed but more for getting some professional support.

'It was my first murder case and I was too late.'

'No worries, you've got two more now. I've got enough invested in parts of this case to justify coming down. I'll see you there or back in Bristol, whatever you say.'

'Thanks, you're wonderful. See you soon.'

Forensics appeared in a large van from which a small team emerged, each of them holding a tool bag.

Hugh Cranston came over to Mavis.

'You're keeping us busy, DS Mavis Smith. This is a rum do, but don't worry or despair, we'll have something for you – some today, some tomorrow and some back at the ranch.'

'Thanks, Hugh, at a bit of a loose end here. Do you need me?'

'No, you get back and start your detecting. Leave enough security here until we can finally lock up the premises. Thank you for prompt action. Goodbye.'

She left security in the hands of Roy and Rob who, to her surprise, showed real fellow feeling towards her. She texted Clive: "See you Bristol Station. M", and drove back.

Two

Clive went into Bolton's office to tell him what had happened. Because of his involvement with Faulks, the bank theft, Damon Head, and now Penny and Ricky, he asked to go down to Bristol and help develop the next stage of the saga. Bolton just wafted his arm and told him to get on with it.

'I want the whole thing sorted and over and done with.'

Clive slipped out and was soon on the road speeding down the M5. He and Mavis arrived at the Bristol Station only half an hour apart.

Celia took the lead and got them fresh coffee, asking them both what was going to happen next.

'We'll have to see. Thanks for coffee, just the way I like it,' Clive responded. After she had gone back to her desk, Clive grabbed a chair near Mavis's desk and turned it towards her.

'What's your thinking, Clive?'

'It's odd, isn't it? Least expected outcome, probably. Someone or some people appear to have taken the law into their own hands. Who would want to shut them up?'

'Can I go one step further and add that it could be a revenge killing?'

'I like it, yes, the bank, contacts of Faulks, Head and Underwood, and anyone else who had a grudge against them.'

'Do you kill if you have a grudge against someone?'

'Not usually, but there are all sorts out there.'

'I think it's a dead cert. It's someone with connections to Faulks or Underwood, or conceivably Head. They have big reasons for a revenge killing. I suppose we should wait to see whether Forensics find anything incriminating.'

'You're right, I agree, but that doesn't stop us looking for contacts of Faulks and Underwood.'

Mavis called Adrian and Celia over to her desk for a debrief. She formally introduced DS Clive Drewett to them, knowing that they had already met him before. Mavis gave an account of the earlier part of the day at the house that they had both been to previously.

'While we are waiting for anything to come back from Forensics, who are taking the place apart as we speak, we're going to look into the contacts, family members and colleagues of Geoffrey Faulks, Frank Underwood and Damon Head. All seem unlikely, but we may have overlooked something. Can you make a start on that, please?'

'Please, er, Mavis, we know that Faulks has disappeared. Shouldn't we find him first?' asked Adrian.

'Alongside other searches, yes. He may have died in seclusion. There are no reports of any sightings and I agree we should step up the effort to find him.'

'He may or may not be dead, Adrian,' added Clive, 'and I agree with you both that if he is alive and active, then he becomes a prime suspect, yes.'

'The last we knew of him is that he discharged himself from convalescence and disappeared. He would not be in good shape.'

'Just drive a car and pull the trigger twice – that's all it would take,' Celia said. 'Anyone could do it.'

'Okay, back to your desks and phones and screens. We'll know more tomorrow.'

Clive and Mavis chatted about the case and the likelihood of finding Faulks. No one had tried particularly hard since he had disappeared, he'd just been reported as a missing person. Now the search was on, it would need photos and an artist's impression of Geoffrey, somewhat older and maybe somewhat scruffier and bearded. It seemed like discovering who Frank was all over again.

Mavis assumed that Clive would be staying over; Clive didn't want to assume, so they had a silly chat about that. Clive phoned Giovanni's for a table and they relaxed over pasta and wine.

'I'm a bit of a spare part down here in Bristol and I need to get back to base. Anything I can help you with?'

'Clive, you're part of the case now and we only know about Faulks because of you and your boss. It's great you can go back to him and tell him that Faulks is prime suspect; he was right that Faulks was a bad apple etc etc.'

'Agreed, but don't lose sight of it being somebody else. Can I crash out at yours tonight?'

'I'm not going to answer that.'

Three

Cranston reported in to the Bristol station and asked to see Mavis with Robertson. They crammed in to Robertson's office and Celia brought in tea, coffee and biscuits. Robertson kicked off.

'Welcome, Hugh. Don't get to meet so often these days but I know Smith here is keeping you busy. What have you got?'

'She is, and it's fascinating, but this one is rather less so, I'm afraid. There's nothing on the front door, which would have been opened by one of the victims, and nothing in the hallway or the house. So, I deduce that as soon as the front door was opened, he shot them both and left. He did pull the front door to, but no trace of prints. Wearing gloves. The only evidence is the four bullets – they were each shot twice – and tracks in the drive. The bullets indicate a short range gun, the usual model has a silencer. It's a small comfort, but they would have died instantly. They were holding hands. The type of gun is available at most gun shops. All purchases have to be registered and signed for, so that may be a help. I'll let you have details, Mavis. The tracks on the gravel drive give nothing away, normal width tyres and obviously no tread marks. Sorry, it's not my greatest.'

'Could it have been two people?'

'No evidence, but it would be most unlikely as their positioning on the floor implied no time delay. There could have been someone else in the vehicle, obviously. Sorry, forgot to mention, we were able to take prints and DNA from both the deceased, and I have no doubt about being able to match them and one of the cars to what evidence we have of the Underwood murder. There will have to be processes and procedures, of course, but effectively that case is now closed.'

They chatted on sociably, and Cranston left.

'Well, Smith, it looks like you've got a search on your hands.'

'Yes, Sir, and I haven't yet ruled out that it could be Faulks.'

'Good luck with that, keep me posted.'

Mavis went back to her desk and beckoned to Adrian and Celia.

'Nothing from Forensics – only the type of gun and bullets used, which may or may not have been purchased recently. Adrian, can you explore recent gun purchases anywhere in the UK, please, and, Celia, we need to get hold of a mugshot of Faulks. I'll try Clive and West Midlands first. Then it's got to be mass circulation. What do we think about it not being Faulks?'

'They don't seem the sort of couple to have antagonized folk along the way, do they?'

'I agree, but we have to keep an open mind.'

Mavis phoned Clive back in the West Midlands.

'Thanks for dropping by. How about a trip to Devon this weekend? You must meet my folks.'

'Sounds wonderful. I can pick you up en route and head straight down.'

'Now Clive, this is Mavis talking. Please come down Friday evening and we'll set off in our own time Saturday morning. Okay, DS Drewett?'

'Yes, Miss!'

'Any chance you have a mugshot of Faulks there? As your boss has been so pre-occupied with Faulks throughout his career, I reckon he must have.'

'He must, agreed. I'll send it over but it might be from some years ago.'

'We've found an artist who does ageing, so anything would be helpful; and, of course, absolutely anything else you have to help us find Faulks.'

Mavis walked back to her flat and ruminated on the case. They should be able to find Faulks if only through Social Services, the Salvation Army, or such like. But he's most likely seriously disabled and probably not looking after himself too well. Would he really drive his car or a rented car to rural Gloucestershire, getting there early in the morning, confront two fit adults and shoot them twice at point blank range? It doesn't sound like him; he is, or was, a gambler, his game was for money, and there was no sign that he was starting to blackmail again. What would he gain by murdering Penny and Ricky, even if he got away with it? Revenge did not seem to be in his make-up. So, who else?

She settled on her sofa with a tray of ravioli and a glass of white wine, and phoned Clive. He was back home. She discussed all of her thoughts with him, and he his, with her, and they came to a conclusion about the weekend which would be a very acceptable away-day for them both. They even booked into a hotel somewhere along the way.

'But Devon first, Clive.'

Four

Clive drove down Friday evening to Mavis's flat, and they continued their discussions on the case until Clive said that was enough. TV and bed, ready for an early start. Mavis phoned her parents and said she would be in the area tomorrow – could she take them out to Saturday lunch? Usual resisting response of 'You must come here!', but Mavis persisted. She booked lunch at 1 pm at the Soul Muscle Place. They packed lightly and booked into a three-star hotel near Exeter for the Saturday night.

They set off early the next morning and drove down the M5 and on to the Devon coast, coffee en route, and were seated at the lunch spot in Torquay at 12.30 with a bottle of house Chablis, nicely chilled. A quarter of an hour later, Mr and Mrs Smith walked in, both sporting Bermuda-style tops. Clive stood up, and Mavis did the greetings and introductions. Her dad shook Clive's extended hand warmly with both his hands.

'Well, Mavvy, you never said you would be bringing a young

gentleman with you,' said Mrs Smith. 'May I call you Clive? We are rarely honoured to meet Mavvy's friends, so you must be special.'

'Mum, don't embarrass the chap. We are old friends and have worked together, and we are just getting to know each other.'

'It's a long way from Birmingham for you to have dragged him down all this way.'

'Believe me, Mrs Smith, the pleasure is all mine, and since getting to know Mavis better I've been looking forward to meeting you both. Let's get drinks and the menus.'

'And you are staying near Exeter, I believe? I'm not going to ask about accommodation.'

'Mum, stop being embarrassing. Everything's just fine.'

Mr Smith and Clive chatted about the area and cricket, and what life in the police force was really like and what being a travelling civil servant had been really like, and so on. Mavis and her mum were much more personal in their chat.

Of course, the lunch and a stroll afterwards was a great success. There was plenty of warmth in the late summer sun until it was time to go. Mavis said that they only had to drive up to near Exeter, so there was no hurry. They took tea and scones in a cosy side street. Mrs Smith said it was a pity they couldn't stop over, but their house was only small and … you know. They said their farewells and Mr Smith lent into his daughter's ear.

'He's okay by me, good luck.' Mavis punched his arm and kissed him. Clive kissed Mrs Smith on both cheeks, and they drove off.

'That went well. Thanks for coming to see them.'

'No problem, they are a delightful couple. I hope I didn't disappoint.'

'Stop fishing, Mr Clive, they approve of you. Normally they are very critical of anyone I introduce to them.'

They checked into the hotel and freshened up in their room. They decided on supper in the hotel and, after that, a glass of wine or two. Clive sat closer to Mavis.

'We get on, don't we?'

'Yes.'

'I don't just mean at work. I mean both socially and when we're on our own.'

'Yes.'

'So, are we an item?'

'Clive! We've been up close and personal more than a few times. I'd hate to think we weren't!'

'Yes, but in today's world, some people seem to just drop in and out of relationships without it meaning very much.'

'Agreed, but I'm not some people and I don't think you are, either.'

'No, I'm not. I can't imagine being with anyone else other than you.'

'Clive, I know, me too, but let's end this particular conversation right now. It's not the right time and I mean that positively and sincerely; another time, my love.' They kissed and Clive suggested a TV drama they both liked before turning in.

The next day, they drove back up to her flat in Bristol, and Clive said his goodbyes with a kiss or two and drove back to the West Midlands. He had enjoyed his weekend, not without stress, he admitted to himself, but he wouldn't have wanted it any other way. He and Mavis were quite definitely an item – a new world for him.

Five

Clive reported in to Bolton on Monday morning and gave a full debrief. The whole game had changed now. Penny and Ricky were proved to have been the killers of Frank Underwood and by association with blackmail were implicated in the death of Damon Head and the attempted murder of Geoffrey Faulks, now disappeared. He would get back to Neil Poole about the original bank theft. Faulks now became one of the suspects, if not the central suspect, for the shootings in Gloucestershire. Bolton intervened.

'I knew he was a bad lot and now we see that he can be driven to cold-blooded murder. He's guilty of a lot of things and this proves a lot more.'

'But how do we find him? Bristol are looking at gun purchases and crying out for a photo. Do you or we have any photos or images?'

'Janet will have mine, and you've got that newspaper cutting taken in front of a pub dartboard. We'll struggle to find anything more recent. Driving licence?'

Clive returned to Janet, who looked through the files. There was nothing to match the newspaper cutting and present driving licence, if there was one. He phoned Megan Morgan in Cardiff to see if there was any news.

'It's Clive Drewett from West Midlands Police. How are you? Have you had any contact with Geoffrey?'

'Thank you for phoning, Clive. I'm much better and hoping that no news is good news. Nothing in particular, but I did have a phone message about two weeks ago, number unknown. All the message said was, "All okay, Meg, don't worry." But I knew it was Geoffrey.'

'Could we have the exact date and time of that call, please, Megan, and also the latest photo you've got of him? If you could go to your nearest police station and ask them to send it to me, they'll sort it, oh, and please remember the date and time of that call.' They signed off. Clive thought the call she mentioned was promising and if it could be traced, they should be able to work out the location.

He then called Neil for a complete debrief. He was shocked and surprised, and immediately latched on to the name of Faulks.

'I could revisit the pub and see if anybody has heard back from him, but with Head gone, it's not likely.'

'Agreed, but only if you're passing.'

'By the way, there is movement on the two roughings up. The gang I suspected are being interviewed and they have revealed that they were operating under instructions from a certain Ricky Villiers, who they knew from way back, and clearly want to shift the blame on to him. They admit to the two beatings up and are, or were, hoping that identifying Ricky would help reduce any upcoming sentence. For info, if any use. How's Mavis?'

'We're getting on just fine and I hope we can all meet up sometime. And yourself, who never says anything?'

'Emma and me are just fine, to quote somebody. Bye.'

Clive smiled.

Six

Adrian had made some progress on chasing up gun purchases. Yes, there was a registration process with the police but it was always updated in arrears. Recent purchases could take a while to be recorded. He had a list of purchases in Bristol, Gloucestershire and Somerset, and wondered what to do with it.

Celia had tracked down an old driving licence photo of Faulks. Clive's newspaper cutting was on file, and both gave a picture of how Faulks looked many years back. A more recent photo of Faulks was coming through from Megan Morgan. Mavis said she'd get their friendly artist to portray Faulks as he was then and also age him to today, with and without facial hair.

Mavis thought it was time for another Press briefing; Robertson agreed. The story of Ricky and Penny had come up through the local Press in that area, and it was surely time for wider coverage. They would wait till the artist's impressions were completed.

These came through two days later, together with a more recent photo of Faulks from his sister, plus the date and approximate time of the phone message left by Faulks to his sister in Cardiff. The several depictions of Faulks harmonized well together.

Robertson called the Press briefing for that afternoon. He and Mavis outlined the events in the village of rural Gloucestershire, filling in as much detail as they could, and confirmed that Villiers and Norton were the likely perpetrators of Underwood's demise, and that a certain Mr Geoffrey Faulks was now regarded as someone of significant interest to the police. The photo and depictions were displayed, and much photographed by the Press. The phone call was not briefed, and the most awkward question from the Press referred to why they did not suspect any possible revenge attack on Villiers and Norton. Robertson smoothly batted that one away.

Celia was on to the phone companies with, inevitably, mixed results. Megan Morgan's phone company was able to give the mobile number calling Megan but it was a from a different phone company. Celia rang the number, getting neither a reply nor a voicemail. She tracked down the phone company and asked for full details. They could not give location, but the name was G Faulks and the address was c/o Megan. They did not have phone tracking. 'But we do!' shouted out Celia to the general office. She had to get authorization, which was forthcoming, and off she went. The phone had been physically stationary for some weeks in a deserted part of central Wales. She went over to Mavis who suggested she contact the local police there, even if they were several miles distant.

Celia described the location of the phone, hastily adding that it was in connection with a recent double murder case, and asked what was there.

'Not a lot, love; it's hills and sheep, and the odd farmhouse and a nearby village.'

'Anything bigger or smaller than a farmhouse?'

'There's the community centre and many small stone cottages.'

'Is the community centre a hostel of any sort?'

'You know you're right, love, it does double up as a youth hostel, with one bedroom of bunks for guys and another for the girls.'

'Please, Officer, would you mind visiting it and asking if a Mr Geoffrey Faulks has been around recently? As I said, this is in connection with serious crimes in Bristol.'

'My pleasure, love. Owen and I can drive over there when we're less busy and get back to you. You're very welcome to visit, you know.' Celia signed off. That was enough loves for a while.

Seven

Mavis drove up to Clive's for the weekend, early on Saturday morning. She wanted to discuss this other possibility in private, and he was threatening badminton with Anna and Ray. Their meeting was a matter of enveloping each other.

'I've fixed up badminton at three this afternoon. That'll get us hungry for some local curries which I've been tempting you with for far too long now. It's up to you if you want Anna and Ray to join us, see how you get along.'

'Okay, either way is fine by me. Can we have a bit of culture some time?'

'I haven't got tickets to anywhere this trip, but there's live jazz and blues in some nearby pubs and restaurants. Suit?'

It did. Over Saturday morning coffee, Mavis raised the other matter.

'The trouble is, Clive, that it's out of area and a long shot. I feel that you and I have a nose for this sort of thing going way back to when we first worked together. Feelings don't count in police work. It's facts and evidence and verification. Internally, I've worked up quite a case that is more than plausible.'

'Me too, and ditto on the internal thinking. Look, it's a free country and we're not always on duty. Why don't we have a weekend away there and take the temperature, case the joint, see how the land lies, whatever cliché comes to mind.'

'Agreed; two weeks today, okay?'

'Done.'

They changed into their badminton kits at Clive's flat, and met Anna and Ray at the leisure centre.

'Hello, you must be Mavis, heard a lot about you. I believe you're good at badminton, or so Mr Clive says.'

'Nice to meet you two, too. I try to keep it up, but have been busy these summer months so it'll be good to get back on court for the winter.'

'Yes, I've worked out that you and Clive have been busy. It's a good word. Come on, let's warm up.'

They changed partners after each game and Clive rediscovered that he tended to be on the losing side unless he was paired with Mavis or Anna. Nevertheless, some of the points and games were keenly played. It was good to relax with lagers all round afterwards. Clive initiated.

'I want to show Mavis some live music, with a curry, of course. Are you up for that place that has jazz and blues with the restaurant to one side?'

'Definitely count me in,' said Ray.

'Me too.'

'Me too.'

'It's the one with the strapline Hot'n'Cool for Notes'n'Nosh, but it's Caribbean, not Asian. Is that okay?'

'Stop talking; it's sounds great! I'll choose the food, I mean nosh. Can't wait.' Mavis felt in her element.

They went back to his flat, showered and got changed, Clive in typical male dress-down mode and Mavis spectacularly so. Clive found words difficult to find.

'Mavis, you look just wonderful, I don't know what to say.'

'Then don't, mister. I want you to be proud of me up here.'

'Proud is an understatement. Come here.' Kisses can be long.

They met inside the club where Ray had secured a corner table for the four of them. Ray gave a view to Clive.

'You need to hold on to her because otherwise someone else'll grab her. I include tonight as well as the hereafter. I've organized a tab; settle up later, okay?'

'Thanks, and, yes, I intend to. Anna's wonderful too, you know.'

'I do. I owe her a lot.'

They drank; they ate (as selected by Mavis); they listened, and they danced. At every level, Clive was in awe of his partner. They left at just gone one am, piling into a taxi.

'Must do this again,' was said several times. Anna and Ray dropped them off at Clive's flat and they helped each other up to his floor.

'Clive, that was such a marvellous, wonderful evening! Thank you. It's been one of the best evenings for a very long time.'

'Me too, and you made the evening; it wouldn't have been the same without you, thank you.'

'But you made it happen, Clive. You got us going there, thank you. Come here, my lovely man.'

They collapsed into bed and slept forever.

Eight

Barry Williams from Central Wales Police returned Celia's enquiry a few days later. He said that he and Owen had been over to the village the previous day.

'We crammed it in to our busy schedule as there were rumours of some sheep rustling nearby. You were quite right, lady, about the hostel incorporated into the community centre. I asked the warden about a certain gentleman called Geoffrey Faulks, and she went all peculiar.'

'What do you mean?'

'I had told her it was in connection with important investigations and obviously we were in uniform. She wriggled a bit and said she had been sworn to total secrecy about divulging his name and whereabouts. I said, go on, Miss, we're not here to arrest you, you can tell us in confidence. She then revealed that this Geoffrey chap was doing some sort of penance; he goes to chapel, asking for forgiveness every morning, then walks the moors in the afternoon, then cooks a small meal in the evening and reads in the community lounge, sometimes the Bible.'

'What does he say he's done wrong?'

'She said he mumbles that he's not been a good person, he's not been fair in life, but he's done nothing that can't be put right. I think you've got to meet him.'

'So, he continues to live there … By the way, what sort of physical shape is he in?'

'Yes, she said he's here indefinitely and, no, he's not in good shape. He limps around with a stick that he calls his shepherd's crook. All a bit weird if you ask me.'

'Thank you, Mr Williams, but if you don't mind we'll take it from here. We'll keep you in the loop but would you mind if we paid him a visit some time?'

'No, that's fine, pop in for a coffee, that's if we're not too busy, mind. Bye, love.'

Celia said goodbye, noting that she had escaped with only one love.

Celia and Adrian went over to Mavis at her desk. She recounted the phone call.

'How do we explain this turn of events?'

'It may be true; he's committed sins, had a serious brush with death, every day from now on is a bonus and he is seeking redemption while he's alive. "Nothing that can't be put right" suggests financial compensation to me rather than bringing Penny and Ricky back to life. And physically he doesn't sound like a dawn raid type in a Gloucestershire village. If this is the same person, it throws complete doubt on him shooting P and R. How is the response to the artist's impressions and photo?'

Adrian had nothing to report. Megan Morgan had phoned in and thanked them for their effort.

'Thank you both, now let's get on with work.'

Mavis knew exactly what she wanted to do and what needed to be done, but no practical idea how to proceed. That evening after mackerel and rice and a large glass of wine, she settled on the sofa and phoned Clive.

'Clive, missing you. Wish you were here. Have you got an hour or two?'

'I've got a lifetime.'

'Ho ho, maybe. Clive, I know everything about this case and I understand everyone's part in it, and I've cracked it, but I don't know how to resolve it in an official way. I want and need to do some sleuthing, preferably with you, but it will cut across official lines. How do I do it?'

'Well, shall we try to unravel it first? Simplification always helps clarification.'

'That PhD in the post must have been delivered by now. Okay, we've traced Faulks to a retreat in Wales and it seems he's turned to

God. He's a physical wreck and could hardly have shot P and R. Matheson and Underwood were very close, and Stanley was outraged by P and R getting rid of one of Frank's best friends, Damon, and then, brutally killing Frank, he went and shot them out of extreme loyalty to his dear friend. No other explanation works.'

'That's a brilliant analysis but is it true?'

'We have an account of Faulks which I would like to go and verify, and more information has come to light on Matheson and his past that would justify his outrage. I want to go on one of his walking trips and get the measure of the man. I want to go to both with you – that's Wales and Chester. There.'

'Wow and wow. Let me think: how many days holiday are we due, and how many do we need?'

'Clive, that's brilliant and obvious; let's do it.'

Next morning, they each booked the following Friday and Monday off as holiday. Celia winked at Adrian, and Janet smiled knowingly at Clive.

Nine

Thursday evening, Clive drove down to Mavis in Bristol. They packed walking gear and social gear, just in case. Mavis herself had checked that there was a CHAPS walk on Sunday and had applied as a couple to join the walk to see if the club was right for them. No problem.

That evening, they discussed in some detail the logistics of the extended weekend. They were both excited and a little on edge, not with each other but with the venture. They could both see problems back at the ranch that would need careful handling.

Friday morning, they set off early, with Clive wondering about his greasy spoon visit en route. Mavis said that he should go for it, as they didn't know what the day would hold. It was back up the M5, turning left at some point into central Wales. They approached the village just before noon and went straight into The Red Dragon for a drink and a sandwich, and maybe some chat with locals. They sat there in their walking gear, looking for all the world like a couple on a hiking holiday. There were a few locals sitting quietly over pints, and Clive did his friendly chat bit.

'Turned out okay today. What are the best walks round here? I've got a map but never as good as local know-how.'

He received some grudging advice, one even saying why not follow the hikers from the hostel, they've got to get back here. The hostel was pointed out to them. Clive thanked them and they went back to their car. Clive drove near to the hostel, and they sat and waited.

'Neither of us has met Faulks but we should recognize him from the photos.'

'If he goes for his walk, I suggest we follow him from a distance and wait till we're in open moorland on our own.'

'He will think that's threatening but I don't see an alternative. Agreed.'

They waited for over an hour until a man came out of the hostel dressed for a hillside walk and assisted by an outdoor walking pole. He was below average height, late middle-age, stooped in posture, and walked with a pronounced limp. A small day pack was on his back and a beanie on his head. He was unaccompanied and did not look round as he headed up a side path in the direction of the nearest hilltop. They caught a glimpse of his face and both nodded that it had to be Faulks.

'Let's give him ten minutes at that pace; it won't take us long to catch him up,' Clive said.

'I don't think we should be adversarial, more empathetic, though not forgetting that he is a criminal, of course,' added Mavis.

'Let's start off by chatting and see where it goes. We have plenty in reserve.'

They set off up the same path, keeping him in sight a few hundred yards ahead. They slowed their pace to allow Faulks to get clear of outlying cottages and outbuildings. Then they caught up with him.

'Not used to these climbs; it takes some puff to get up here, but worth it in the end. You a regular?'

'You could say that. Most days I'm out if it's fine. Don't hold back on my account, you're younger and fitter than me.'

'No, it's fine, we can enjoy the view if you don't mind the company.'

'There's company and there's company, depending on your attitude.'

'Our attitude is positive and empathetic as we know a little bit about you, Mr Faulks. We'd rather not say who we are but we would like to hear your side of the story.'

Mavis gulped as Clive plunged in with both feet. No time like the present.

Faulks stopped for a breather and calmly looked both of them up and down.

'You the Press?'

'No, I promise.'

'You the police?'

'Not today. We know about your miraculous recovery, but tell us about it.'

'Well, I suppose I've got nothing to lose. I've not been as good as I should have been, my mum and dad would be horrified by my exploits and, as for my poor dear sister, I've put her through hell. Because of the silly things I did, some nasty people came after me and shoved me off a cliff down on the coast along from Cardiff. I shouted out on the way down and then everything went blank. If I'd had any understanding at that time, I would have said I was dead and in hell. When I came round, I was in a hospital bed with my dear sister crying over me. That made me determined to get better. When I was let out of hospital, I stayed with her for a while and I could see I was holding her back, however much she loved me. So, I took to the hills in these lovely parts, staying at various hostels. I have an arrangement to get cash whenever I need it through an old pal and I keep going by walking and praying, and basic eating. When you've seen death, each day here is so valuable.'

'Do you get out and about beyond here at all?'

'No, I've been in these hills ever since I left Meg's house. I wouldn't know how to get anywhere else.'

'It's a grand word but do you have any remaining objectives in life?'

'I do, but I don't know how I will ever achieve them. My objectives can only be achieved with money and I don't know how I'm going to get any more than the small income I have.'

'What would the money be for?'

'I've got to use an ugly word: blackmail. I blackmailed two people because I thought they had robbed a bank. And now I think they probably didn't and they paid because they didn't want any exposure. Then I heard that my old friend Damon had been done in. It's all too much.'

'I think we might be able help you a bit with that, maybe later. How did you get to hear about Damon?'

'Old friends who have been kind to me and kept me in touch, though I haven't been kind to them. You've no idea what the effect of being thrown off a cliff has had on me. I guess it hasn't happened to either of you. Well, quite. In me, it induced redemption which is a word I never recognized before. The people I have wronged just would not recognize me now. I certainly don't.'

'I think we've trespassed enough on your time and exercise, Mr Faulks. We'll leave it there. Your words are safe with us. Can we assume you'll be staying at this hostel for a while yet?'

'Nice to meet you; yes, I'll be here till it gets colder then I'll come down into the valley or see Megan for Christmas.'

'I strongly advise that; she'll be pleased to see you.'

They veered off his track and took a short cut back to the car.

'Clive, you were really good, but do you believe all that? Remember, he's a clever chappie.'

'I'm not usually gullible, but strangely I do. Do you see him renting a car or getting a lift to Gloucestershire, doing the business, and returning back here? I don't think he's capable of it.'

'I agree, that's my hypothesis too, but all that redemption stuff?'

'Have you ever been thrown off a cliff?'

'Sorry … let's make tracks north and find somewhere to stay.'

They drove halfway towards Chester and found a gastropub with rooms.

Mavis took two or three items of clothing out of her bag, plus accessories, and made yet another transformation. Clive changed his shirt. They had drinks and dinner in the restaurant while they chatted over the events of the day and what to do tomorrow. The basic plan was to stake out Matheson and follow him round. He had not seen either of them before so there was no risk of being identified. Even on the Sunday walk, they could chat to him. That left Monday for any action. So, they talked personal stuff.

'How do you think our careers are going? This will be a feather in your cap to have sorted out what led up to Frank's death and the consequences.'

'And yours! You've bottomed out Faulks, or hopefully have, and also the bank robbery.'

'That's still supposition, but it's highly likely. No way will we ever find out how they handled the money between stealing it and buying that place in Gloucestershire. No, I meant more personally in our careers. Next promotion is way off for me, could be five, ten years or never. You're on a steeper curve, I would say, and it could be anywhere in the country and you'd accept.'

'Clive, you're doing that poor me stuff. You're a good man and a good detective, of course you'll get a promo. And it could be anywhere in the country and you'd accept, to quote somebody. I want you and I to work, whatever happens. One of us can ask for a transfer and I might want a career break. Ho ho!' She smiled.

'Moving on, that steak was excellent. Are we having pudding? I seem to drift into a STP every time.'

'Maybe you've earned it this time; for me, it's tiramisu.'

'Okay, and then an early night, don't you agree, Miss?'

Ten

Clive made tea for two first thing, and downstairs tackled a full English, though here it was called a full Welsh, maybe with a very subtle difference. Kedgeree for Mavis.

'Shall we stay two nights in Chester, or see how we go?'

'Why not? We can always cancel the second night depending on developments.'

They decided to see what Matheson was up to and do the tracking by the book, as learnt in college. First up was to find his house. Celia had previously given Mavis his address. It was a semi in the Chester suburbs, a short walk into the city. It backed on to the back of other houses so the only way in and out was at the front. They parked fifty metres away on the other side of the road, with his house in full view.

They continued chatting while they waited for something to happen. It was Saturday morning so not a work day. At 11.30 a middle-aged man appeared and started strolling towards the centre. He was clearly about Frank's age, tall – over six foot – a full head of hair, dressed in jeans, sports shirt and donkey jacket. Mavis followed him less than fifty metres behind, and Clive a similar distance behind Mavis. There was no objective at the moment other than trying to gauge the fellow. He didn't look around and seemed intent on wherever he was going. He bought a newspaper, then a takeaway coffee, and later went into a pub where he joined some friends. Clive and Mavis went to the other end of the bar and got engrossed with each other.

'Clive, this is almost boring. What's the plan now?'

'Yes, it is boring but it would be good to get a photo of that lot. Can you try coming out of the Ladies?'

'You mean and not get noticed?'

'Yes.'

Mavis waited until they were all busy sorting out the next round of pints and got a snap in.

'We can sit here or over the road at that café.' They went over the road and ordered coffee and croissants and read the paper.

Matheson emerged after two o'clock and walked back home.

'This is silly; he's probably going to watch the football or rugby or cricket, or whatever now for the rest of the afternoon.'

'Okay, please can I request another half hour?'

Matheson came straight out of the house, got in his car in the drive and drove off. They followed, keeping some way back.

'See what he's done with the number plate, Clive.'

'I had noticed; I've got my own views about people who flaunt their number plates. He must either have bought it or got it off a friend or family. Quite ancient now.'

The number was 505 TAN and Matheson had personalized it to look like SO STAN with a little exclamation mark at the end. *SO STAN!*

'Probably best if you keep your views to yourself.'

He stopped at a house and went in. They parked as before, some fifty metres away on the other side of the road.

'Clive, that's Frank's house, I recognize the address.'

'What's he doing there?'

'Well, they were supposed to be best buddies; let's check Frank's Will first thing Monday. Just a thought.'

'It's a good thought; he might have had a key before Frank's death, anyway, and he kept it, whether or not Frank left him anything. You'd think the house would be left to Emily to sell but maybe their longstanding friendship was deeper.'

An hour later, Matheson came out of the house with a hold-all, obviously stuffed full, and drove off. They followed him back to his house.

'Can't do any more, can we? If he socializes this evening, we can hardly intervene. Let's begin our holiday in Chester and start again tomorrow on the walk.'

They walked round the city walls, took in the cathedral, a little shopping with Clive asking ahead what she might like for her birthday and even Christmas, then tea and a scone and back to the gastropub. They enjoyed a long evening of drinks, dinner, a crime TV drama in their bedroom and … other things.

Over breakfast the next morning, they discussed the walk.

'They might introduce us as possible new members so I suggest we are John and Jenny from London, having an extended city break in the lovely Chester, okay?'

'I had a best friend at school called Jenny, no problem. Don't forget, I've interviewed Matheson. He couldn't see me but I could see him; he has heard my voice, though.'

'Try a lower voice with a London accent. He won't be suspicious.'

'I don't know about that; don't forget, I interviewed him about Frank's murder. He's bound to be on his guard; yes, I agree the interview was weeks ago. How does this sound?' She growled at him and they burst out laughing. A family two tables away smiled indulgently at them.

In view of a potential Sunday roast, Clive limited himself to a kipper and Mavis had poached eggs. Back in their room, they got togged up for a town and country walk: boots and old anoraks, with Clive taking a small back pack for two bottles of water. They joined the group of walkers assembling outside the city walls. A few couples were drinking coffee out of a vacuum flask.

'Ah, you must be the visitors, interested in joining our little walking group. Hello, I'm Cedric.'

They introduced themselves as John and Jenny from down south, enjoying a weekend city break.

'You'll love it; it's so different from all the congestion you have to put up with down there. It's a short walk out of the city and then you're in marvellous country, proper fresh air. Let me introduce you to a few folk.'

"John" and "Jenny" entered into the spirit of Cedric's gung-ho style, saying how much they were looking forward to the walk and the lunch. They caught sight of Matheson's car turning up and noticed one or two comments like, 'Oh, here he is, has to be last,' and, 'Oh, Sir Stanley has graced us with his presence.' Mavis thought it best to chat to the ladies, leaving Clive to the menfolk, including Matheson.

Cedric gave a briefing on the route and the lunch place, and casually mentioned how nice it was to have two visitors who may join the club. They set off, first down the road and then abruptly turned immediately left to a footpath tracking the river.

Mavis spoke about domestic things: her childhood, her sister, while noting that most of the walkers were couples, with Cedric and Matheson on their own. She made a subtle comment about it. Cedric was easy – his wife had died ten years ago and he'd thrown himself into everything to do with the walking group, such as prospecting new walks and new lunching places for this predominantly middle-aged group. Stanley Matheson was more unknown, they didn't seem to know much about him. Sometimes a girlfriend joined for the lunch but it was a different one each time. He was a keen hiker, going on long trips away, there was the odd joke about the number plate on his car. He belonged to a rifle club and some of them had been to a few of his matches, oh, and for work he seemed to be some sort of agent going round the country. Mavis was left with the impression that Mr Matheson thought a lot of himself.

"John", or Clive, had a harder time. Apart from Cedric, the male contingent was not that loquacious. The talk was work, sport, politics, the appalling road works in town, and where they had been on holiday. Clive spoke to a few of the guys individually before easing himself next to Matheson.

'Like your car; how did you get the number plate?' He couldn't think of anything else to start off a conversation.

'Bit of a joke, really. It's an old one. My folks bought it for my eighteenth when I had my first car. I've transferred it on every car change since. As an outsider, I'm wondering if you think it's a mite pretentious for my age?'

Clive laughed heartily. 'I really could not presume to comment. You're only as old as you feel and I'm guessing you don't feel as old as you actually are. Sorry, by the way, but just like the rest of us.'

They both laughed. Matheson continued.

'Why join this walk? What's your own line of business?'

'You know, when you're on a short break, it's good to meet different people from the same old tribe, like people who go on cruises. Me, I'm in one of those transport and freight companies that surround Heathrow. Screen work most of the time, but occasionally a client offers a trip abroad, which is a nice bonus. And yourself?'

'I'm an agent for an ultra-modern kitchen and bathroom design company. Yes, screen work too, but sometimes a client really does want to be outrageous and break the mould of British interior design.

The big thing is that technology and design are fast changing and you, kind sir, might think your K and B are the bees-knees but in a few years' time, they won't be.'

'Wow, you're getting into sales mode and I'm not a buyer! Well, at least not yet. My partner over there and I are thinking of combining forces on exactly what you're talking about in a few years. What about outside work – we do badminton, walking, and TV and that's about it.'

'I belong to the local rifle club and have been interested in shooting since school, really. Don't worry, I'm not armed, it's all strictly controlled. The police inspect me every so often.'

'The guns are at the club, presumably?'

'That's right, though most of us members have a gun safe at home. It's inspected by the police quite regularly. The main activity is matches, but in season a few of us help out at the pheasant shoots and get rid of a few pigeons in the woods.'

'The walking group must be relieved to have you as their very own security guy.'

'They might, but I never go out with a rifle, gun or pistol. It's an introspective hobby. Anyway, you must circulate, John.'

Clive moved away and caught up with Mavis.

'I think we're done here. Let's enjoy lunch and go, I've had enough.'

'Me too, found out some stuff, though.'

'Let's compare notes when we're back.'

They enjoyed their Sunday roast, quite conventional, all the trimmings, and nothing odd to report at all. Cedric made a short pompous speech extolling the virtues of the (i.e. *his*) group. They decided they would have to stay with the group for the walk back because taking a short cut might raise suspicions.

Back at the gastropub, they confirmed the extra night, and over a drink in a corner alcove, compared notes and planned the following day.

'The women don't rate him and his flash car; and he belongs to a rifle club.'

'He says the number plate dates back to a gift from his mum and dad on his eighteenth birthday when he got his first car. It does sound perfectly plausible. He's also just starting to wonder if it looks a trifle juvenile. He said he never goes out with a gun or rifle or pistol but he has to say that. Frankly, my dear, we don't have anything on him.'

'Well, he did it, and it was odd that he went to Frank's house. First question to Celia in the morning is the Forensics report on Frank's house and what was in it. Second question is what was Frank's Will and has probate been granted. Third question is what, Clive?'

'Third question is what did the local police here mean when they said that Matheson was known to them, implying some sort of record?'

'Yes, I suppose we have to confess to a busman's holiday in Chester. Tomorrow, while we're here. We'll have to make it sound like it was all unexpected and it happened when we were here.'

'Okay, end of work, start of play. Come here.'

'That's very direct, Mr Plod. No, you come here.'

By seven o'clock, it was time to get dressed again and go down for supper. They both chose the fish of the day and Clive selected a Chablis. Sunday evening there was a TV crime drama which they watched together closely in bed, enjoying pulling the plot apart in most scenes.

Eleven

Next morning was like being back at work. A hasty breakfast plus a request for an extension of the checking out time "due to work pressures", and by 8.30 Mavis was on the phone to Celia with her two questions. 'As quick as you can, while we're up here in Chester,' she said.

Then she put in a call to Chester Police, without identifying her whereabouts. She recalled with them that after she and they had interviewed Matheson, they said that they knew about him and his misdemeanours. What exactly did they mean? Mavis asked them to call her back on her mobile.

They ordered some coffee in their room while they waited for responses. Chester was first. Stanley Matheson did have a record of taking the law into his own hands. It could be by strong verbal abuse, harrowing a victim into agreeing with him. It could be strong arm tactics using his own strength and muscle to coerce the victim to give in. It could be by brandishing a gun and threatening to use it to get his way. There was always an element of right on his side, but he would solve the dispute his way and not through proper police channels.

'That fits in with him thinking he's always right and wanting to get his way,' Clive said.

Then Celia came through an hour later.

'Tricky to get this, Mavis. The Forensics report on the house did not stray into areas that did not seem to matter. His desk contained his papers and details of a few investments. He had been a collector of car badges and similar insignia and there was a list of the scrap yards he visited to collect them. He also was a collector of old-fashioned hand-made tools. These were quite extensive and bulky, not exactly like a schoolboy stamp album.

'Secondly, we have had access to his will as part of police enquiries on his death. Everything is left to Emily, his sister, and the two collections I've just mentioned are specifically left to, quote, "My dear old friend Stanley Matheson with a legacy to enjoy." Will this do, Mavis?'

'Perfect, thanks Celia, see you tomorrow.' She rang off before Celia could ask how they were getting on.

'That explains Matheson going to the house to collect the collections. The house is Emily's. I think we have to assume she gave permission for Stanley to collect his inheritance.'

'Okay, assuming they have been legitimately acquired.'

'Yes, Sir.'

Clive paid up, and they were just putting their bags in the car when Celia rang back.

'Please, Miss, er, Mavis, I've got a message for you to call Hugh

Cranston the pathologist. He said it was urgent.'

'Thank you, Celia, I'll deal with it now.'

She phoned Cranston.

'Ah there you are, Mavis. I must apologize sincerely for omitting something from my report. The deceased in Gloucestershire you will be aware were operating very much a siege-like occupation of their house. They had had a security camera fitted above the front door to monitor and record any comings and goings at their house. We have run the files, and on the early morning of their deaths, a car drives right up to the front door.'

'Hugh, Hugh, stop. Sorry to interrupt, let me finish your sentence: it was a blue two-seater with the registration 505 TAN, looking like SO STAN with a little exclamation mark added?'

'And we both appear to have come to the same conclusion. Well done, Mavis.'

Clive gave Mavis a big hug.

'Intuition can be wrong, you know. Not here.'

They drove to Chester Police Station, explained who they were and asked to speak to someone in authority. They were told Inspector Appleby was available and would be down shortly.

He was down five minutes later, in uniform, and greeted them in what could be described as a somewhat guarded manner.

'Hello, and how can I help?' Mavis let Clive do the talking until she was needed.

'Hello, Sir. I'm DS Clive Drewett from West Midlands Police and my colleague here is DS Mavis Smith from Bristol Police. We happen to be in Chester on what we might describe as a bit of a busman's holiday.'

'Well, you don't look like off-duty detectives – perhaps that's a compliment. What's the problem?'

'We, er, have found ourselves operating in your area without letting you know in advance. We more than half expected our investigations to amount to nothing but, both good and bad, they didn't, and we've cracked a serious crime.'

'Why don't we go into this side office and get some coffee?' Appleby said.

The coffee came and they let Appleby in on the whole story. It sounded more like a confessional but Appleby redeemed himself in their eyes by seeing the funny side of it.

'As you've met this Matheson on your walkies, his brief may well conjure up an argument about unofficial interviewing methods. It's probably best if we pick up the reins on this one and deal with Bristol through, shall we say, official channels. Well done, by the way. We can chalk it up as a crime notified and solved in a single day. I jest.'

Clive phoned Bolton and Mavis phoned Robertson, both also adding that they would be back first thing tomorrow.

'Got to celebrate this one. Here or next weekend?'

'Let's drink now and celebrate back at home, at yours *and* mine.'

'I've got to get you back to Bristol by first thing, I think you said.'

'Ten o'clock's fine. So, shall we make tracks back this evening?'

*

In fact, by setting off directly, Clive was pulling up outside Mavis's flat by 7 pm.

'I could go straight back or, er . . .'

'Clive, you're staying right here; you can leave especially early in the morning for your greasy spoon or you can come into the Bristol Station; which option do you fancy?'

'Always one for a hard bargain. I'll take the greasy spoon option because I think we both have a bit of explaining to do in person, obviously for the success but also the off-duty bit.'

'Agreed. Here's the Italian takeaway menu, please order for two and I'll get pouring the wine. It's great to be back.' And she flung her arms round him for a giant hug.

Twelve

Mavis got to the station at nine o'clock, where Celia and Adrian were waiting for her with coffee and croissants.

'Good stuff, you cracked it! What made Matheson click with you? Did Clive make a difference?' and so on. Twenty minutes later, Robertson called and asked her to come up to his office. Mavis had noted Clive's style with Appleby and hoped it would work on tougher material.

'Come in, Smith.' Mavis kept her poker face on. 'We've had the Chester Chief on late yesterday afternoon and Brandon and I have further discussed this matter. You do understand our dilemma, Smith?'

'Yes, Sir.'

'Brandon and I had to attempt to pretend that we knew what you two were up to. Not something we like doing or expect to do in the course of running this station.'

'No, Sir.'

'It's not exactly a misdemeanour, it's bad form; not good. We'll note it in your records and move on. You can relax, Smith. Chester Chief was quite complimentary about how you two handled yourself at his station, made easier by tracking down this culprit who seems to have taken the law into his own hands. How did you identify him?'

'Thank you, Sir. We met Faulks last Friday and it was not difficult to eliminate him from the shooting. He's on a tricky path to redemption and probably needs personal counselling, even though he's a proven criminal. The only other people who knew Underwood were his family and his long-standing friend, Stanley Matheson. The tie of friendship, perhaps even closeness, must have motivated him to action. We met him on the Sunday ramble and two things stood out. First, he was an experienced shooter, a member of the local rifle club, and secondly his approach was to solve problems directly, physically or otherwise, and not turn to due process. I understand Chester will interview him, maybe already have, and I would like to see a copy of that.'

'That won't be a problem. Write a full report for me and Brandon, and then return to normal duties.'

'Thank you, Sir.'

She wondered how Clive had fared.

Thirteen

CI Bolton summoned Clive into his office.

'I had the Chief at Chester on the phone first thing this morning. I gather you two, and you know who I mean, went off-piste last weekend. You told me it was a holiday, Drewett.'

'Yes, Sir, I did and it was, but it was not only a holiday as you are aware. I had envisaged it would be little more than background investigations but further discussions and further information supplied yesterday morning established without doubt the perpetrator of the shootings in Gloucestershire. As the senior on the spot, I felt we had to take action.'

'Aye, well, you did right Drewett, and the Chief at Chester said good things and a reprimand for being out of area unofficially would be quite inappropriate. I have to say, well done.'

'Thank you, Sir.'

'Now tell me about Faulks.'

'He's a sad case.'

'Not in my book.'

'I know, and you're not wrong. But he's the other side of having been thrown off a cliff and survived. He's a different person from the slippery chancer of the past. He's holed himself up in the Welsh hills, goes to chapel to pray every morning, struggles walking the moors with a stick in the afternoon, and ruminates on how he can get redemption. He actually said that he wants to pay the blackmail money back. Damon Head's death didn't help. I didn't tell him that his targets had been shot dead. It couldn't have been him. My colleague, Mavis Smith, at Bristol thinks he needs personal counselling.'

'Well, that's another matter; at least we know where he is. Write your report and return to normal duties.'

'Thank you, Sir.'

Janet brought him a cup of coffee and mouthed, 'Well done.'

Fourteen

Matheson was brought out of custody to the interview room where Appleby was seated at a desk with a colleague next to him. The duty solicitor had spoken previously with Matheson and sat opposite Appleby's colleague. After the formalities, Appleby commenced by asking Matheson to give an account of his movements on the day that Penny and Ricky were shot.

'No comment.'

'Do you own a blue two-seater car with registration 505 TAN?'

'Yes.'

Appleby produced a photograph of the car in the drive of Penny and Ricky's house.

'This is timed at 7 am on that day, with yourself in the driving seat.'

'No comment.'

'I have to say, Mr Matheson, that a "no comment" will not help you in front of a jury when the evidence is crystal clear. If you are guilty of a double murder, and no doubt you will have your reasons, an early admission may assist the degree of sentencing.'

The duty solicitor asked for a short recess to explain the legalities of the situation.

'Granted, let's return in forty-five minutes.'

During this recess, Mavis phoned and asked if she could view the interview as before, without being seen. This was agreed to on the condition that she did not utter a single word.

Nearly an hour later, the same group had reassembled.

'Mr Matheson, please can I ask you to respond to my earlier question about this photograph? I would add that it is a video so there is a running scene before and after.'

'I accept it was me.'

'Thank you. Did you have in your possession a gun whose bullets fit this technical description which I'm passing over to you?'

'Yes.'

'Do you admit to shooting Penny Norton and Ricky Villiers that same morning?'

'Yes.'

'I don't need to ask, and your trial will no doubt cover this, but would you be prepared to give an explanation of your behaviour?' The duty solicitor shook his head but Matheson brushed him aside.

'Yes, I would because there are bad people in this world and something needs to be done. Let me start. I grew up with Frank from nought. We were toddlers together, we went through school together, we trained together in the kitchen and bathroom industry, we worked together, we've drunk together, we've partied together, we've even swapped girlfriends. In the good old-fashioned sense of the word, we were mates forever. We've stood by each other through thick and thin. So, when someone does Frank in, I'm going to do them in. I hope my trial solicitor and counsel will make something of that. I would also add that I've followed this case ever since Frank was dumped in Bristol Harbour. I've done my own little investigation, with a little bit of help from leaks in the force, and I formed a very clear picture of how the trial might run and I knew they would get off. They would get off not only with the murder of Frank, and others, but also the old bank theft. Yes, I know about that too. Can I go now?'

'Interview terminated at 15.43.' Matheson and the duty solicitor were ushered out. Appleby returned to his office and phoned Mavis.

'Did you get all that, Miss Smith?'

'Mavis, please. Yes, and thank you. He's in his own world, isn't he? I wonder whether he should be checked out.'

'You mean for a personality disorder? That'll be for others to decide but in the room it felt quite natural that he was standing up for his best friend.'

'Were they in a relationship?'

'I very much doubt it. What we have on file for Matheson shows him to be quite the lad about town, if you get my drift. No, he used the word "old-fashioned" and I for one am happy to believe that. If you need anything from us for the shootings in Gloucestershire, please get in touch. We'll treat this double murder through proper channels and due process, so it'll be coming back to you, I guess. Good luck, and come to Chester again. On holiday, I mean.'

'Thanks, I promise.' They ended the call.

Fifteen

Clive phoned Mavis.

'How did it go?'

'I had a mini dressing down from boss first thing, but Chester had already helped things along. I guess you too.'

'Ditto.'

'I watched the interview of Matheson. He denied it at first and then admitted everything. The reason for the shooting was that he thought they would get off and that sometimes you have to take the law into your own hand – especially when his long-term best buddy gets done in.'

'How did Stanley know who captured and killed Frank?'

'I'm working on that. He had access to Frank's house as we know. Frank may have left an account of his dealings with Penny, Ricky and Head and, by extension, Faulks. Frank went to their house, so would have left a note of the address for Matheson to find. Matheson also said he had been following the case very closely because of Frank, and implied useful leaks from the police. Nothing here, or your station, I assume, but could be via the Press and their contacts. I'm desperate to celebrate all of this. This weekend, please!'

'Yes, there's still a volume of tidying up to be done: Penny, Ricky and Faulks, and Neil's gang.'

'Clive, you're infuriating!'

PART IV

Epilogue

Neil reported back to Clive that the gang Ricky had contacted to rough up Faulks and Head was being monitored continuously. They finally tripped up and were arrested. The leader of the gang made a plea that they had told the police about Ricky being behind their dealings with Faulks and Head, and that their instructions were to stop just short of A&E. Regrettably, Head's constitution had not been robust enough to stand up to their interpretation of the instructions. The members of the gang received prison sentences based on their confession that they had assaulted Faulks and Head, with other crimes to be taken into account. The judge noted that they had assisted the police with their enquiries on a related case and, given good behaviour, this would be a consideration in assessing their suitability for parole.

*

When Geoffrey Faulks returned to his sister Megan's place in Cardiff, she arranged for further physiotherapy and also some personal counselling. With his physical and mental health strengthening, he turned himself in to Cardiff Police and confessed his blackmailing of Norton and Villiers in the past, which presumably led to him first being beaten up and secondly being thrown off a cliff, presumed dead. He was both surprised and delighted that they had both been shot. He was nevertheless referred to West Midlands Police for questioning by CI Bolton. Faulks didn't have any recollection of past events at Corinthian Catering or Winning Wines, and the discussion went nowhere. None of Cardiff, Bristol, London or West Midlands could bring themselves to charge him with anything that would stick, and he was released back to the care of his sister with the instruction, 'Stick to darts'.

*

Mavis was required to close the case on Penny and Ricky. The mounting evidence of security cameras, polythene, Jeremy Hyde, Fred and Betty, and finally Celia locating Frank Underwood's car left in a quiet residential road in Newcastle-upon-Tyne was convincing. The forensic search by a local team there revealed prints and DNA belonging to Villiers. Celia added, 'And don't forget the coffee cup.'

Mavis and Adrian had looked blankly at Celia.

'What coffee cup?'

'The coffee cup; the one that was left in the rental car in Birmingham; both their prints and DNA were on it. Mr Cranston confirmed it in an email some time ago.'

*

Richard Villiers and Penelope Norton were found guilty of Frank Underwood's murder at a special Crown Court hearing, recognizing that they had subsequently been shot dead. It was noted that they would have received long prison sentences – Ricky's longer than Penny's.

Ricky's sole dealings with the accused blackmailers, Faulks and Head, were officially recorded and some crafty wording associated Villiers and Norton's involvement with Head's demise and the intention to murder Faulks. No one was left in any doubt about Villiers' involvement.

*

The bank went formal on reporting the theft of used notes some decades ago, and the CPS found Villiers and Norton guilty of the crime. It was recorded as additional to other crimes they had committed in their efforts to hide the theft. The bank was given permission to recover the theft proceeds by taking a charge on the Gloucestershire property with no allowance for accrued interest. Peter Vernon was an important witness in establishing the verdict and the bank not only paid his expenses, but also sent him a surprise case of wine approximating to the current value of his old, unpaid expense claim.

He has told Barbara that he has now finally retired from everything and anything to do with the bank. She has told Peter that the filing cabinets are going.

*

Brandon and Bolton played a hotly contested 18 holes of golf, and the winner paid for dinner for them and their lady wives. A re-match has been scheduled.

*

Adrian and Celia got engaged and married in no time at all, and now live in a semi in Bristol. Mavis was best "man".

*

Mavis and Clive went on a long Caribbean holiday, and came back more than happy with each other. They continued to have long discussions most weekends, evenings and into the night about their futures. Eventually they agreed to propose to each other and had a lot of fun buying rings. Neil has been told he will be best man when they get married … sometime.

THE END

About the Author

N N Wood spent his entire working career in financial services. On retirement, he turned willingly to golf, bridge and writing. *Fake Reward* is the third and final book in the Clive and Mavis saga, with each book in the trilogy wholly free-standing. He enjoys his book club, two walking groups, dubious attempts at the piano and guitar, and the company of good friends. He lives in SW London, has two amazing grown-up daughters and two delightful grandchildren.